CW00507808

CONVICT DADDY

ASTER RAE

Copyright © 2021 by Aster Rae

All rights reserved.

No part of this book may be reproduced in any form or by any electronic or mechanical means, including information storage and retrieval systems, without written permission from the author, except for the use of brief quotations in a book review.

Thank you to B. Rourke for beta reading! I appreciate your help so much :)

Proofreaders: Tammy, Julie, Haylee, and Missy. You are all wonderful and you helped SO much! Thank you for helping me deliver the highest quality book to my readers possible! <3

All characters are 18+. Not for readers under 18 or those uncomfortable with adult content.

Cover design: Aster Rae

❀ Created with Vellum

CONVICT DADDY

DISCLAIMER

Thank you to my sensitivity readers who helped with the belly worship scenes!

PROLOGUE
ROMAN

"You're eligible for work release."

"Excuse me?" I grunt.

"I said you're eligible for work release," my lawyer Antoine says, his eyebrows knitting together. "There's a Christmas tree farm in upstate New York looking for free labor for the next thirty days. If you get through the next month without incident, Judge Barker will grant you parole."

My head spins as disbelief rockets through me.

Eight long years have passed since I came to Rikers Island.

Eight long years have passed since a judge locked me up with the most vicious criminals in the state of New York for defending my family's honor.

Convicts aren't supposed to spend more than one year in Rikers.

I'm one of only two inmates who've ever been there close to a decade.

Now I finally have a chance to be free.

A farm in upstate New York wants to take a chance on me for the next month.

All I have to do is mind my fucking business and cut down Christmas trees.

This is your fucking opportunity to get out of here.

"I'll do it." My voice is gravel as I stare at my lawyer, determination blazing through my chest. "Sign me up."

"Good." My lawyer slides a photograph of an old couple in holiday sweaters across the table to me. "Mr. and Mrs. Johnson are your new hosts for the next month. They're going to keep close tabs on you and put you to good use."

"I'm fine with that." I look at the couple in Christmas sweaters sipping out of mugs in front of a crackling fire, kindness and warmth on their faces. "I've got this, Antoine. I won't fuck this up."

"You'd better not." Antoine caps his pen. "You were lucky as hell to get this opportunity, Roman. You won't get another shot at parole again."

"There's one more thing," Antoine says, pushing the picture to the side and giving way to a second picture underneath.

"What's that?" I grunt.

"Mr. and Mrs. Johnson have a grandson who will be on the Christmas tree farm with you." Antoine taps the picture in front of me. "You'll be spending the next thirty days working with him."

Wait.

...What?

"The owners... Have a grandson?" I ask.

Intrigue draws a finger of heat across my neck.

My lawyer nods. "Bentley."

"How old?"

"Twenty?"

"What does he do?" I ask.

"He's a student at Cornell University. He's going to be sharing the farmhouse with you."

Curiosity beats a drum in my chest as I pick up the photograph Antoine hands me.

I haven't even taken one look at the boy when I nearly faint in my seat.

"Oh... My God," I gasp, my eyes going up and down, the feelings of lust pummeling me so intense I can barely breathe.

No. I *can't* breathe.

This... Is the owners' grandson?

A beautiful boy. An innocent angel.

Curvy. Thick. With a hint of brattiness lurking beneath his Colgate smile.

My cock springs to an erection as my eyes lap up every inch of this young man.

Sapphire eyes. Curly brown hair. Rosy cheeks primed for kisses. A look on his face that screams *I'm waaaaaay fucking naughtier than you think, Daddy!*

My foreskin retracts as my ten-inch cock mashes against my tattooed thighs.

"This is... The owner's grandson?" I rasp, lust tinging my voice, betraying the need welling up within me as a chorus of heavenly angels fills my ears.

"Yes." My lawyer nods. "Bentley has an older brother who's had brushes with the criminal justice system before, and he has a lot of animosity toward the prison system. Barney and Bertha Johnson invited you to the farm because they think you can do some good for him."

No. Oh sweet Jesus no.

His grandparents want me to... *Mentor* this boy?

I count ten million ways this could blow up in my fucking face.

And yet it's been so long since I've been around... A young man.

A man with meat on his bones...

A man like...

Bentley.

"I'll do it," I snap, sliding the picture back to Antoine, adjusting my aching cock in my orange jumpsuit.

Antoine nods. "This has been a hard fight, Roman. But you're on the right track."

Sweat beads on my forehead as visions of Bentley whirl through my mind.

"One last thing," Antoine warns in a low voice, his eyes turning to slits as he stares at me.

"What?" I growl, tendrils of desperation surging across my gut.

"Don't pull any shit with this kid, Roman." Antoine's eyes bore into mine. "You have a great record for being locked up this long and if you uphold your end of the bargain, you'll be eligible for parole. Pull any shit and Judge Barker will send your ass back to Rikers."

Fuckfuckfuck.

This is so goddamn fucking bad.

The owner's grandson is a fucking curvy knockout in every way and his soft little lips are just *crying out* for a Daddy.

But I've seen what excess passion can do.

It's why I was locked up in the fucking first place.

I'll go to this damn Christmas tree farm, but I'm going to avoid this bratty little angel at all costs.

1

Two weeks later
December 1st

"OMG," I yelp in delight, taking in the delicious assortment of Christmas tree and unicorn cupcakes on the counter. "Grandma Harmony is going to *love* these."

Macon, my BFF and world-famous online porn star, makes a pouty face. "Please tell me we're not giving *all* of these yummy treats away to charity."

I roll my eyes to the ceiling. "We already went over this."

"Refresh my memory," Macon drawls.

"We get to keep the unicorn cupcakes," I say, popping a giant bite of a cupcake in my mouth, "but we give the Christmas tree cupcakes to Grandma Harmony because she's a single old lady who needs a little love and cheer to tide her over until her grandson returns home next week."

"Rude," Macon snaps, putting his hands on his hips. "Maybe I want a Christmas tree cupcake too. Or maybe your next-door neighbor Mrs. Harmony would prefer unicorns. Ever think of that, Bentley? Not everyone fits into the neat little box you want to smush them in."

Uhhm.

Did this boy really just talk shit about the way I want to spread love around the neighborhood this holiday season?

"You're lucky I'm ascending Jacob's ladder to a heavenly sugar high right now," I say, savoring the yummy pink frosting in my mouth.

"What's that supposed to mean?" Macon demands.

"If I weren't so loaded up on sugar, I'd dump this container of pink frosting all over your head for your rudeness."

"You wouldn't dream of it," Macon groans, flipping his blond hair back over his ears. "I need to stay clean for my video I'm filming with Aleksei this afternoon so if you screw up my look you'll get a swift cupcake to the face."

I nearly choke on frosting. "Video with Aleksei?"

"Yes," Macon says with a proud smile. "Aleksei's going to rail me underneath a Christmas tree when he arrives this afternoon. It's going to be the most fabulous video on Fans4Camz of all time."

A mammoth groan escapes me.

This boy can't be serious.

"You can't have sex under a Christmas tree," I say, glaring at Macon.

"I don't see the problem," Macon says with a laugh.

"This is my *grandparents's* Christmas tree farm." I slap Macon's forehead with my palm. "I invited you here to get away from the city. Not to get railed by your boyfriend beneath a Douglas fir."

"Fiancé," Macon corrects sassily, rolling his eyes as he puts his hands on his hips. "Aleksei's my *fiancé* now. And it's not my fault that you said your grandparents were super accepting when you invited me here last month. You should've known that I was going to get up to something sexual."

This boy seriously has zero conception of boundaries.

A mammoth groan escapes me. "You didn't say you were going to film a Fans4Camz video under a tree."

Macon rolls his eyes. "I shouldn't have to tell you beforehand that I'm going to get up to something kinky," Macon drawls. "Aleksei and I are the most in-demand online models in the world right now. You should've known we were going to have some naughty fun."

Wow. Just wow.

This boy is a total loon.

Last month, Macon got engaged to his Mafia boss-slash-beautiful growly alphahole boyfriend Aleksei at my friend Christian's ice cream parlor in Midtown.

The video blew up online and transformed Aleksei and Macon into instant internet sensations.

Fans4Camz, the premier adult at-home entertainment site, inked a deal with them and they became joint shareholders in the brand.

They get up to kinky shit in bathrooms, alleys, and even ice cream parlors for the site.

But a kinky video beneath a Christmas tree takes exhibitionism to an entirely different level.

And it's totally unacceptable to me.

"Quit pouting, bitch." Macon winks as he smears frosting on a Christmas tree cupcake and raises it to his mouth. "Aleksei and I will be stealthy and you won't even know that we're getting it on in every possible location."

"Put that cupcake down," I snap. *This guy.* "And you're not having sex underneath a Christmas tree on my farm."

"Why not?"

"If my grandmother sees you and Aleksei using tree sap for lube, she'll have a heart attack."

"Spoilsport," Macon says, popping the cupcake in his mouth.

I try and fail to smack the cupcake out of his hands. "No Christmas cupcakes. Those are for Grandma Harmony."

"But I *waaaaant* it," Macon whines, rolling his eyes as he munches his pastry. "You're totally stereotyping Grandma Harmony by assuming that she only wants to eat Christmas trees."

If there was an award for brattiest twink of the year, Macon would take first prize.

"Are you done now?" I groan, flipping my brown hair over my ears.

"Where do you have to go that's so important?" Macon asks.

I let out a groan. "Away from you, bitch."

To a sweet old lady who really needs some holiday cheer this season.

Macon snorts as he puts down his cupcake. "You're stuck with me, sweetie."

"I don't want to be," I pout.

"You should've thought about that before you invited me and Aleksei up here for Christmas."

Macon walks over to me. "Are you still going to try to find a Daddy over break?" Macon asks.

Wow.

Little bastard.

Does he really think that I won't notice he's trying to change the subject?

"Changing the subject, much?" I snap, glaring at my nine-teen-year-old bratty ass friend who, though only a year younger than me, doesn't act a day older than thirteen.

Macon laughs. "Forgive me for trying to get the mental image of Aleksei rearranging my insides out of your mind."

Ugh.

Well, at least he's self-aware.

"No." I pick up an extra-large sized bag of Skittles and pop a few in my mouth. "I wanted to find a Daddy, but now I just want to help my grandparents out with the farm."

Macon furrows his brow. "Why? You were pretty gung ho about finding a Daddy in Manhattan."

"Plans changed," I say with a shrug. "Grandpa Barney and Grandma Bertha are getting up in age and I'd hate to miss these special moments chasing after a man."

"What kind of Daddy would you be interested in if you didn't have to worry about your grandparents?"

"Well, I'd want him to be tall, dark, and sexy as fuck to start," I drawl with a wink.

"That's a given," Macon agrees.

"I'd also want him to be muscular as hell and covered in tattoos," I continue, envisioning this beautiful dream Daddy in my mind.

"Obviously," Macon adds.

"And lastly," I continue, my heart fluttering as I stare out the window, "I'd want him to be ruthless and rough as he manhandles the hell out of me in bed. I'm a big boy with a giant thick ass, Macon, and not too many guys have what it takes to be with me. I need a man who can give me the ass lovin' that I need."

Macon lets out a snort. "So the men at Cornell didn't do it for you this past semester?"

"Oh please." I check my nails. "I'm a thick bitch with a lot of junk in my trunk. Those *boys* at Cornell can't handle these fabulous curves, honey."

To be perfectly honest, I'm totally avoiding telling Macon the real reason why I'm not looking for a man over winter break.

The truth is that I just found out last week that my older brother who I haven't seen in eight years is in Rikers Island.

He's been locked up for something that happened when I was barely twelve years old.

I haven't seen or spoken to him since *the incident* and it's going to take a *lot* of mental energy when I visit him next month after eight long years.

"You'll get back in the dating spirit eventually," Macon drawls, stealing my bag of Skittles.

"I hope so," I say, rolling my eyes. "If I don't get fed up with you and Aleksei having dirty sex all over this farm first."

Macon laughs. "Want to take pictures in a naughty Santa hat?"

Ugh.

This boy.

"I had a funny feeling you were going to ask me something like that," I snap.

"Yes or no, sis."

"I feel like you'll keep bothering me until I agree," I say reluctantly as Macon eats another forbidden cupcake, "so yes. But let's make it snappy. I'm getting hangry for one of Grandma Bertha's Skittle cookies."

That's when the doorbell rings.

2

ROMAN

I STAND in front of the farmhouse with a tattered duffel bag in my left hand and my rescue puppy in my right.

Today's the day I finally fucking break free of my chains.

The day I put the bullshit that happened to me eight years ago behind me and start my new life.

It was hell getting out of Rikers this morning.

Two men jumped me in the showers when they realized I was leaving the prison behind.

Rikers has a culture where inmates who don't get out on sweetheart deals viciously attack those who do and these men wanted to make me pay for abandoning them.

But my focus was elsewhere and I refused to let them get to me.

I smashed their heads against the tile and gave them black eyes to send a message to every other inmate that they'd better not fuck with me on my way out.

I'm a fucking ruthless motherfucker who nearly killed a man with his bare hands which is why I was in Rikers in the first place and I didn't let them forget it.

No one can fucking come between me and my freedom.

No one can fucking prevent me from following through on my deal with Antoine to make sure I never step foot in Rikers again.

I forced myself to focus on Tura Lura, the rescue Corgi I trained in Rikers for therapy sessions with the *Paws For Prisoners* program, and ignored the inmates who taunted me and goaded me to attack them before I left for the Christmas tree farm this morning.

The inmates and officers were taking bets on how fast I'd end up back behind bars but I didn't listen to a goddamn word they said.

The officers and wardens gave me three weeks.

The inmates gave me one-and-a-half.

I didn't take their goddamn bait.

It'll be a cold day in hell before I wind up back in Rikers Island.

My duffel bag shifts in my hands when the door in front of me swings open.

The chubbiest, most angelic twenty-year-old face pokes out from behind it. "Uhhhh. You're not the deliveryman."

A grunt escapes me as I stare at the boy. "Bentley, right?" I growl, ignoring the tidal wave of lust washing over me.

Oh sweet mercy me.

It's the same beautiful angel from the picture.

Bentley looks even better than he did in the snapshot Antoine showed me two weeks ago.

He's curvy and sexy and thick in all the right places.

His skin is soft and smooth and his eyes shine with youthful excitement.

His lips are red and bee-stung and they make me want to pull him close and crush my mouth to his.

I feel like I could fucking transcend the metaphysical constraints of the universe staring into those blue eyes.

"Yeeees," Bentley says cautiously, his brows knitting together as he turns his blue eyes up to me. "I don't mean to be rude, but... Do I know you?"

"No, you don't." I let my duffel bag shift in my grip to cover up my aching hardness. "My name is Roman, and I'm going to be spending the next thirty days with you until Christmas."

Bentley curiously looks me up and down. "I think you've got the wrong address, Sir."

I steal a look at the address on the side of the farmhouse and then direct my gaze back to Bentley. "1843 Hickoryville Drive?"

"Yeeees," Bentley says, his gaze migrating to the puppy in my left hand, before flitting back to me. "But clearly, you've mixed something up. My grandparents aren't expecting visitors, and no one's spending the holidays with us for the next thirty days. It's just me, my friend and his fiancé, and my grandparents. No tattooed six-foot-eight men were scheduled to swing by... And something tells me you're not a caroler stopping here to spread holiday cheer."

Just then the door swings open all the way and two lovely faces appear in the space behind Bentley.

"Roman," the woman says, who I recognize at once as the sweet old lady with the Christmas tree sweater from the picture. "I'm so glad you made it here safely. Thank you so much for agreeing to come up here this holiday season."

"You came just in time for Christmas," a male voice booms, and I glance up just in time to see the burly man with white hair and the matching white beard named Barney walk out from behind Bertha. "It's nice to finally meet you, Roman. We're excited to put you to work this season and get to know you better."

Bentley's jaw falls to the ground. "Wait, Paw Paw and Maw Maw... You *know* this man?"

Bertha nods. "Yes, dear. Roman agreed to help us this Christmas season."

"Roman's on work release from prison," Barney grunts, patting Bentley's back. "These are the busiest times for us at the tree farm, boy. Roman's going to help us chop down trees and do all the menial tasks I can no longer do on account of my back. He's also going to work alongside you to make sure we sell all of our trees this holiday season."

"Hold up." Bentley freezes in the doorway. "You... Brought a *convict* here for Christmas?"

"Ex-convict," Barney explains, glaring at his grandson. "When Roman finishes with his work release here, he'll be out on parole very soon."

"Thank you, Barney," I growl in a growly voice. "I'm ready to put my past behind me and make a positive impact on society. I've served my time and suffered enough."

This is the speech I rehearsed before I left Rikers this morning.

The goal is to make myself appear remorseful and safe so the Johnson family isn't scared of me.

I whisper a prayer to the Mnemosyne, the Greek goddess of memory, to help me remember the rest of my lines.

Bentley puts his hands on his hips and glares at me. "I wasn't speaking to *you*, Sir. I asked my *grandparents* a question."

"Forgive our grandson," Bertha says with a laugh, shaking her head in amusement as she pats Bentley's head. "We decided it was best if we didn't mention to him that you'd be staying with us during the holidays this year. Bentley can be a little... Overprotective, and we didn't want him to put a wedge in our plans before you came up."

"I can't believe you, Maw Maw." Bentley lets out a groan. "You invited a freaking convict into our family home and you didn't even think to consult me. This is unbelievable."

"Ex-convict," I bark again, adjusting my puppy in my arms, who licks my tattoos. "I'm not a convict anymore, boy. Watch your mouth."

Little brat.

Who does he think he is, sassing me in front of my new hosts?

He might be the cutest little thing in the world with all those curves and his chubby cherub cheeks, but he isn't going to tarnish the image I'm trying to create in the minds of Barney and Bertha, that's for damn sure.

I've worked too damn hard for some angel to sabotage my work release and I'm not going back to prison anytime soon.

A sigh escapes Bentley as he stares at my puppy. "What's your damn name again?"

"Roman," I growl, a fierce glint in my eyes as I drag my suitcase up to my side.

"Well, *Roman*," Bentley says, digging his hands into his hips even more, "you can take that suitcase and head back to whatever institutional corrections facility you came from. You're *not* welcome here and I won't have you intruding on my Christmas."

Bertha sighs as she taps Bentley's shoulder. "Roman is from *Rikers Island*, Bentley. That's another reason why we invited him here."

Bentley doesn't move. "Rikers Island?"

Bertha nods. "Roman can tell us about Jericho's living conditions and get us ready for our visit to Rikers next month."

Bentley freezes in the doorway.

I can see everything in Bentley's mind whirr to a halt as he processes his grandmother's words.

"You mean... Where my brother is staying?!" Bentley sputters at last.

"Yes," Barney grunts, patting Bentley's shoulder. "Roman will teach you about Jericho's life behind bars. He doesn't know

Jericho personally, but his expertise will help you prepare for when you finally see him next month."

Bentley can barely believe what he's hearing. "I'm still not buying it. Felons are dangerous people, Maw Maw. Jericho's only in prison because of what he did to protect me. But Roman looks like a stone-cold killer who deserves to be behind bars."

"Don't be such a bratty pants," Bertha coos, hugging her grandson. "Roman's not a bad person, Bentley. We read his file."

"You read my file?" I bark, my fingers curling into fists as I stare at Bertha before I quickly calm myself down. "My apologies," I hedge. "I'm glad you looked at my record."

Bertha laughs. "Yes, dear. We wouldn't just let anyone into our home, as I'm sure you understand."

"Roman trained therapy dogs in prison and he didn't get into a single altercation in his incarcerated life," Barney explains, cuffing Bentley's shoulder. "He was an upstanding inmate which is why we felt comfortable letting him into our home."

Well, except for the inmates I maimed in the showers this morning. *Thank fuck that wasn't in my file.*

"Is that why Roman has that dog in his hand?" Bentley says, cocking an eyebrow at Tura Lura.

"Roman," Bertha says encouragingly, winking at me. "Would you like to answer that?"

"Yes," I grunt, holding Tura Lura up. "Tura Lura is my pup. She's a teacup Corgi who helps prisoners with PTSD."

"See, dear?" Bertha says, hugging her grandson. "Roman brought a therapy dog he trained. You still have issues with nervousness relating to *the incident* eight years ago, and Roman's puppy will help you get over that."

Bentley takes one look at Tura Lura and shakes his head. "I can't freaking believe you did this, Maw Maw and Paw Paw. You're both insane."

"They're not insane," I snap before I can stop myself, allowing Bertha to remove Tura Lura from my hands. "They read my fucking file, boy. I have a clean record and I've never done anything dumb."

"Yeah," Bentley gripes, glaring at me. "Besides the *crime* that landed you in prison."

Hmm.

Touché, brat. Touché.

"Quit being a brat," I bark, glaring at Bentley. "You don't know me, boy, and I'll teach you a damn lesson you won't forget if you talk like that to me again. I'm here for the next thirty days to work *gratis* for your grandparents, meaning that they're getting free labor out of this too. We don't have to speak to each other at all."

Bertha squeals. "Did you hear that? Roman's just like the men on *Scared Straight*."

"He's perfect for Bentley," Barney barks in agreement. "Roman's exactly what he needs to learn about life inside Rikers Island."

"Y'all are so annoying." Bentley rolls his eyes and retreats inside the farmhouse. "This guy is a ticking time bomb. Don't blame me when you all wake up dead."

"You can't *wake up* dead, Bentley," Barney chastises. "And Roman's not going to pull any dumb shit with us, so you can drop the attitude now."

"Come on, Macon," Bentley snaps to someone inside the house. "We're going to deliver these cupcakes to Grandma Harmony."

Bertha sighs as Bentley scurries away from us into his grandparents's house. "I'm afraid that wasn't the most congenial welcome."

"Don't worry about it, ma'am," I growl at Bertha. "I'm a grown ass man who's dealt with prisoners with PTSD for eight years behind bars. I can handle the occasional bratty college kid every now and then."

"Why don't we get your puppy a treat from the kitchen?" Bertha says to me. "I just made a fresh batch of whipped cream for a pie this morning. I imagine Tura Lura would love a taste."

Wow. Just wow.

This is the sweetest thing ever.

This woman and her husband have shown more kindness to me in three minutes than anyone has in the past eight years combined.

Save for their annoying ass little gorgeous grandson, this is the sweetest household I've ever entered in my life.

It's much better than the billion-dollar castle where I grew up in Russia with my father who screamed at me whenever I held my gun wrong.

I pat Tura Lura's floppy ears. "You hear that, girl? Let's go inside. It's time for a treat."

"Everything will be fine, dear," Bertha says, wrapping her arm around mine as she pets Tura Lura. "Bentley has a bratty exterior because of *the incident*, but he'll warm up to you soon enough."

"Thanks, Bertha," I grunt.

But I have no plans to speak to Bentley again.

As long as I stay clear of that bratty angel, my work release plans will go swimmingly.

And then I'll be out of prison forever and I can finally start my lawsuit to change the corrupt legal system that put me behind bars.

3

UHHH. So *that* just happened?

"I can't believe it," I wail as I exit the farmhouse and drag Macon to the little dirt road next to our white picket fence.

"What's the problem?" Macon asks.

I tug my gold bicycle out of the bush where I hide it when I forget to lock it up and sit on the seat. "There's a man staying here for Christmas that my grandparents didn't tell me about. It's insane."

"Oh." Macon's brow furrows. "That is weird."

Sheesh.

Ya think?

Anger clouds my mind as I think of Roman.

Roman was tall. Dark. Sexy as sin.

He was covered in menacing tattoos and his jaw was sharp enough to cut steel.

Every cell in my body sprung to life when I saw the burly patch of chest hair tufting out from beneath his collar, rough and matted as hell.

Holy shit.

I answered the doorbell and I was smacked in the face with a gaze full of *man*.

Hairy. Ass. Man.

I wanted to fucking sink my teeth into that chest hair and latch on for dear life.

A colossal wave of lust rocketed through me when I saw his giant calloused hands clasping his tiny puppy in front of him, giant and unwavering.

What. The. Fuck.

This man's hands were big enough to slam my face into a wall headfirst but he held that adorable puppy with the tender loving care of a true protector.

This is bad, dangerous, and freaky AF.

Roman's a horrible distraction from the perfect Christmas I'm planning with my grandparents.

Roman has no right to barge into my life like this and make me toss out all my carefully constructed plans.

"The stranger is an ex-convict," I groan, placing my foot on the bicycle pedal and gripping the handlebars tightly. "He's huge and scary and covered in menacing tattoos. He looks like he could smack my face into a wall and beat me into a pulp."

"That sounds like something your grandparents should've told you about before they invited him over for Christmas," Macon surmises. "You have a right to know who you're spending the holidays with."

"Damn right I do," I snap, rolling my eyes.

Ugh.

Grandma Bertha didn't even *consult* me before she invited this convicted felon into the family home.

What kind of freaking grandma does that?

She probably has it out for me because I ate all of her apple tarts this fall.

Vindictive granny. Sabotaging my perfect Christmas by inviting the literal Daddy of my wet dreams over to taunt me.

I lean on my gold bicycle's handlebars and turn to Macon. "There's something else I'm not telling you. Something personal about me."

Macon hops onto the spare bicycle I'm lending him. "Let me guess. You have a fetish for convicted felons."

"It's not sexual, dumbass," I snap, glaring at Macon.

Of course this boy would think that my confession is something kinky right away.

He's a freaking walking sex machine and his libido never slows down.

Macon rolls his eyes. "Fine. Tell me."

"Okay, good." I lean on my handlebars. I take a sharp breath. "My brother Jericho is in prison. He committed a crime when I was in seventh grade and he's been stuck in Rikers Island ever since."

"Oh really?"

I nod. "His court-appointed lawyer was a dumbass and never helped him get out. We didn't even know which prison he was in after he aged out of juvie because we couldn't afford proper representation."

"I'm sorry, Bentley." Macon makes a sad face. "I had no idea."

"That's why I'm so mad at this Russian asshole," I say at last.

"Why?" Macon queries.

"He waltzed right out of prison and came to stay at *my* Christmas tree farm," I say, slamming my fist on my handlebars, "while my brother suffers inside Rikers Island in silence."

Macon nods. "How did this man even get out of prison in the first place?"

"I don't know," I confess, spitting the words out. "I'm assuming he scored one of those sweetheart deals that only rich people with well-connected lawyers get. I mean, seriously. A month at a Christmas tree farm and then he's eligible for parole? This isn't exactly a conventional deal."

"I agree," Macon agrees.

"I'd bet my left foot that his lawyer bribed his judge," I grumble. "He also had a Rolex on his left wrist and a pair of diamond cufflinks on his shirt cuff. He had a gold chain around his neck. This is a man with connections and money. It's disgusting."

"What's disgusting?"

"That men with powerful lawyers get sweetheart deals while goodhearted people like my brother suffer without recourse," I say. "If Roman truly got a sweetheart deal, then I hate him for it."

I don't care that my grandparents only invited Roman here so that I could "prepare for my visit" with Jericho and "find out what life is like" inside Rikers Island.

Roman represents everything that's wrong with the criminal justice system.

It doesn't even matter that he has a sexy Russian accent and stunning tattoos.

It doesn't even matter that he's the dream man I want to bend me over my grandfather's kitchen table and take my virginity.

Roman's lawyer probably bribed his freaking judge to let him out early and he can take his adorable puppy right back to Rikers and shove it up his ass.

He's corrupt and disgusting, and he needs to go, no matter how much he makes my dick scream.

"What's his name again?" Macon asks after a beat.

"Roman." I shrug. "Or at least that's what he said. I don't know what to believe anymore. How can I trust anyone when my grandparents didn't even tell me that I was spending Christmas with a felon?"

Macon's jaw drops to the ground. "You said *Roman*?"

Uhhm.

Did I stutter, bitch?

"Yes," I snap, rolling my eyes at my friend's inability to keep up with the conversation.

God.

Where the hell is Macon's brain today? Thinking about Aleksei boning him beneath a pine tree?

"My fiancé has an older brother named Roman who's also in Rikers," Macon says excitedly, his eyes widening. "I'll call Aleksei right now."

Macon pulls out his phone and FaceTimes Aleksei. "Hey, Daddy. How's your day going?"

Aleksei answers on the first ring. "Good, boy," he growls. "Just uploading our latest video onto Fans4Camz."

"You're so sweet." Macon blows Aleksei a kiss. "Hey, I have a question for you, if you're not too busy."

Aleksei lets out a grunt. "I'm never too busy to answer a question for my baby boy. Ask away, angel."

"You have a brother named Roman, right?" Macon asks.

"Yes." Aleksei nods.

"Where's Roman locked up again?"

Aleksei chuckles. "Rikers Island in New York. It's the most overcrowded prison in the world."

"Errrr," Aleksei continues, correcting himself, "Roman *was* in Rikers Island, but our new lawyer scored him a killer supervised work release arrangement to get him out. He's at a Christmas tree farm in upstate New York."

Wow. Just wow.

So Roman is my friend Macon's fiancé Aleksei's fucking brother who's a criminal billionaire.

The entire family — including their extended family here in New York — is rich as shit with connections to powerful people in high places.

I knew Roman was a corrupt worthless piece of shit.

"You piece of shit," I say, glaring at Aleksei.

"What did I do?" Aleksei feigns innocence.

"You used your billionaire connections to get your brother out of prison," I snap. "You're corrupt."

Aleksei rolls his eyes. "I know it's kind of shitty, Bentley. But Roman isn't a bad guy."

"His lawyer bribed a judge."

"Roman helped stop a man from destroying our family's honor," Aleksei says with a growl. "And he didn't bribe anyone. It's not illegal to hire a lawyer with connections."

"This is such BS." Anger thrums in my temples. "Why should someone like Roman be allowed to waltz right out of Rikers Island when regular people can't even get a hearing? It's so gross and unfair."

Macon sighs. "I know it's BS, Bentley. But Roman's suffered long enough."

"Suuure." I glare at my friend. "I'm sure Roman cries himself to sleep every night and dries his tears with his family's billions."

"Roman didn't just waltz out of prison, bud," Aleksei snaps. "He could've left earlier if we bribed the judge. But Roman wouldn't have his legal freedom that way. He's doing this the same way that everyone else is so he can get his rights back."

"Why did Roman even go to prison in the first place?" I demand, glaring at Aleksei through Macon's phone.

Aleksei makes a zipping motion over his lips. "I can't tell you the specifics."

"Give me a hint."

Aleksei sighs. "Something happened eight years ago on Christmas Eve when Roman helped his sister out. We don't talk about it much. Roman was never supposed to be involved in the first place. But he cared a bit too much and he's paid the price for it ever since."

Everything in me grinds to a halt.

The world spins in slow motion.

Eight years ago? Christmas Eve? No, it must be a coincidence.

I nip the urge to ask more about Roman's case in the bud.

It's not my fucking job to get involved.

I just need to get through the next thirty days and then Roman will be out of my hair and I'll never speak to him again.

Although it is pretty strange he went to Rikers on the same day as my brother.

"Thanks for the lackluster explanation," I snap, turning away from Aleksei. "Tell your brother he can march straight back to Rikers now."

Aleksei lets out a growl. "You have no idea what you're talking about, Bentley. You need to watch your fucking mouth and stay in line."

Macon lets out a laugh. "Stop, Daddy. You're only supposed to talk to me like that."

"What's that supposed to mean?" I demand.

Macon winks at me. "Aleksei is my Daddy, so he must save his naughty words only for me."

"You're never invited to my Christmas tree farm again," I snap when I swipe Macon's phone out of his hands and kill the Face-Time call.

"Tell that to your grandparents," Macon drawls, putting his foot on his pedal and bicycling past me to head to my friend Preston's farmhouse so we can deliver the cupcakes to his grandmother. "Apparently, you don't have final say in who gets the invitations around here."

Oh. My. God.

This is going to be the worst Christmas ever.

4

ROMAN

One hour later

"AND THESE," Barney says, leading me to the barn where the various power tools sit, "are your tools for the job."

I let out a grunt. "Fuck, this looks complicated."

"You have pruning shears and shearing knives to get the trees ready to sell this week," Barney explains, gesturing to the tools. "And you'll distribute sharpened hand saws to customers when they come to cut down trees for Christmas."

My head spins as I take in the information Barney gives me.

Holy. Fucking. Shit.

This is a *lot*.

I studied my ass off before I left Rikers with a giant textbook on Christmas tree farming to learn everything I could but clearly I came up short.

The giant book I used to study didn't go over the day-to-day activities involved with running a successful Christmas tree business.

"It's a fucking lot." I take in the various blades spread out before me. "I won't deny it. But it's nothing I can't handle."

Barney barks out a laugh. "I know that, son. It's a lot to keep track of your tools and manage everything so that the season goes off without a hitch."

"You can say that again," I growl. "Pardon my French, but this looks complicated as hell. It's way more intense than the book on Christmas trees I read in Rikers Island made it out to be."

"I completely understand, Roman." Barney chuckles. "But Bertha and I read your file and we're confident that you can handle this."

"We'll find out," I bark.

Barney claps my shoulder. "Chop down trees and guide customers through the farm when they come next week and you'll be golden. It's not rocket science, Roman. Bertha and I believe in you."

I let out a sigh.

It's not going to be easy learning this new skill.

I worked my ass off to learn new skills in Rikers Island but this has more moving parts than anything I've ever done.

Barney cuffs my shoulder. "Can I tell you something, Roman?"

I'm still trying to figure out the difference between a pruning shear and a shearing knife when Barney's words register in my mind.

I nod as I lean back against a wall. "Go for it."

"I wanted to... Apologize once more for our grandson's attitude at the door this morning."

I shake my head. "I'll stop you right there, Barney. The apology is nice but it's unnecessary."

"Oh?" Barney asks.

I nod. "I've dealt with a lot of convicts with PTSD. Bentley is just a bratty twenty-year-old who's pissed at me for barging into his home. He's a walk in the park compared to them."

He's also a sexy-as-fuck curvy angel with an ass that goes on for days.

Seriously, the boy's sexy hips need to come with a fucking warning sign.

WARNING: *Hotness ahead! Do not proceed unless you have ten fucking inches to pleasure me!*

I COULD BARELY CONTROL the log in my briefs when Bentley snapped at me in the doorway.

I tried to hint that I wanted to "teach him a damn lesson" and "punish him" but I couldn't get too detailed in front of his grandparents.

Bentley's even more fucking hot than in his photographs and I don't know how I'm going to keep my mind off him.

The worst part is that my feelings are *so* much more than sexual attraction.

Bentley's the type of boy you want to bang senseless and then cuddle all night in your tattooed arms.

He's only a brat because it's a defense mechanism and he needs a man to break down his walls.

Can I be the man to break down his walls?

I'm tempted to bark out a laugh but I keep quiet.

A boy like Bentley is the last thing I need right now and it'll only end in flames.

Barney lets out a grunt. "Let's be fucking honest. Bentley's a total brat."

I snort. "A brat?" *Like I didn't know that.*

"Bertha and I spoiled him like hell after the incident," Barney says. "He never learned to respect others who shared different views."

My eyes tick up as my pulse slows. "The incident?"

Barney turns his eyes to me.

"Bentley was only twelve when his parents passed away," Barney confesses at last.

Concern funnels through me. "I'm sorry to hear that."

Barney nods. "Bentley and his parents were... Driving back from a performance of Tchaikovsky's *The Nutcracker* when a man leapt out of an alley and carjacked them."

My jaw drops. "You're kidding."

"No." Barney shakes his head. "Bentley's parents stood up to him but the man pulled out a gun and fired into the car."

"They died?" I ask for clarification.

"Yes," Barney says. "Bentley was in the car with them. He saw everything. We took Bentley in with us after the incident but the damage was done."

Holy shit. "Bentley mentioned that he had an older brother. What happened to him?"

Barney rubs his chin. "Bentley's older brother Jericho took matters into his own hands. Jericho made the carjacker pay the price. He's been paying for it ever since."

"Did Jericho try to kill the carjacker?"

"Yes."

"And that's why Jericho's been locked up in Rikers?" I ask.

"Yes," Barney says. "We only discovered that Jericho was in Rikers two weeks ago. We didn't know where he was before. His court-appointed lawyer dropped the ball after he aged out of juvie. Bentley's still processing this."

"How long has Jericho been in Rikers?"

"Eight years." Barney nods. "It happened on Christmas Eve. The same as you, at least according to what we saw in your file."

Something suddenly shifts in the atmosphere.

I try to take deep breaths to steady myself but I can barely get the air into my lungs.

Jericho's case sounds so familiar to mine and yet... There's no way in hell the two are related.

Christmas Eve.

Men bursting out of an alley.

Two men who defended their family's honor and paid the price.

It must be a coincidence.

I grit my teeth and force myself to stop thinking about this.

This is *not* going to help me get parole.

I have one job on this farm and that's to help Barney and Bertha pull Christmas off without a hitch so I'll be free of the court system forever.

Then I can start my lawsuit.

Bentley's brother doesn't factor into that plan.

Caring too much has only gotten me into trouble in the past.

I refuse to go down that road again.

"This is actually why we invited you here." Barney's voice fills with hope. "We glanced at your file and saw many similarities to Bentley's brother's case."

"How so?"

"Both of you were sent to prison for defending people close to you. Both of your incidents occurred on Christmas Eve. And both of you wanted to avenge your families and protect yourselves from further harm."

Barney stares at me. "We thought that bringing you around Bentley could help Bentley make peace with the part of himself that feels responsible for what happened that night with his brother."

Holy. Fucking. Shit.

This... Is too much.

Barney and Bertha are the first people in eight years to check out the details of my case and try to discover the other side of what happened that fateful night.

But instead of feeling overjoyed that someone finally is interested in the truth, I'm fucking overwhelmed.

I'm not ready to discuss this right now.

Not when my parole is right around the corner.

Not when I have so much at stake.

"Thank you." I force a nod, then set down the power tools that I'm holding. "I appreciate everything you've said, Barney. But I need to process this first."

"It's a little much," Barney barks, staring at me man-to-man. "Is that what you're saying?"

"Yes." I don't mince words. "I respect what you're saying and I'm going to try my best to help Bentley. It won't be easy because it sounds like he hates me. But I want to help him in any way I can. I'm going to head to my room to unpack now but I'll think this over and see how I can break down his walls."

Barney nods. "That's fine, Roman. There's no pressure to talk about this right now. You and Jericho have both been through a lot these past eight years and the last thing I want to do is push you to discuss this before you're ready. Let me know when you're ready to talk."

Jesus Christ.

This just got complicated as fuck.

5

BENTLEY

The next morning

"Good morning, Maw Maw."

I kiss my grandmother's cheek as I step into the kitchen for breakfast.

Maw Maw is making apple cinnamon pancakes which are basically my favorite thing in the entire world.

They're my older brother's favorite breakfast and I never liked them much as a kid but I started eating them after he went to prison.

The apple pancakes are the first thing I ask for now whenever I come back to the farm.

"Good morning, Bentley." My grandmother hands me a mug of steaming hot chocolate with a fresh dollop of whipped cream on the top. "I made special *Yum Yum Cocoa* for your big day today."

"My big day?" I query, my tummy rumbling as I take the hot cocoa in my hands.

Yum.

Maw Maw calls this *Yum Yum Cocoa* for a reason.

It basically makes me feel like a little kid again and it's the yummiest thing in the world.

"Yes." Maw Maw winks at me as she dishes up an extra-large serving of fluffy pancakes for me. "Grandma Harmony tried one of the unicorn cupcakes yesterday and she loved it."

"How did she get a unicorn cupcake?" I groan, sipping my hot chocolate.

"Your friend snuck them into her Tupperware container."

"You're kidding," I groan, taking another big sip of cocoa. "I specifically told Macon to only give her Christmas trees."

"I'm afraid he didn't listen to you," my grandmother says with a laugh. "Mrs. Harmony said the unicorn cupcakes were so delicious she wants to pay you to whip her up an extra batch."

"Macon had no right to give her a unicorn cupcake," I lament, wrinkling my forehead. "I was saving those for a play date next week."

"You can make another batch for your play date, dear." Maw Maw chuckles. "Your friend Preston is coming back next week. You can make some for him."

My jaw drops.

Wait. Hold the phone.

"My childhood best friend... Is coming back from California?" I ask.

Maw Maw smiles. "Yes, sweetie. Preston's world tour ended last month in Chicago. He's coming up to spend Christmas with his grandmother before he heads back to LA."

"You're joking," I say, disbelief rocketing through me.

"I'm not." Maw Maw shakes her head. "We're going to spend Christmas Eve together and have lots of holiday fun."

Anticipation crashes through my chest.

Preston is my closest childhood friend who grew up on the farm next door.

He's the lead singer in the boy band *Wonder Rection* and he has crazy fans all around the world.

He got a record deal from a YouTube video he posted his freshman year in high school and his entire life changed.

We keep in touch every now and then but we only see each other once a year.

It doesn't matter that he's a couple years younger than me because we've always been best friends.

We share everything together, even the fact that we're both littles.

Preston can't tell anyone about his kinky side yet, because his entire career would explode into smithereens if anyone found out that he secretly likes cuddling stuffed animals and sleeping in onesies in his tour van, but he knows he's safe with me.

He also has a raging crush on his bodyguard Sasha — who I'm pretty damn sure is Roman and Aleksei's brother — but this is taboo to discuss because Preston isn't eighteen yet.

Luckily, Preston turns eighteen next month, and he's excited to finally tell Sasha his true feelings.

"I'm so excited," I shout, licking the whipped cream off my hot chocolate. "Preston's so cool. I'm so excited he hasn't forgotten about me. I can't wait to have a playdate with my friend."

Maw Maw dishes me up another pancake. "I'm sure Preston feels the same way, dear. You were always so close growing up, and I'm sure he's just as excited to see you as you are to see him."

I lift my fork to dig into the fresh pancake that my grandmother puts on my plate.

But I've barely jabbed my utensil into the yummy breakfast treat when two loud footsteps thunder into the kitchen.

Roman.

Oh for crying out loud.

This man is... Still here?

I'm preparing to verbally belt Roman with words of fury when something gives me pause.

I glance at Roman and... I completely forget how to breathe.

Roman's muscles bulge in his checkered pajamas and his biceps stretch the fabric of the shirt Maw Maw lent him last night.

His giant pecs mash against the thin fabric and his chiseled jawline is sharp and fierce.

I can barely control the wave of lust that courses through me when I see the enormous bulge in the front of his pajama pants.

Holy. Fucking. Shit.

That's not morning wood... That's just the size of Roman's meat when he's flaccid.

My mouth waters as I stare at Roman's midsection like a whore in church, completely forgetting to eat my breakfast that's cooling in front of me.

Roman turns to face me. "Morning. My eyes are up here, Bentley."

Welp, I'm busted.

But damn, I refuse to give myself away this easily.

I cross my arms over my chest. "I'm not sure what you're still doing here."

Roman lets out a grunt. "Getting breakfast, dumbass."

"Hmmph." I take a sip of my hot chocolate and glare at Roman. "I'm guessing that my grandmother promised you breakfast before she sends you packing."

Maw Maw is cross when she turns around to face me. "For the love of God, Bentley."

"What?" I snap, forcing myself not to look at Roman, who's standing in the middle of the kitchen with a smirk on his face.

"Say good morning to your new house guest," Maw Maw chastises, brandishing her spatula at me. "You were nothing but rude to Roman yesterday and it's time to treat him with respect."

"Come on, Maw Maw," I say, curling my fingers around my mug of cocoa as a bolt of annoyance surges across my gut. "This man shouldn't be here. It's completely unfair and you didn't even ask me if he could come."

"Roman's doing a lot of work for us around the farm," Maw Maw begs. "We're getting up in age and we need Roman to help us run everything this year."

"Why couldn't you have hired someone from the local Home Depot?" I wail, drawing my eyes away from Roman, who's beautiful package just won't stop begging me to stare at it. "This is a beautiful farm and you're both amazing employers. You could get any employee you want to work here."

"It's an employee's market right now, boy." Maw Maw shakes her head back and forth. "Businesses across the country right now are desperate for help. We put out feelers at the local farmer's market but no one was willing to come up to Hickoryville during Christmas."

Damnit.

I should've known my grandmother would swing some made-up BS about a bad labor market back in my face.

I'd bet my entire allowance that she doesn't even know what she's talking about.

Damn Grandmas. Always making up excuses to force you to be nice to the sexy felons they invite home.

"I know this is hard, Bentley," Grandma Bertha says, walking over to me, "but Roman's only here for the next thirty days. He can also help us understand Jericho's situation better before we visit him next month."

"I don't want to learn about Rikers," I pout, crossing my arms over my chest. "Especially not from a man who cheats his way out."

The atmosphere in the room suddenly tenses.

Roman's eyes turn to slits.

"What does that mean?" Roman grits out.

"I said what I said," I say sassily, "and I meant what I meant."

"I went to prison for defending my family's honor, boy," Roman grunts. "I didn't cheat my way out."

Lust feuds with annoyance within me as I stare at Roman's face.

He's seriously the sexiest man I've ever had the misfortune of laying eyes on in my life.

But I refuse to back down, despite the fact that he makes me hornier than a dog in heat.

Roman's lying to me.

Time to confess everything that I learned on my phone call with Macon's partner Aleksei yesterday.

"I know that you got a sweetheart deal from your judge," I say to Roman, sticking my chin up in the air as I ignore his mouth-watering pecs. "I spoke to your brother Aleksei on the phone yesterday with Macon. You come from a filthy rich Russian family who probably has connections to the legal system. Your lawyer was well-connected and probably paid your judge off to give you this opportunity."

Roman cocks an eyebrow at me. "Do you really believe that?"

"Yes." I nod emphatically. "You're related to my friend Macon's fiancé Aleksei, which means that you're a member of one of the most ruthless Russian crime families in the world. You probably bribed your judge to let you off. You don't deserve this work release, Roman. You're a cheat and a liar."

I want to tell Roman that he's basically everything that's wrong with the criminal justice system in this country.

He's the reason that my brother doesn't get a fair shot at

parole and has to tiptoe around bullshit bureaucratic rules to even get a meeting with his lawyer.

Roman's feeding into a system of corruption and that's why he's so odious to me.

"You're so wrong I don't even know where to begin," Roman snaps, helping himself to a mug of hot coffee that my grandmother hands him. "I didn't bribe a judge, moron. You need to ask these questions to my face before gossiping about me behind my back."

That's exactly what a liar would say.

"Me thinks ye doth protest too much," I say, crossing my arms over my chest. "You probably waltzed into your new judge's office and bribed her to let you out." I shake my head in disappointment. "Well, that doesn't fly with me, buddy. Some people work years and years to get a meeting with their judge and they don't have well-connected lawyers to get them off."

"You should be ashamed of yourself," I dish out, trying with everything I have not to stare at Roman's delicious tattoos on his forearms.

Oh my God.

He even has a family crest tattooed on his left bicep beneath two bolts of lightning.

I gulp loudly and press my thighs together so that nobody can see my erection.

Because right now, I'm rock hard.

I never thought that sticking it to a filthy rich gorgeous muscular billionaire would do it for me but apparently, my dick is telling me that this is my new kink.

Just then a tiny adorable puppy bursts into the room and walks over to Roman.

I recognize her at once as the same puppy from yesterday that Roman was holding in his giant hands.

Roman lets out a grunt and scoops the adorable pup into his arms.

"Good morning, Tura Lura," Roman growls in a manly voice, scratching his tiny pup behind the ears with his manly knuckles. "You're the only one who knows the truth around here. Kindly tell this privileged little fuck to do more research before he accuses people of crimes they didn't commit."

"Roman knew you had a problem with nervousness, dear," my grandmother says, petting the dog. "He brought his therapy dog to help you out."

"And?" I snap, trying and failing to ignore the cute dog in Roman's arms.

Damn, Sir.

Is Roman really trying to convince me to like him by cuddling a dog?

I mean, he's not wrong, but this is not the time, man.

I'm way too mad at Roman for stealing opportunities from people like my brother to be swayed by puppies and cuteness.

"Tura Lura's helped quite a few prisoners with PTSD on the inside," Roman barks, his lips tightening in annoyance. "I brought her here to help you with your nervousness relating to the incident with your brother. But you can kindly fuck off."

"If you let Roman stay on the tree farm this month," my grandmother begs, staring pleadingly at me. "He'll let you cuddle Tura Lura to help you with your feelings about your brother. Please give Roman and his puppy a chance. It'll help us get ready to visit Jericho next month."

I stare at the dog.

My heart melts in my chest when I realize for certain that Grandma Bertha only brought Roman here to help me cope with seeing my brother next month.

Ugh. So Roman is kind to animals.

Humph.

Yeah, Roman's hot, and he's good with animals and convicts with PTSD, but he's still corrupt AF and my brother is still suffering because of people like him who feed into a system of corruption.

"I don't care about Roman's adorable dog," I lie, rising from the table as I avoid staring at the Corgi puppy that I just want to cuddle. "No one asked me if I wanted to spend my holidays with the literal embodiment of corruption in the criminal justice system. I apologize for my attitude, Roman, but what your lawyer did is unacceptable. M-My brother—" A breath tears out from my lips. "Forget it. You should've left prison the right way."

"And what is the right way?" Roman growls in a thick Russian accent. "Enlighten me, Bentley." He walks right up next to me and presses his enormous palm against the wall next to my head. "What did you want me to do? Rot in Rikers Island until I die?"

I stare Roman dead in the eyes. "Wait your turn until you finished your sentence like the rest of us. Like the people without fancy lawyers do who can't bribe judges to let them out."

"Come on," I grumble as I exit the kitchen and meet Macon in the hallway, taking my friend's hand. "Let's go get our Tupperware back from Grandma Harmony's house."

"Did she like the unicorn cupcakes I gave her?" Macon asks hopefully.

"Now is not the time," I snap, glaring at my friend.

Sheesh.

Not a damn thing is going my way around here.

6

ROMAN

That afternoon

WHY IS it so hard to expel curvy boys with terrible attitudes from your head?

"Come on, girl," I grunt, beckoning Tura Lura to follow me into the farmhouse.

I had a long ass day today shearing Christmas trees and pruning bushes on the Johnson Christmas tree farm.

Barney showed me how to trim excess branches from trees with shears this morning.

We inserted fertilizer sticks into the soil and prepared sapling trees for winter by covering them with frost-resistant burlap.

We made wreaths and garland from Frasier fir trees by cutting off bows and looping them with wire.

My first wreath looked like a bomb went off in Santa's workshop and sent shards of limbs scattering everywhere.

My second wreath was better but Barney tells me I'm lacking a certain feminine touch.

I thought I had what it took to work on a Christmas tree farm thanks to the giant book I checked out in the Rikers Island prison library but there's still so much I'm shit at.

Who the hell would've known that it was so much work to run a tree farm?

A sigh escapes me as I walk up the driveway and enter through the garage door.

Tura Lura follows me into the house and I guide her to my bedroom next to Bentley's.

After pouring her a bowl of doggy food in the little heart-shaped bowl I keep next to my bed, I strip off my clothes and grab my towel for a shower.

Normally I fight ten men off at every turn in the showers because everyone wants a piece of me but I'm not thinking of that now.

But I'm not thinking of the solitude in the shower I'll enjoy for the first time in eight years.

I can only think of one thing.

"Bentley," I groan, lust smacking me from every direction.

Bratty, beautiful Bentley.

Such a sexy little brat to me this morning.

I sort of figured he'd warm up to me when he saw me today.

I was dead wrong.

Bentley doesn't want me in his farmhouse for a second longer and he was pissed as hell that I was ruining his special breakfast.

"I know that you got a sweetheart deal from your judge."

"Your lawyer probably paid the judge off to give you this opportunity."

Bentley thinks I'm a remorseless criminal who bribed my judge to let me out of prison.

He couldn't be more wrong.

"I didn't bribe a single motherfucker to get out of Rikers," I growl as I dip my head beneath the stream, hot water scalding my back. "I got out fair and square. It's not illegal to hire a lawyer who knows how to look for opportunities that other lawyers miss."

It's true.

I didn't do anything illegal to spring myself out of Rikers.

My lawyer specializes in getting wealthy criminals out of prison and a big part of his job is finding avenues for work release that other lawyers overlook.

It sucks that Bentley's brother wasn't afforded the same opportunities but I didn't do anything wrong.

My lawyer is merely savvy and he found a loophole to get me out on work release.

But Bentley had one less-than-informative conversation with my brother -- who's apparently intertwined with Bentley's friend Macon -- and now he's convinced that I cheated my way out.

Bentley fucking hates me.

He'd beat me up if my muscles weren't so huge and enormous.

I know I must force myself to remember the wisdom I acquired in the prison library when I had hours and hours to myself (it was actually quite nice to have so much free time to read.)

Dogs bark at what they don't understand — Heraclitus

Like a dog that barks at the mailman, Bentley is reacting to my presence out of fear because he doesn't understand the true reason why I'm at his house.

My giant uncut Russian cock rises between my legs.

I glance down and groan as my foreskin retracts and gives way to the shiny head that I only want to bury inside Bentley.

"Oh sweet Jesus," I groan, clenching my fingers in a tight fist and ramming my giant man meat through them.

I've been celibate for nearly a decade.

The men in Rikers didn't have what I was looking for.

I wasn't into giant hairy bears or stick-thin meth twinks looking for their next fix.

They accosted me in the showers and tried to get me to have dirty sex with them but I was never interested.

I like curvy boys.

Beautiful angels with thick juicy hips and asses that don't quit.

I need a man with meat on his bones, someone with sexy love handles that I can grab as I ram myself into him over and over again.

Someone I can spoil with delicious treats and then bring to the heights of pleasure in my bedroom.

I want to buy Bentley every delicious treat known to man and watch him lose himself as he eats every bite.

I'm not a feeder — that's horrible — but I want my partner to feel comfortable enough to be their true self around me.

I want to adore every inch of Bentley's curves and tell him there's nothing wrong with having thick sexy thighs.

Bentley's beautiful and curvy and thick in all the right places.

Bentley's my dream boy come to life, and every inch of his body begs to be dominated by me.

I saw the tent in his pajamas as he stormed out of the kitchen to meet his friend Macon and the way he tried to hide his erection by tucking his thing into his waistband as he passed me.

Bentley can only hide himself from me for so long.

I'm a ferocious beast who's been deprived of the objects of my lust for eight long years.

I shouldn't think of Bentley in this way because I need to avoid him at all costs.

But I can't stop myself.

A groan escapes me as I cup my giant shaft in my palms, wrapping my firm fingers around my meat.

My dick is ten inches, and I strangle every inch as I grit my teeth and think of Bentley.

I picture beautiful thick Bentley in this shower with me, his sexy curves on full display as I press him against the tile walls.

"That's right, boy," I growl in my fantasy, squirting soap into my hands and rubbing suds all over Bentley's backside. "You've been such a naughty boy. Daddy's going to teach you a lesson, boy. He's going to spank those perfect curves and teach you how to behave."

Bentley clenches against my fingers. "Yes, Daddy! I was so naughty to you and I need you to turn me into a good boy!"

"Damn right." A growl tears out of me as I smack Bentley's thick ass, bringing my palm down hard on his right cheek and leaving a mark. "You deserve a fucking spanking for taunting me in your grand-mother's kitchen, boy. I wanted to slam you on the kitchen table and take you in front of that sweet little old lady. A twenty-year-old boy like you can't strut those hips in front of a grown man who hasn't seen a boy with curves in eight long years."

"I only did it because I want you inside me, Daddy!" Bentley spreads his cheeks and presses his forehead against the tiles. "I'm naughty because I want you so bad! Teach me how to be good, Daddy!"

A deep growl sits on my lips as I grip Bentley's firm hips and tease his opening with my dick.

My cock head brushes against his soaped-up hole and I groan when Bentley wiggles his cheeks against my shaft.

A bolt of inexorable passion claims me as I rut my tip against Bentley's opening, unable to stop or slow down.

The waves of need that Bentley stirs within me hit me deep in my loins.

I've been locked up for eight long years and I've been dreaming of a man like Bentley every moment of my incarceration.

I'm an addict who finally has his fix in front of him on a silver platter within these bathroom walls.

How could I control myself even if I wanted to?

My vision blurs as I spear Bentley's walls with my giant cock, burrowing myself deep into his sexy tight hole.

Bentley's curvy perfection opens for my dick, and he whimpers as I impale his channel.

His defenses fall to the wayside as I pin him down with my manly palms under the hot shower, flattening myself against his sexy cheeks as I jam my cock even deeper into his body, so desperate to access the wells of pleasure he stores for me inside.

I push harder against Bentley's natural defenses, and a deep cry of pleasure bursts out of Bentley's lips when I finally press down hard against his spot.

"Oh Daddy," Bentley cries, pinching his walls around my cock and grinding hard. "You're hitting it, Daddy. I've never been able to fit something inside there before but you're getting it inside!"

"Damn right I am, boy. This is Daddy's hole from now on."

I slam Bentley's curvy hips against the tile, the need to dominate and possess every inch of his perfect body welling up inside me.

I crush my lips against his silky smooth neck, sweat beading on my forehead as I stroke harder and harder inside his channel walls, my mushroom head grinding against his pleasure points, flames of need ravishing me.

Bentley bites down hard on my thumb as I buck into him even harder, and he whines and flexes his asshole around my cock as he gives himself over to pure unadulterated need.

"I-It's happening, Daddy!" Bentley screams at the top of his lungs, pressing his palms against the tile as he trembles before me. "I'm all yours, Daddy!"

I plunge into Bentley with wild abandon, thrusting my dick into his private parts like a fucking caveman.

Pleasure clamps down on my throat and a series of unintelligible grunts escapes me as I bulldoze Bentley's tight virginal walls.

Bentley spreads even further for me and his crazed screams let me know that I'm about to take him over the edge.

"Oh Daddy!" Bentley whines, staring down at his cock between his legs that's spurting shot after shot all over the shower. "Look what you did to me, Daddy! You're making me spurt!"

"Damn right I did, boy," I roar, tearing my dick out of Bentley's ass and forcing my angel to his knees.

I thrust my fingers through Bentley's hair, ramming his jaw up as I smear my cock against his lips.

I prod his wet mouth with my giant erection, nearly losing control when my enormous man meat dirties his pristine lips.

Bright blue eyes stare up at me.

Oh sweet Jesus.

This is what Apollo felt when he held Hyacinthus in his arms.

This is what Zeus felt when he threw the maids out of his Olympian mansion and took Ganymede in the middle of the hall.

I nearly cream all over Bentley's face as I stare into those perfect sapphire eyes, my heart tumbling to my feet below.

That's when Bentley says something that surprises me.

He opens his mouth and sticks out his tongue.

"Messy, Daddy." Bentley licks my tip with his tongue. "I'm a messy boy for you tonight. Do what you'd do to me in Rikers Island."

The temptation is too much to bear and I roar with primal adrenaline.

A carnivorous moan escapes me as I blast my seed all over Bentley's parched lips, gluttonous grunts ushering out of me as my hardness juts out shot after shot onto Bentley's mouth.

Hot white come smears across Bentley's cheeks, and Bentley whimpers as he rubs my seed into his skin.

I slam my fist into the tile behind Bentley's head and cause the bathroom to quake as Bentley licks my come from his face.

His eyelashes bat at me when I finish spurting.

"You did it, Daddy," Bentley moans, licking my shaft over and over again. "You treated me like only a big protective man can. You weren't scared of my beautiful curves at all. You're my everything."

I reach a new plane of existence as Bentley's words wash over me.

Scooping Bentley into my tattooed arms, I crush my lips against his, a desperate grunt escaping me as I pierce his mouth with my tongue, the need to kiss him overwhelming.

Passion overflows in my chest as our mouths mate in spiritual union.

My boy. My angel.

Bentley's full of rainbows and curvy perfection and he's what I've been looking for my entire life.

As I drain the hot water from the basin and clean my load off the shower walls, I can't help but think how fucking dangerous this is.

The fantasy was amazing but I can't let it happen again.

Bentley's a ticking time bomb and even if he's a sexy fuck, I must focus on my work release.

Acting on my attraction to Bentley will fuck my work release plan right in the ass.

I'll be damned to hell if I head back to Rikers Island.

The next morning

WELP. That was interesting.

"Argh," I groan, prying myself out of bed and walking over to my dresser.

I had the most interesting night I've had in a *long time* last night.

Macon and I had a sleepover in my room because Aleksei was delayed in his commute up to the farm.

We shared a bed and played a cool game with my favorite reindeer stuffy named Señor Antlers and Macon's unicorn stuffy Mr. Rainbow.

But halfway through the game, I heard an odd noise emanating from the bathroom.

It sounded like a bunch of grunts and groans coming through the pipes like a ghost was in the house or someone was dying.

I told Macon I was going to check it out and walked into my bathroom to listen.

The noises were coming from the room next door and they were only getting louder and growlier.

I remembered that my brother and I used to have a secret hole in the wall where we talked to each other after we were supposed to have gone to bed and curiosity got the best of me.

I popped the secret lid of the hole off and poked my eye against the wall.

Holy. Fucking. Abs.

I figured that the noises were probably coming from Roman but never in a million years did I anticipate seeing what he was doing in the shower.

Roman was having a pleasure shower in the place where my brother and I used to bathe together when we came home for Christmas vacation.

The man was going at it like he hadn't touched himself in years.

Ripped muscles and glistening tattoos bulged in all the right places as Roman beat his meat.

His enormous frame jutted and jolted as he furiously pounded his clenched fist and let out unintelligible garbles.

My cock rose like nothing else in my snowman pajamas and I couldn't stop myself from slipping my hands into my undies and stroking my cock.

I jerked myself off as I watched this huge specimen of a man pleasure himself in front of me, forbidden lust circling through my veins.

Then a giant shadow suddenly blocked out the hole and scared the hell out of me.

I yanked my hand out of my pajama bottoms and sprinted back to the bed with Macon before Roman could catch me.

Sheesh.

I didn't plan on spying on Roman because I seriously hate the guy.

But I didn't realize he was *so fucking hot* while jerking off.

It was seriously like he hadn't touched himself the entire time he was locked up in Rikers Island and was just getting a chance to blow his load.

What was Roman thinking about while he masturbated?

Was Roman thinking about someone that he met back in prison who was super hot?

Did Roman have a prison wife behind bars who serviced him when the wardens weren't looking?

Or was he thinking about me?

It was a mystery that plagued my dreams when I fell asleep.

I woke up with a giant puddle of wetness in my special sleepytime snowman pajamas.

I guess wet dreams are the body's natural way to finish fantasizing about what you couldn't during the day.

"Hey, Bentley." Macon yawns and stretches his limbs in the bed beside me, cuddling his unicorn stuffy under his arms.

"Hey, Macon."

"Did you have a good sleep?" Macon asks, turning to face me, a smile on his face as he brushes a strand of blond hair from his forehead.

"Yes," I say, letting out a snort as I roll over and face my friend. "I dreamt about someone who's supposed to be totally off limits to me. Someone I've vowed to hate for the next four weeks."

"Ugh," Macon says with a laugh, shaking his head in amusement as he props himself up on one elbow. "Let me guess, you had a dirty dream about your Paw Paw. Well, I hate to say it, Bentley, but sometimes incest dreams indicate that you're stressed, so you'd better light some incense before you go back to sleep."

Uhhhhm.

This fool really thinks I had a wet dream about my grandfather?

Somebody call WWE, because this boy needs a smack down.

"You're disgusting," I say matter-of-factly, picking up Señor Antlers and smacking Macon over the head. "You watch way too much porn and you need to get your head out of the gutter."

"Liar," Macon drawls, poking my arm. "You were totally thinking about your Paw Paw. Don't hate me because I'm the messenger, Bentley. I've been through way too much fucked up shit in my life to ever judge you for that."

"It wasn't Paw Paw," I snap, adjusting my pajama bottoms and rearranging *the thing between my thighs* as thoughts of Roman fill my mind. "It was a secret stranger, and I'd rather you not mention it ever again because I've already vowed never to speak to this person again in my life."

Also, I totally shouldn't have been spying on Roman, which would probably give him grounds to report me to my grandparents.

I'd much rather let sleeping dogs lie than deal with a lecture over watching a felon beat his meat.

Macon pokes my thigh with his index finger through my pajama bottoms. "It was totally your grandfather. Who else could get you this hard?"

"You're the worst," I drawl, turning away from my friend. "I'll tell you about it when we go bring a fresh batch of unicorn cupcakes to Grandma Harmony this afternoon."

"I thought she only ate Christmas tree cupcakes," Macon says, withdrawing his hand and slipping it into his own pajama bottoms and jerking his own shaft. "At least that's what you been giving me shit about all week."

I roll my eyes. "Apparently I was wrong. I guess there are little old ladies who like unicorns just as much as you."

"Come on," I drawl, prying myself off the bed and pulling Macon's hand out of his pajamas. "Stop being a pervert and help me bring some holiday cheer to a little old lady."

"Grandma Harmony!"

A smile washes over my features as I enter Grandma Harmony's kitchen with a bag of treats.

I'm so happy to see my childhood friend's grandmother who I always visit whenever I come to the farm during Christmas.

She's a sweet old lady with gray hair who loves to bake reindeer cookies and she has a true heart of gold.

She helped give her grandson Preston a place to stay when his parents were going through a messy divorce when he was nine and she always treats me like family.

Grandma Harmony welcomes Macon and I into her kitchen. "Hi, Bentley boy. It's so nice to see you this holiday season."

I let out a snort. "We just saw each other the other day, Grandma Harmony. We're here to drop off another batch of those unicorn cupcakes that you loved so much."

Macon lets out a groan. "I'm the one who came up with the idea for the unicorn cupcakes, buddy. If you're going to tell her about them, you at least have to give me credit."

"Come here, bud." Grandma Harmony buries Macon in a hug. "I figured that Bentley had a little friend who helped him out with the treats. He couldn't have come up with those delicious unicorn cupcakes on his own."

I put my hands on my hips. "Well, that's not very nice, bitch."

"It's the truth," Macon drawls.

"I'm very creative when I put my mind to it," I snap, giving Macon the bird.

Grandma Harmony rolls her eyes. "You bring me Christmas tree cupcakes every year, dearie. I was just thinking to myself, *Gosh, Bentley's baked goods are always so delicious, but he needs to switch it up every now and then. Not every little old lady likes Christmas cupcakes during the holidays. Maybe he could bring me a cookie shaped like a teddy bear.*"

Macon nudges my ribs with his elbow. "See?" he gloats. "Grandma Harmony is obviously very open-minded and doesn't mind deviating from the norm."

"It's not that I don't mind deviating from the norm, Macon," Grandma Harmony says. "I love breaking barriers whenever I can. My grandson Preston is a testament to the fact that I welcome diversity in every form."

"What do you mean?" Macon asks Grandma Harmony as she leads us into the kitchen where she sets two steaming mugs of hot cocoa on the table.

"My grandson isn't exactly normal, but I accept him for who he is inside," she explains. "He's quite kinky, you know."

Macon snorts out a laugh. "Did you just call your grandson kinky?"

"Yes." Grandma Harmony doesn't miss a beat. "He likes to cuddle with stuffies and suck on pacifiers to chill out after shows. Kinky is the most apt descriptor of his personality."

"You'll see that for yourself when Preston comes up here next week," Grandma Harmony says with a smile. "He wrapped up the last leg of his world tour in Chicago this past weekend. He'll be here as soon as he finishes sleeping his tiredness off."

I nearly squeal in anticipation of seeing my friend.

"I'm so excited!" I gush at last, shaking my head in disbelief. "It's been two whole years since I've seen Preston last. I can't wait to play with him."

"You don't see him often?" Macon asks, taking a sip of cocoa.

"Nope," I say, shaking my head. "My childhood BFF is always traveling the world or chilling with his bandmates in LA. We text pretty frequently but it's been a while since I've seen him in person."

"That's so sweet," Macon gushes. "It sounds like you really value his friendship."

"I do," I say, nodding eagerly. "It's super important to me to maintain my friendship with Preston. It doesn't matter that he's a world-famous singer who's always gracing the covers of tabloid magazines. He's still my BFF from the farm."

"You nailed it, Bentley." Grandma Harmony flips her phone around to show Macon and I a text. "Preston sent me this text this morning and told me to show you."

I scoot across the room on my chair and read the text message.

PRESTON: Damn, Bentley! It's been so long since I saw you last. Have you found a Daddy yet at Cornell? I can't wait to catch up with you when I get home next week. My grandmother's done nothing but brag about your unicorn cupcakes so I expect to see a fresh batch waiting on the steps when I get back ;)

LOL.

Looks like being a world-famous celebrity hasn't changed my childhood friend a bit.

"I'm so glad Preston wants to see me," I gush, my heart melting.

"Preston can't be his true self when he's on the road," Grandma Harmony says, shaking her head. "That's why he wants to see you so badly."

"What do you mean?" Macon asks.

"Preston's bandmates know that he's a little," Grandma Harmony explains, "but they never want to play with him."

"Oh." Macon furrows his brow. "That's not cool."

"That's why Preston loves Bentley," Grandma Harmony continues. "Bentley's one of Preston's only friends who knows about his little side and won't spill the beans to the media. He can be his true self around Bentley and not worry about being judged."

Macon lets out a snort. "And it's not weird or anything that you know about Preston's little side too?"

Grandma Harmony cocks an eyebrow at Macon. "Why?"

"I'd feel pretty weird if my grandmother knew I was into age play kink," Macon says, taking another sip of hot chocolate.

"Not me, dear." Grandma Harmony lets out a laugh. "I accept my grandson for who he is. Preston's still my little boy inside, and he needs a place where he feels safe and comfortable to be who he is. I'd never turn him away because of who he is."

I turn to Grandma Harmony. "Has Preston told you anything else about Sasha yet?"

Grandma Harmony chuckles. "No, dear. He keeps that to himself."

"Who's Sasha again?" Macon asks.

"Sasha is Preston's bodyguard," I drawl, sipping cocoa. "Preston's been obsessed with Sasha ever since Sasha started protecting Preston last year. Preston was going to rescue a monkey on Sunset Boulevard and Sasha beat up a paparazzo taking pictures of him. It was basically a whole thing."

"Why is it a problem?" Macon asks.

"Preston's still seventeen," I explain, exhaling a breath. "He refuses to make a move on Sasha until he turns eighteen in one month. Preston knows that it could mess everything up and

Sasha would have to quit being his bodyguard and he doesn't want that."

Macon chuckles. "It sounds complicated."

"It is," Grandma Harmony says earnestly. "But Preston knows that he needs to wait until next month when he turns eighteen to confess his true feelings to Sasha and I'm so proud of him for thinking this through. That's the only way this will be acceptable."

I turn back to Grandma Harmony. "Thank you so much for inviting us over again today."

"For sure, Bentley." Grandma Harmony grins. "You're welcome to swing by the farm anytime."

"I'm glad you like the unicorn cupcakes," Macon sing-songs, winking at Grandma Harmony. "I'd be happy to bring more over anytime."

Grandma Harmony laughs. "I'll enjoy them, dear. I can't wait for Preston to see them when he flies in from California."

8

BENTLEY

Two hours later

I'M LUBING up my bike chain with WD-40 after my visit to Grandma Harmony when I get the text.

MAW MAW: This is Roman. Your grandfather ordered me to spend the day with you. I'm going to meet you in the garage this afternoon so we can cut down a Christmas tree.

"OH HELL NO," I groan, nearly dropping my phone onto the closest workbench.

Paw Paw wants Roman... To spend the day with me?

To *spend hours* with the man I've vowed to avoid at all costs?

For crying out loud, I only stopped home to fill up my bike tires and get something to eat before Aleksei arrives this afternoon.

I wanted to eat some cookies and read on my Kindle Oasis on a hill I like to go to and spend the afternoon lost in thought.

But apparently my grandfather wants me to spend the afternoon with my forbidden object of lust instead.

Oh. Hell. No.

I hear his voice before I see him.

"Hey, Bentley."

I let out a groan as Roman walks over to me. "Look," I say preemptively, already dreading confronting this man. "I know what my grandfather told you, buddy, but forget it. I just got back from a visit to a neighbor and I'm going on a bike ride this afternoon. Cutting down a Christmas tree right now isn't in the plans."

Roman lets out a snort. "It's not my fault your grandparents signed us up for an afternoon of activities together."

I raise my eyes up from the can of WD-40 I'm using to lube up my bike chain and try not to think about Roman beating off his ten-inch dick in the shower. "Forget it, bud. I'm going on a bike ride."

"I'm taking you to cut down your Christmas tree," Roman grunts, shoving his fists in his pocket. "Believe me, I wasn't thrilled to get the news from your grandfather either."

The fiercest wave of annoyance I've ever experienced crashes through me.

I drop the can of WD-40 on the ground and turn around to face Roman with my hands on my hips.

"Like *hell* you are," I groan, sticking my hips out to the side and scorching Roman with a menacing glare. "Cutting down the Christmas tree is something *I* do with Paw Paw every year."

"You're not invited," I say, whipping around to show Roman that that's the end of this conversation.

Well, that was easy.

I imagine he'll leave me alone and stop teasing me with those giant pecs and menacing tattoos now.

"You won't shake me that easily." Roman props himself up against the garage wall next to me, his firm muscles bulging out of his checkered shirt as he crosses his arms over his chest. "Your grandfather gave me explicit instructions to cut down this tree with you. I'd be going against the terms of my work agreement if I disobeyed him."

"I find that hard to believe," I say.

"I'm serious." Roman nods. "Your grandfather said his back hurts too much to cut down a tree this year. That's why he needs me to cut it down and bring it back to the house with you. Then you and he can bond while decorating it."

"I'm sorry. I'm booked all afternoon."

"Booked?" Roman cocks an eyebrow at me. "How can you be booked when there's literally nothing to do around here?"

Oh hell no.

Does this man not know there are a million things to do in Hickoryville?

Like skinny dipping or suntanning by the lake.

Oh wait... I forgot it's not summer.

"This," I say, snagging my canvas backpack from the floor and fumbling in the biggest pocket for my trusty e-reader, "is my Kindle Oasis. I'm going on a bike ride to read on my Kindle before the first snowfall comes. It's why I'm booked and can't accompany you."

"Kindle Oasis?" Roman grunts.

"I have a Kindle because I love to read," I explain. "I read constantly in between my classes at Cornell University. Reading is a pastime of mine and an amazing stress relief. It's what I'll be doing this afternoon alone, thank you very much."

Roman sighs. "I know what a Kindle is, dumbass."

"You said you didn't," I say, thrusting the device in front of Roman's eyes. "You need to get your story straight."

Roman snatches the device from my hand. "I've been locked up in federal prison for the past eight years, bud. I was around when the Kindle came out. But I've never heard of a Kindle *Oasis*."

"And besides," Roman continues, "we didn't have electronic reading devices in prison. We only had real books. Thick ass paperbacks you could take out from the prison library."

Oops.

I guess I forgot that you can't exactly keep up with technological advancements behind bars.

"You should still know what a Kindle Oasis is," I dish out, crossing my arms over my chest. "It's kind of the best invention of the twenty-first century."

"I don't need to," Roman counters. "I have real books."

I roll my eyes. "That's mildly offensive to us members of the e-reader community."

"I'm serious," Roman says. "I read tomes of Russian literature in prison. That's the only thing that distracts me from life."

"Mmhm." I sigh. "What kind of books did you read?"

"Tolstoy, Dostoyevsky, Nabokov, and Chekhov's shorts. Also Propertius' love elegies and Ovid's *Amores*. I checked them out at the prison library."

"I had no use for a..." Roman clears his throat as he taps the device in his hands. "What is it called again?"

"A Kindle Oasis," I snap, reaching out and making a grabby motion with my fingers. "It's Amazon's premium reading device that allows you to download books from the cloud. It's the best thing anyone's ever invented and I find it extremely hard to believe that you've never heard of it."

"I'm not convinced." Roman jerks the Kindle away from me

and flips open my leather case. "What the fuck is the cloud? I don't think you know what you're talking about."

It takes everything in me not to snort.

Seriously?

This man doesn't know what the cloud is?

I sit my ass on the closest workbench. "I wasn't born yesterday, buddy. We both know damn well that you know what the cloud is. You can stop pretending to be technologically illiterate now."

"I really don't know what it is." Roman shrugs.

"They definitely have *the cloud* in prison."

"Not that I'm aware of."

"It's more isolating inside the prison than you think, Bentley," Roman explains as he returns my precious Kindle to me. "Some prisons may have access to the cloud — whatever the hell that is — but Rikers is different. We're the most underfunded and overcrowded prison in the USA."

"Whatever."

"I'm serious." Roman glares at me. "We don't get much of anything inside. We have access to TV Friday and Saturday nights if we don't murder anyone in the lunchroom during the week. We have access to the library and the outside gym where we can go one hour a day to breathe fresh air. But we spend the rest of the time in Rikers by ourselves in the common areas or in our cells. Rikers is one of the most overcrowded prisons in the world and we're completely cut off from modern technology as a result of underfunding. So no, I don't know what the fucking cloud is, little brat. You'd better watch your fucking mouth around me."

I snatch my Kindle out of Roman's outstretched hand and stow it away in my backpack.

"I still think you're full of it," I say. "But I'm probably not going to get the truth out of you anyway since you're a convict and all, so I'll just let it go."

"Quit being a brat," Roman growls. "I'm telling you the truth."

"I'm not a brat," I retort, sticking my nose in the air and glaring at Roman. "I'm a merely poking holes in your fabricated story because you're messing with me."

Come on.

It's 2021.

Everyone knows what the cloud is.

Even Grandpa Barney uploads his phone pictures to the cloud.

Anyone who doesn't is just faking it for attention.

"With this attitude, I'm going to throw you over that work-bench and give you a spanking," Roman says at last, a vein throbbing in his forehead. "Keep mouthing off to me and you'll get what you deserve."

"Mmmmhm." I roll my eyes. "We both know you can't lay a finger on me."

"Why not?"

"You'll get sent back to prison and you won't be eligible for parole in January."

"Goddamnit."

"That's right." I blow Roman a kiss. "You'd better watch *your* mouth around me."

"Maybe I'll murder you and feed your body to Tura Lura."

"You wouldn't dare."

"They didn't call me *El Malo* in prison for nothing."

Roman presses his fingers to his temples. "Are you coming to cut this Christmas tree down with me or not?"

"I'm not."

Roman lets out a growl. "Your grandfather's going to kill you."

"Let him try." I check my nails. "He should've thought about that before he invited you here without consulting me. Chopping down our annual Christmas tree together is *our* tradition, not yours. You have no right to butt in."

"Brat." Roman brings his massive fingers to his chin and ponders something. "If you come with me to cut down this Christmas tree, I'll let you play with Tura Lura tomorrow."

Hmmm.

The offer is tempting.

I glare at Roman. "As if I'm going to be swayed by a cute puppy."

"I mean it." Roman nods. "You can play with her all day tomorrow. I won't even come to check on her once. She'll help you with your anxiety."

Hmmmph.

Okay, well, I do like dogs.

"Fine," I agree, ramming my hands in my pockets. "I'll go with you. But don't think we'll become friends just because we're spending time together today."

"I wouldn't dream of it."

"And I want a helluva lot more than one measly afternoon with Tura Lura," I continue, zipping up my backpack and pushing it to the far side of the workbench. "I'm a very troubled boy with nervousness problems and I have lots of issues with feeling abandoned. If you let me bond with your dog and then yank her away from me the next morning, there'll be hell to pay."

"I wouldn't dream of it."

Roman stares straight into my eyes. "Tura Lura and I helped convicted murderers get over their issues with PTSD. We're not going to let you down."

A grunt escapes Roman as he stomps out of the garage.

My eyes widen as I watch him march out into the trees with a giant chainsaw on his back, like an enormous lumberjack.

A flutter of something I can't quite place surges through me.

Hmmm.

Well, this is certainly interesting.

But I'm not going to let it sway me.

I'll give Roman one tiny itty-bitty chance this afternoon, then I'm going straight back to the sassy little bitch I've always been.

Roman might have a nice side, but he's still a corrupt SOB who bribed his judge to get out of prison, and he's ruining my Christmas.

9

ROMAN

"HERE YOU GO, BENTLEY."

I hand Bentley the smoking chainsaw as I gesture for him to stand back.

"Timber," Bentley bellows as the enormous Douglas fir tree that I just finished sawing down comes crashing down and thuds on the barren ground with a smack.

Bentley yelps as a cloud of dust assaults him in the face.

"Jesus, Roman," Bentley shouts, coughing wildly as he spits out dirt.

"What?" I grunt, brushing a pine needle from my flannel.

I savor the site of Bentley getting what he deserves after being such a brat to me in the garage.

Bentley lets out a whooping cough. "Are you trying to freaking kill me?" He bangs his chest with his fists. "This is dangerous. Grandpa Barney never would've done it this way."

"Your grandfather isn't here right now."

"This is seriously a breach of protocol," Bentley says, sneezing wildly as he waves his hands in the air in front of him. "I agreed to help you cut down a Christmas tree, not give myself whooping cough."

Uhh.

Well, I guess a near-death experience isn't enough to banish the brat out of Bentley after all.

"You're being dramatic." I walk over to Bentley. "It's just a little dust."

"You're giving me asthma."

"You've done this before with your grandfather a million times," I say. "You should've known what you were getting into."

"Grandpa never cut down trees without giving me a safety mask first," Bentley shouts, tossing the chainsaw on the ground. "You nearly killed me. You should be ashamed of yourself."

"For what?"

"I have very sensitive lungs. You could be giving me a respiratory infection."

I let out a groan. "You could've grabbed a fucking safety mask when we were in your garage, Bentley. You're not helpless."

"Grandpa always does that for me."

"Well, I'm not your grandpa. I'm an ex-convict who you should be thanking for doing all the grunt work while cutting down this tree."

"Respiratory infections are no laughing matter. I should report you to the Rikers Island police."

"You're so annoying."

"Well you should've researched how to cut down a Christmas tree before you attempted to do it," Bentley shouts, glaring at me. "You've been locked up in Rikers Island for the past eight years. What the hell do you know about this? How do you know I won't get an incurable lung disease?"

Ahh.

This couldn't have come at a more opportune time.

"I know more than you think," I growl, staring straight into Bentley's eyes.

"Enlighten me," Bentley spits out.

I smirk. "There was actually a giant book on Christmas trees that I checked out of the prison library two weeks before I came here."

"Sure."

"There was," I say. "I read the whole thing front to back. I learned all about the different varieties of Christmas trees."

"Mmmhm." Bentley crosses his arms over his chest. "Well then I bet you wouldn't mind taking a little pop quiz."

Uhh oh.

Pop quiz?

I didn't sign up for that.

"Fine." I cross my arms over my chest. "Quiz me. I'm sure I'll pass with flying colors."

Bentley chuckles. "Okay. How many types of Christmas trees are there in the United States?"

Ahh. I got lucky.

"Sixteen," I say without pause. "Sixteen common varieties, that is. Although most people just go with whatever type is on the lot at the local Home Depot."

Bentley rolls his eyes. "What are the most common trees?"

"The Douglas fir, the Frasier fir, and the Balsam fir tree," I retort, rolling my eyes.

Duh. Everyone knows that.

"Name the most common type," Bentley demands sassily, putting his hands on his hips.

Phew.

Thank fuck I skimmed this chapter right before I left Rikers.

"The Balsam fir," I say proudly. "Also known as the *abies balsamea* in Latin. It's the most widely sold Christmas tree in the United States."

"What are its characteristics?"

"It has hints of silvery white and it's frequently used for

wreaths. It has an amazing Christmasy scent and it's small enough to stand inside people's homes."

"Hmm." Bentley mulls this, then shrugs. "You passed the first test."

"Of course I did."

"Don't get so cocky," Bentley snaps. "What's the second most popular variety? And what's its Latin name?"

"The Frasier fir," I say smugly, nodding at Bentley. "Also known as the *abies fraser*. It's a yellow-green fir tree that's extra sturdy and is the type of Christmas tree you want if you have lots of heavy angel decorations to hang on it. It's amazing for garland to spread around your mantel or fireplace during the holiday season."

Bentley rolls his eyes. "What are its drawbacks?"

"It can grow up to seventy feet tall so you'd better make sure you have lofty ceilings."

"Okay, buddy," Bentley snaps. "If those two are the most common trees, then why did we go with this Douglas fir? Why not a Frasier or a Balsam?"

Ahh.

Time to let my knowledge shine.

I smirk. "The Douglas fir tree is the ultimate statement tree," I explain, placing my steel-toed boot on the brown trunk. "The *pseudotsuga menziesii* is enormous and has the best Christmasy scent of all the fir trees. A full-grown Douglas can range anywhere from two-hundred feet to over five-hundred feet tall and they account for nearly three-quarters of all Christmas trees grown during the holiday season. The annual Christmas and New Years celebrations in New York use Douglas fir trees shipped in from Nova Scotia because they're the best in the northern hemisphere."

"Why does my grandfather want one?"

"Your grandfather wants to put this tree smack in the middle of the driveway to show off to all the visitors who stop by when you open up shop in two weeks," I explain. "The *pseudotsuga menziesii* is the type of tree that will astound his clientele."

Bentley taps his foot impatiently on the ground.

"Well," Bentley huffs after a spell, checking his nails. "You're not *completely* illiterate in the ways of Christmas tree farmers. But you're still completely overlooking the most important thing of all."

I roll my eyes up to the sky. "What's that?"

"How the hell are we supposed to get this tree back to the farmhouse?!" Bentley shouts, shooting me a death glare. "That's the most critical part of Christmas tree farming, bozo. When my grandfather and I come here, we always pick a tree we can both lug back to the farmhouse on a sleigh. Sometimes we even call our neighbor Mrs. Harmony who has a horse-drawn carriage to help us out. But you didn't even think to bring a sleigh before you chopped this sucker down."

"I'll chop you down if you don't quit mouthing off to me, boy."

"You didn't even think about the logistics of tree transportation," Bentley roars, stomping his little angel feet on the ground. "You just walked up and grunted, *Let's chop down this giant tree and someone else will figure it out.* That's the fucking problem with people like you. You don't think about how your actions affect others. It's no different than how you got that bullshit sweetheart deal to come up here in the first place."

Mmmh.

Well, now I know what this attitude is all about.

"Okay, Bentley. Calm down."

"Don't tell me to calm down," Bentley snaps.

"Grab the trunk of the tree so we can get to the farmhouse and get you some warm cinnamon milk," I say.

Bentley glares at me. "I don't drink milk."

"Drop the attitude and help me with this tree."

"You chopped it down, you carry it back. Those are the rules."

I glare at Bentley. "It's too heavy for one person."

"You should've thought of that before you cut it down."

"Come on, boy."

"I can't," Bentley says. "I'll hurt my nails."

I roll my eyes. "You don't even have nails. You're just saying that to get out of doing any work."

"Fine," Bentley says, sticking his middle finger up at me — which is entirely devoid of polish, as I suspected. "But I still won't help you cart the Christmas tree back to the farmhouse."

"Why not?"

"I'm deathly allergic to working out."

I let out a groan. "Quit being annoying."

"I'm serious." Bentley sticks his backside out and wiggles his ass to tempt me. "I'm a thick boy, Roman. Lugging this tree to the farmhouse is too much cardio for me. I'll burn too many calories. I need these curves to ward off men."

Holy. Fucking. Shit.

Lust pounds me as I drink in the sight of Bentley's curves.

What the hell? Is it even possible to be this sexy?

I picture spreading Bentley's cheeks and diving into his juicy ass.

I want to pound every delicious inch of that buffet and then bring him to the heights of pleasure.

"Ward off men?" I ask in a warbling voice. "Don't you mean... *Attract* them?"

"Nope." Bentley's voice is sharp. "I have zero interest in men harassing me for dates. If I stay thick, I can avoid that conversation before it even happens."

I let out a groan as visions of Bentley's *curvy perfection* flash through my mind.

Holy shit.

Bentley's... Insecure about his body.

He makes self-deprecating jokes to hide that fact.

Has Bentley... Ever even been with a man?

Or has he been saving those juicy curves for the right man who knows what to do with them?

"Forget it," I grunt, squatting next to the tree as I suddenly realize what I must do.

"Forget what?" Bentley asks.

"Don't help me carry the tree," I snap, securing the trunk in my giant palms. "I'll do it myself and you can head back to the farmhouse and get some fresh cookies and hot chocolate."

"You say that like it's a bad thing."

"It's whatever the hell you want it to be."

I heave the giant tree into my arms and hoist it over my shoulders.

"Ahhhh," I grunt, my muscles screaming under the weight of the Douglas fir.

Bentley's jaw drops to the ground. "You're actually carrying that thing?"

"Yes," I grunt, my muscles begging for me to drop it. "I've lifted way more in prison."

"You look like you're about to have a heart attack."

"I'm not."

"You look like you're about to have an aneurysm."

"I'm not."

"Then you're going to have a stroke," Bentley says exasperatedly. "When's the last time you got your blood pressure checked? This can't be healthy for a man your age."

"I've lifted dead bodies in Rikers that weigh more than this." I shoot Bentley a death glare over my shoulder. *Age shaming bastard.* "I'll manage."

Bentley lets out a groan. "Fine, fine. I'll help."

"Don't even dream about it," I snap. "Just head back to the farmhouse and eat your cookies in peace, little boy. I wouldn't want you to burn any precious calories."

"Look," Bentley snaps, taking a branch of the tree in between his fingers as he marches through the forest with me. "I'm helping. See? I'm supporting the rear end."

"I'm not giving you a round of applause."

Bentley lets out a groan. "You're a jerk. I'm not sharing my cookies when we get back."

"Don't," I snap, a vein popping in my neck. "But you could do me one favor."

"What's that?" Bentley says eagerly.

I turn around and stare straight into his eyes. "Walk in front of me and shake those sexy little cheeks while I walk. It'll distract me from this burden."

"You're disgusting." Bentley's cheeks turn pink.

"Do it, boy. I need some motivation to get back to the farmhouse in one piece."

Bentley gives me the finger. "You're a pig."

But Bentley drops the twig he's holding and walks in front of me to strut his stuff.

His ass jiggles in his sexy pants as he leads the way back to the farmhouse.

Ahh fuck.

Keeping my hands off this boy is going to be harder than I thought.

10

The next day

Uʜʜʜʜ. So that was... Weird?

My head is a whirlwind of conflicting emotions as I walk over to Grandma Harmony's house with Macon the following day.

Preston is finally here after a long plane ride and we're going over to surprise him with freshly baked unicorn cupcakes and stuffies.

But I'm not thinking of Preston, Grandma Harmony, or the silly hijinks we're going to get up to while we're playing.

I've only got one thing on my mind.

One big, tattooed, growly Russian thing... Who apparently likes men with meat on their bones.

Roman.

"Holy shit," I groan as I step into Preston's grandmother's

farmhouse, thoughts of Roman lighting up every dopamine receptor in my brain.

Yesterday, Roman showed me a different side of himself.

I was as pissed as a squirrel who's had his stash of nuts stolen when I found out that Roman was butting in on the tradition I normally have with my grandfather.

It was just one more piece of evidence of who Roman is inside, a big, growly A-hole who doesn't care about respecting anyone other than himself.

But then Roman busted his ass to chop down the tree and he didn't disappoint me at all.

I sat on the sidelines and mouthed off to him to see if he could really prove himself to me but Roman went above and beyond.

He led me out into the patch of Christmas trees with a giant chainsaw over his shoulder and took control of the situation at once, picking out a giant Douglas fir tree and walking me through all of the steps to cut it down.

"Squeeze those boughs tight and make sure it doesn't fall."

To be frank, I was shocked that Roman knew what he was doing.

I figured that Roman was the type of man to let others do the grunt work for him because he comes from a family with so much money.

In the back of my mind, I expected Roman to treat me like a servant.

But Roman actually did the work for me.

He didn't let me get my nails dirty, and he made sure that I didn't exert myself too much.

And he even showed me that he studied his ass off to learn about my family's way of life.

He rattled off factoids about trees that *I* barely knew and passed my pop quizzes with flying colors.

Roman even knew the Latin names for the trees here on my farm.

Pseudotsuga menziesii. Abies fraser. Abies balsamea.

It was crazy.

He didn't know that *abies* means "rising one" in Latin and that it was originally used to describe tall ships but that doesn't matter.

Roman researched fir trees before he came here and proved that he was so much more than some privileged asshole who expects everyone to drop what they're doing for him.

And he likes that I'm curvy.

That should count for something, right?

"Don't get your panties in a wad," I grumble to myself as I follow Macon into Preston's grandmother's house. "Roman might be into curvy guys, but he's still a corrupt asshole who only cares about himself and he'll leave the second he's eligible for parole. Then he'll never think of my grandparents who were so nice to him ever again."

"Bentley!" Preston shouts when I step inside.

I snap my head up and nearly melt with warmth when I see my childhood friend sitting at Grandma Harmony's kitchen table.

I shake my head in amazement.

Preston's wearing a t-shirt with monkeys on it and he has a pet lemur that he always takes Instagram pictures with on his right shoulder.

His eyes are bright and blue and his pointy nose accentuates his high cheekbones.

The lemur's name is Scooter and he's the band's mascot and Preston takes him wherever he goes.

OMG. I can't believe Preston's actually here.

I'm so damn excited to finally see my friend.

"Preston," I yelp, removing Tura Lura's leash and rushing over to Preston's side. "I'm so glad you made it here safely."

I bury my BFF in a hug and squeeze him tight as Grandma Harmony snaps a picture of us for Instagram.

"You can loosen your grip now, bud," Preston groans, freeing himself from my tight embrace and giving me the stink eye.

"Sorry," I say, shaking my head in amusement as Tura Lura peppers Preston's ankles with kisses. "I'm just so excited to see you after all this time."

"How long has it been?" Grandma Harmony asks, grinning as she accepts the Tupperware container of unicorn cupcakes from Macon and brings the hot chocolate on the stove to a boil.

Preston lets out a whistle. "I'm thinking it's been at least two years since I last came up here."

"Two whole years?" Grandma Harmony gasps.

"Unfortunately, yes," Preston confesses, his cheeks turning pink. "I tried to come up last summer but my tour dates didn't allow it so I had to stay in Los Angeles and hang out with my bandmates. They're a lot of fun, don't get me wrong, but it's not the same as coming home. This is where I belong."

Macon waddles up to us and nudges my ribs. "Have you told Preston about your new Daddy yet?"

Preston's jaw drops. "Wait. Seriously? Bentley has a Daddy?"

"Yes," Macon gushes, winking at Preston. "He's six foot eight and covered in menacing tattoos. He's the perfect compliment to Bentley's sassy persona."

"Quit lying," I groan, picking Tura Lura up from the floor and giving her a kiss. "I don't have a Daddy."

Preston sets his pet lemur on the kitchen counter so it won't throw a cupcake at Tura Lura. "Don't lie to me, buddy. We used to tell each other everything and I want to know if you have a Daddy right now."

I shoot a nasty glare at Macon.

I'm seriously going to murder this boy the second we get back to our farmhouse.

A sigh escapes me. "The man that Macon is talking about isn't my Daddy."

"Then who is he?" Preston prods, rubbing Tura Lura's ears.

"He's a sexy — if not incredibly irksome — ex-convict that my grandparents invited to our farm for Christmas break," I lament.

"That sounds promising." Preston rolls his eyes. "I don't see the problem with that."

"Well," I hedge, secretly preparing to dump a mug of hot chocolate on Macon's head, "there's more to the story than that. The man's name is Roman and he's related to Macon's fiancé Aleksei... As well as your bodyguard."

Preston's eyebrows shoot up. "Roman's related to Sasha?"

"Yes," I say, savoring the much-needed sugar in my cupcake. "He's Sasha's brother who's been locked up in Rikers Island."

"OMG," Preston squeals, feeding his lemur a bite of cupcake. "That's so exciting. I had no idea Sasha had a brother in prison."

"He's going to be out on parole as soon as he finishes his work release," I continue, letting out a sigh. "He won't be in prison much longer."

"*But*," I say at last, removing the stuffy that I brought for Preston from my backpack and plopping it down at the kitchen table, "he is *not* my Daddy."

"Mmhm."

"He's a growly billionaire criminal who doesn't have a protective bone in his body," I snap. "I want nothing to do with him this holiday season."

"You're being a brat, Bentley," Macon snaps. "Roman's a nice guy. You just need to give him a chance."

"He's cruel," I groan, pulling Señor Antlers, my favorite stuffy in the world, out of my backpack, and setting him next to the unicorn cupcakes. "He took me out to cut down a Christmas tree yesterday and didn't even compliment me once when I showed him my voluptuous curves. I wiggled my ass in front of him and he didn't even tell me that I looked sexy. I don't need that kind of negative energy in my life."

This is a bald-faced lie but my friends don't need to know it.

Roman was... *Very* interested in my curves.

But I'm not going to give him the satisfaction of admitting this to my friends.

Preston leads me and Macon into his bedroom and shuts the door behind us. "And he's staying on your farm until Christmas?"

"Yes," I say, rolling my eyes as I take off my big boy shirt and slide into my pajamas. "He popped up this past week unannounced while Macon and I were decorating cupcakes. Apparently, my grandparents invited him here for the month without telling me."

I fill Preston in on everything he needs to know.

Preston listens and changes into his onesie when I finish giving him the deets.

"Roman doesn't sound horrible to me," Preston says, sliding into the Christmas slippers I brought him as we all plop down on the floor. "He doesn't seem like he's bad to look at either."

"He's sexy AF," I confess, rolling my eyes. "I can't deny that. I definitely noticed the way his muscles bulged when he heaved a heavy Christmas tree over his shoulders to bring back to the farmhouse," I groan, munching on a unicorn cupcake. "And I could've sworn he got a boner when I strutted my stuff in front of him, but he didn't admit it. Roman's been locked up so long he's probably just going crazy over the first man he sees, i.e. me."

"I actually met Roman at Lucas's wedding last month," Macon says, puffing his chest out.

"Lucas's wedding?" Preston asks.

"The one where you hid behind your bodyguard Sasha and gave him bedroom eyes the entire time?" Macon drawls.

"Of course," Preston groans, hiding behind his elbow. "I was so stressed because it was in the middle of my world tour. How did I forget?"

"Hey." I turn to Preston. "Let's change the subject and talk about how you're wildly in love with your bodyguard."

"Nooo," Preston groans, hiding behind his elbow. "I don't wanna."

"Too bad," I say with a snort. "You forced me to talk about Roman. Now I'm going to do the same to you."

"Sasha's been my bodyguard since I turned seventeen last January," Preston confesses with a sigh. "I always make little comments around him and put secret signals in my songs for him but he thinks I'm too young for him."

Macon snorts. "You *are* too young for him."

"No I'm not," Preston snaps.

"You're only seventeen," Macon retorts.

"And?"

"You're too young."

"I'm the lead singer in a boy band who was forced into the spotlight at an early age," Preston snaps. "I might be seventeen on paper, but I grew up fast in this industry and I know what I want."

"That's not how it works."

"It is," Preston maintains, glaring at Macon. "I've been doing shows around the world since I was fourteen. There's not a single psychologist on this planet who'd argue against the fact that that makes you mature faster than your peers."

"And besides," Preston continues, "Sasha isn't even remotely into me. I've tried to hint that I'm interested in him but he shuts me down at every turn. He wants to protect me, but he swats everything that goes beyond that away with an iron fist."

"Whatever," I say, rolling my eyes. "You turn eighteen next month anyway, so this won't even be a problem then."

My phone buzzes.

Maw Maw: Send a picture of Tura Lura for Roman. He's worried she's feeling anxious

My grandmother's message gives me pause.

I turn my eyes up to Preston. "Hey... Is it okay if I send a picture of Tura Lura to my grandmother for Roman?"

Macon chuckles. "I don't see a problem with that."

I make a face. "Roman will probably nag me for letting Tura Lura get into the unicorn cupcakes," I say.

Tura Lura chomps down on a big bite of a cupcake and turns her beautiful dog eyes up to me.

"Do it," Macon drawls. "What do you have to lose?"

I roll my eyes. "I'll do it, but Roman won't be happy."

Me: She's covered in unicorn cupcakes, but she's alive and well

My phone buzzes at once.

Maw Maw: This is Roman. Thanks for the pic, sweet cheeks. Now show us what you're doing with your friends

I let out a snort as I read Roman's message. "Roman stole my grandma's phone."

Macon peeks over my shoulder. "What does he want?"

"He wants to see what we're getting up to," I say.

Preston snorts. "Maybe you can take a picture of me in my reindeer slippers and tell Roman to send it to Sasha. Sasha would really like that."

I roll my eyes. "Sasha isn't into you, Preston. And you need to wait thirty more days before you make a move."

"They're just slippers, moron," Preston snaps, wiggling his toes. "It's not anything lewd. And besides, I'm way too paranoid about getting my pics leaked to the paparazzi to do that."

"Do you want to be in a picture for Roman or not?" I demand.

"It depends if you want to let him know that you play with stuffies," Macon says.

I mull this but not for very long.

I'm proud as hell of my little side.

For fuck's sake, I started the Age Play club at Cornell last semester.

I'd never shy away from being confident about who I am.

I raise my phone to take a selfie.

Me: We're on an ADULT PLAY DATE, Roman. So if that makes you uncomfortable, it's probably time to get your Russian ass off our farm

Me: *sends pic*

My phone buzzes.

Maw Maw: That's adorable
Maw Maw: Tell your reindeer stuffy I say hi, sweet cheeks

"Oh my God," I groan, rolling my eyes as my cheeks flush pink.

"What is it?" Preston asks.

"Roman complimented my reindeer stuffy." I smack my forehead. *And he called me sweet cheeks.*

"And?" Macon snorts.

"I thought Roman was going to be freaked out that I was on a grown-up playdate," I lament. "I thought he was finally going to quit bothering me. But he's not."

Macon shrugs. "Send him a close-up of Señor Antlers. It wouldn't hurt to see what he says."

Me: *sends pic of reindeer stuffy*

Me: This is my stuffy Señor Antlers and if u never want to speak to me again, that's fine w/ me

My phone buzzes again.

Maw Maw: Awww that's so precious

Maw Maw: Your stuffy and my stuffy should be friends

My fingers hover over the message. Is this man serious?

Me: You have a stuffy?

Me: I find that hard to believe

Maw Maw: I've said too much

Me: Liar

Me: ...do you rlly have a stuffy

Me: RESPOND TO ME

Maw Maw: Honey, it's your Grandma. Roman had to go chop lumber and help me with a batch of strawberry dumplings

Me: DOES ROMAN HAVE A STUFFY OR NOT

Maw Maw: You have to ask Roman when you get back *rolls eyes*

I let out a mammoth groan.

Roman has a stuffy.

And apparently he's also chopping wood and helping my grandmother in the kitchen.

Ugh. Can you say dreamy?

So this guy isn't all bad... But still.

I'm not going to let him sweep me off my feet.

11

Saturday morning

MY COCK IS an iron rod when I wake up the next Saturday morning.

I'm just waking up from a dream where I'm back in prison and Judge Barker is lecturing me that I won't be eligible for parole.

Sweat drips down my body as I tear off my blanket to slow down my thinking.

Judge Barker said that I was spending too much time obsessing over men in my dream.

She said that if I don't stop spending time with Bentley, she'll strike down my work release deal and send me back to Rikers Island for the rest of my life.

But oh my God.

There's no way I can fucking follow her commands.

There's no way I can force myself to forget the bratty angel who's literally sleeping in the bedroom next to me.

"Ugh," I groan, letting my giant Russian cock spring up against my abs.

The thoughts I've had about Bentley since we texted about his stuffies are too horrible to even admit out loud.

When Barney and Bertha forced me to spend the afternoon with him the other day, I was certain that Bentley was going to smack me across the face and tell me to never speak to him again.

I thought Bentley was going to lecture me about intruding on his time with his grandfather and tell me to get the hell off his farm and never come back.

Bentley did lecture me.

At first.

(And actually he lectured me throughout the entirety of our afternoon together.)

(And for many hours after that.)

But then I sensed something inside of Bentley that he wasn't showing me, something he cloaked in sarcasm to avoid discussing out loud.

Bentley's vulnerable.

He's hurt and upset that he can't afford a top-tier lawyer to get his brother out of Rikers.

He's hurt and upset that I'm benefiting from billionaire privilege and living in his grandparents's farmhouse, sleeping in his brother's old bedroom, while his brother can't even get a hearing with his judge.

And I mean, yeah, I haven't accessed my billion-dollar bank account since before I went to prison — the Russian authorities froze it when I got locked up — but my family still has loads of money and connections to lawyers and judges.

I'm benefiting from privilege which allows me to gain opportunities that people like Bentley's brother can't have.

But there's something else Bentley's insecure about.

Something that Bentley will never admit out loud.

His body.

At first, I was pretty damn sure Bentley was cocksure about his sexiness.

I mean, how could anyone be ashamed of sexy curves like that?

Thick. Juicy. Beautiful in all the right places.

But the comments Bentley made during our outing the other day cast that into doubt.

He made self-deprecating jokes at his own expense to cover up the fact that he's secretly embarrassed about his body.

"I'm a thick boy, Roman."

"I need these curves to ward off men."

Something tells me that Bentley's had bad experiences with dating in the past because of his weight.

It doesn't help that Bentley doesn't even have facial hair, which only adds to the "chubby virgin" thing he's got going on.

Bentley's comments were to encourage me to lose interest before I could reject him first.

But there's one thing Bentley doesn't know... He's exactly my type.

There are no sexy-as-hell curvy boys in Rikers Island.

He has perfect curves and the bratty glint in his eyes drives me to the brink of insanity.

I'm a thirty-seven-year-old man who's desperate to taste the most luxurious nectar of the curvy boy kingdom.

I'm also ninety-nine percent sure that Bentley's a virgin and that only makes him so much hotter.

He's curvy and thick in every way and the need to bury myself inside of him is overwhelming.

But then I get a phone call on the landline that Barney installed in my room, and I have to force my thoughts about Bentley to the side.

Riiiing.

I pick it up and answer the call on the first ring.

"*Privet?*" I grunt. Hello?

"*Roman,*" a low voice barks. "*Eto Sasha. Ya s nashimi dvoyurod-nymi brat'yami Nikolayem i Igorem u Igorya pristani.*" It's Sasha. I'm with our cousins Nikolai and Igor at Igor's wharf.

I slip the towel that I'd picked up from my bedpost back onto the bed and sit on the mattress, gripping the phone tight in my palm.

Thank fuck Barney and Bertha let me give their landline number to my brother.

"*Chto eto?*" I ask. What is it?

Sasha blows out a breath. "*Ya koye-chto obnaruzhil vchera. Chto-to o vashey situatsii. Ya ne znayu, khotite li vy, chtoby ya rasskazal vam, chto eto, ili net.*" I discovered something yesterday. Something about your situation. I don't know if you want me to tell you what it is or not.

My brow furrows.

Sasha... Discovered something about my incarceration situation?

"*O chem ty, Sasha?*" I bark, my jaw ticking as I stare out the window in my bedroom. I see the Christmas tree farm that stretches on to infinity beneath the blue sky in front of me. What are you talking about, Sasha?

I need to know what my brother's talking about right now.

If it's something relating to my incarceration, I must hear it.

I pray to God that my nightmare about Judge Barker didn't come true and that she hasn't nixed my potential eligibility for parole before my hearing.

"*Eto o vashey situatsii v tyur'me,*" Sasha growls in a low voice.

"*Vy khotite, chtoby ya vam rasskazal, chto eto takoye?*" It's about your incarceration situation. Do you want me to tell you what it is?

I exhale a breath of relief and nod even though Sasha can't see me.

"*Da,*" I demand, my fingers gripping the phone and an iron grip. "*Podskazhite, chto eto seychas, Sasha. Prekrati vozit'sya.*" Tell me what it is right now, Sasha. Stop fucking around.

"*Eto o sem'ye Richchi.*" Sasha's voice is slow and steady. "*Vchera vecherom my obnaruzhili, chto ikh podchinennyy - vedushchiy upravlyayushchiy khedzh-fondom bogatykh milliarderov N'yu-Yorka. On sostoit v zagorodnykh klubakh s vashim predydushchim sud'yey, i oni druzhat godami.*" It's about the Ricci family. Last night we discovered that their cousin is a top hedge fund manager for wealthy billionaires in New York City. He belongs to country clubs with your previous judge and they've been hobnobbing for years.

My chest goes numb. "*Chto yeshche?*" What else?

"*Etot chelovek vse eti gody skarmlival vashemu predydushchemu sud'ye lozhnuyu informatsiyu. On solgal sud'ye o vas. Yesli by on ne uchastvoval, vy by otsutstvovali meneye chem cherez shest' mesyatsev, yesli by Richchi ne solgali.*" This man has been feeding false information to your previous judge all these years. He lied about you. If he hadn't been involved, you would've been out of Rikers in less than six months.

Sasha's words are a punch to the gut. "*Chto on skazal moyemu predydushchemu sud'ye?*" What did he tell my previous judge?

"*On skazal, chto vy pytalis' ubit' byvshego parnya Anastasii, potomu chto on ugrozhal obratit'sya v politsiyu i razoblachit' nashu sem'yu. On takzhe vse eto vremya oplachival chlenstvo sud'i v zagorodnom klube Khemptona. My ne uznali ob etom, poka vash novyy advokat ne otkryl vse dela i ne podkupil sotrudnika investitsionnogo bankira v Germanii, chtoby tot prosmotrel dela sud'i.*" He said that you attempted to murder Anastasia's ex-boyfriend because he threatened to go to the police and expose our family. He also was paying the judge's country club membership in the Hamptons this entire time. We didn't find this out until your new lawyer got the complete case files unlocked and bribed an employee at an investment bank in Germany to look into the judge's files.

My heart stops dead in my chest.

No. It can't be.

The judge on my case... Was paid off by the Ricci family this entire time?

No. I refuse to believe this is true.

"*Spasibo, Sasha.*" My voice is a guttural growl. "*Ya pogovoryu s toboy pozzhe.*" Thank you, Sasha. I'll talk to you later.

"*My naydem sposob spravit'sya s etim, Roman. My vsegda tak delayem.*" We'll find a way to deal with this, Roman. We always do.

I kill the call and the set the phone back in the cradle.

Oh. Fuck. No.

I have three new missions... Focus like hell so I can finally break out of the system the legal way and start my case against the New York judicial system.

Track this motherfucker down.

Then find a way to make Bentley know that I adore every inch of his sexy curves and make him mine.

12

So THAT WASN'T the *worst* day ever.

I roll over in my cozy sheets and let out a yawn as I hold Señor Antlers to my chest.

I just had the craziest dream where I was walking through the woods and a wild lumberjack was sawing down Christmas trees wherever I went.

I think it's because during my play session with Preston and Macon we pretended that our stuffed animals were chopping down wood to build toys in Santa's workshop.

It was the best play session ever.

Tura Lura was so cute and she planted kisses all over my face when I opened up to Preston and Macon about my older brother.

And Roman even checked up on me when I came home later that afternoon.

He asked me if Tura Lura had a good time at the play date and I couldn't help but tell him yes.

We talked briefly about me being a little and Roman said that he didn't mind.

He's seen kinkier shit in Rikers Island and stuffies are small potatoes compared to some of the crazy shit he saw in the showers.

Hmmm.

Maybe my dream about the lumberjack in the forest wasn't because of my play date after all.

I roll out of bed and step onto the hardwood floor.

The floor is chilly this morning and I can't help but shiver as I slide into my reindeer slippers to warm myself up.

I hold Señor Antlers in my hand as I walk to the giant window overlooking the beautiful Christmas tree farm.

Pride swells in my chest as I see the clusters of Douglas firs and evergreens.

"Gosh," I say, shaking my head as I press my nose against the window. "I'm so proud of Maw Maw and Paw Paw. They always do such a good job."

It's true.

My grandparents are the epitome of first-generation immigrants who achieved the American dream.

They arrived from Germany two generations ago and didn't have a single penny to put food on their table.

A sweet old lady who went to their church owned a bunch of land and sold them plots so they could survive.

Her name was Violetta Harmony Sr. and she came from a large family of traveling singers who performed and put on shows for people.

She sold the land to my grandparents at a low price and helped them survive their first winter.

At first, my grandparents tried to grow crops and raise animals like other farmers, but they quickly realized that the honeoye soil in New York wasn't optimal for traditional farming.

They quickly discovered that Christmas trees were booming industry and threw in their lot with Christmas tree farming.

The operation took off and they raised a daughter to help them with the logistics of the business.

Everything went swimmingly for decades.

Until one night, when everything changed forever.

Until that fateful night in December eight years ago when an unexpected carjacker ruined everything.

"Stop it, Bentley." A shiver rakes down my spine as I press my stuffed animal to my chest. "That was a long time ago and you need to forget it now."

But I can't no matter how hard I try.

I've tried to forget the night that a carjacker ended my parents's lives in a Toyota back from *The Nutcracker* in Manhattan for many years.

I've tried to attend therapy and work on my problems with anxiety so I can put that part of myself in the past.

But it's so hard to truly move on from something so traumatic.

My parents were everything to me and their death rocked me to the freaking core.

They accepted me from an early age and they never sought to impose their will on me.

They put me in theater and dance classes where they knew I'd shine instead of tossing me into bullshit sports they knew I'd hate.

My brother joined the hockey team but my parents realized that wasn't the path for me and they never pressured me.

They let me do my own thing and I was so grateful that I had them for parents and not other parents who tried to live vicariously through their kids like the mothers on *Dance Moms.*

And my parents always pushed me to bond with my brother whenever I could.

My brother was freaking everything to me, the brother who

cared for me, protected me, and made sure that I always felt comfortable and okay.

He protected me from bullies and never once judged me for eating too many sweets in bed.

And now he's been locked up for eight years on bullshit charges that he incurred for avenging my parents's death.

Stop it right now, Bentley.

You promised yourself that you wouldn't think about this during Christmas.

I let out a sigh as I remove Señor Antlers from my chest and walk away from the window.

I tiptoe out of my room and creep down the hallway to my brother's bedroom.

"Roman?" I ask, pressing my ear against the door, even though I'm not sure what I'm doing.

I guess I want to see my brother's room to bring back all of those memories from eight years ago before the carjacker changed our lives forever.

I knock on the door again. "Roman? Are you in there?"

No response. Hmmm.

Curiosity grips me, so I tentatively place my hand on the doorknob and hold Señor Antlers to my chest as I open the door.

Wow.

A wave of memories washes over as I look around my brother's room.

I haven't stepped foot in here in eight long years.

This bed is so familiar and these sheets are the same ones that he slept on.

My brother and I would have snuggle forts in this bed and read stories together all night.

On Christmas Eve, my brother would hold me close and keep me company while we waited for Santa Claus.

My brother was the first person who knew I liked stuffed animals even though I was too old to still be into them.

He told me that he loved me just the way I was and that I shouldn't change for anyone.

"There's nothing wrong with liking stuffies, Bentley."

"Some people can't let go of their childhood and there's nothing wrong with that."

But then everything changed.

Everything was fucking ripped away from me when I was still so young and just starting to understand who I was.

My brother going to prison tore out a central part of me and I couldn't deal with it.

I started eating more in my bedroom at night and cuddling with my stuffies more and more for comfort.

It wasn't right that this happened to my family.

It wasn't right that we were torn apart.

"Roman?" I say, louder this time. "Are you sure you're not in here?"

I step further into the room... And that's when I see it.

The tiny stuffy on the bed.

Wait. What?

Roman wasn't lying when he said he had a stuffy of his own?

Tiptoeing across the room, I spot a tiny teddy bear with a gold inscription on the heart.

Spasibo vam za vse, toy noch'yu na chto vy sdelali v Sochel'nik vosem' let nazad, Roman. Mne ochen' zhal', chto vy tak mnogo let stradali iz-za etogo. YA ne dolzhen byl pozvolyat' tebe vmeshivat'sya. Vy etogo ne zasluzhili — Tvoya sestra, Anastasia

I pull out my phone and translate it at once.

Thank you for everything you did that night on Christmas Eve, Roman. I'm so sorry you've suffered for so many years because of it. I shouldn't have let you get involved. You didn't deserve that — Your sister, Anastasia

My phone jolts in my grip.

My head spins so fast I can barely keep my thoughts straight.

Wait. Roman went to Rikers Island... Because of something he did to protect his sister?

And it happened on *Christmas Eve?*

I vaguely recall Aleksei telling me this over FaceTime with Macon but I'd forgotten it until now.

"Oh no," I gasp, barely able to keep my phone steady in my hand.

I get the weird feeling that... I may have misjudged this man.

Because right now it feels like there's a lot more to Roman's story that I don't know.

It feels like there's something tragic and sad about his past, something that goes a lot further than a petty crime that landed him in Rikers Island.

My body prompts me into action before I can think.

I set down my stuffy and climb into Roman's bed.

"Oh my God," I groan.

I bury my nose in Roman's pillow and inhale and moan.

I unbutton my pajamas and slide them down to my thighs, forcing the fabric down.

I'm wearing a secret pair of Christmas panties that have little candy canes all over them.

But I'm not thinking about the panties that actually make me feel sexy in my body for once or the naughty nature of what I'm doing.

I'm only thinking of one thing.

One noble, brave man who I've apparently misjudged from

the very second he stepped into this farmhouse, who I've been rude to for no reason.

Daddy.

"Oh Roman," I moan, rubbing my hard cock against Roman's pillow and crying out.

I let out a moan as I slide my thumb into my asshole, sick pleasure coursing through me as my member throbs on the pillow where Roman sleeps.

I think of Roman.

Powerful. Sexy. Strong.

His firm hands are so goddamn huge they look like they could slam me into this bed and choke the life out of me.

His body is so toned and sexy and he looks like he could pummel me with his giant cock for hours without ever tiring in the least.

Roman could actually handle a boy with my body type unlike the losers that rejected me because of my weight in college.

I can only think of one man.

Sexy, tattooed, ex-convict Roman, who apparently went to prison for protecting his sister from something horrendous.

Roman's firm hands slam me into the mattress in my fantasy as he nudges his hard member against my trembling opening.

"So thick and curvy for Daddy, baby boy. The Lord didn't give you a body like that to mope around with a sleeve of Oreos in your room."

Roman slides his thick hardness into me, penetrating my walls as he rams my hips into the mattress, bucking into me harder and harder.

"Yes, Daddy! Just for you!" I cry out.

"That's right, curvy princess." Roman smacks my ass and rams even harder into my passage, deep grunts tearing out of his mouth as he makes love to me. "This is what you wanted since I stepped foot in

here, isn't it, Bentley? You took one look at me and begged me to bury myself in you balls deep. Tell me you need this ten-inch cock. Tell me this is what you think about when you beat your perfect dick off in your room at night."

"It's what I think about, Daddy. You. Your big cock inside me making me feel so perfect."

I press down against Roman's pillow and sink my teeth into his bed frame, letting Roman fuck me harder as I widen my passage opening to give Roman's dick the entrance it needs.

Roman rams himself into me even harder, hot guttural moans escaping his greedy lips as he pumps into me with unhinged abandon.

He threads his fingers through my hair and slams my forehead against the bed frame, then heaves his chest against my back while he pumps into me as hard as he can.

"That's right, boy," Roman growls like a caveman, dragging his giant callused palms down my tummy and jerking my quivering cock while he takes me from behind. "Only your Daddy can fuck that tight virgin ass like this. The boys at Cornell can't give it to you like your Daddy can."

"N-No, Daddy." I bite the wooden bedframe and moan.

"They can't hoist you up and rail you in their arms," Roman growls, picking me up. "They're too weak to do this. They're not strong enough to pick up this thick and beautiful body."

"Yes, Daddy," I cry out, my asshole spasming against Roman's cock. "They're weak compared to you."

"They're just little boys compared to me, angel," Roman growls, breeding me hard and passionately as he supports me with his firm arms. "You know damn well only I can give you the ride you need. Ride this felon's cock, boy. Clap those thick cheeks around my shaft and let out a scream."

I cry out over and over again as Roman makes love to me in my fantasy.

I burst all over my Christmas panties and soak them wet, my

vision blurring as Roman takes me to the precipice of pleasure itself.

I'm a walking ball of pure feeling as Roman guides me through every step of my orgasm.

When I pull my thumb out of my ass, I'm fucking shaking from head to toe.

I stare at the drenched panties that are flooded with come that soaks into Roman's pillow.

Oh. My. Fucking. God.

Never in my life have I come so hard before.

Never in my life have I had a fantasy that's taken me so far over the edge.

I pry myself off Roman's bed and slip out of the room before anyone can catch me.

Luckily Macon invited me to *Little Land* with his friends this morning, so that should provide me with *some* type of distraction.

13

ROMAN

"THANKS, BARNEY," I grunt, handing my host a plate with the remnants of my apple pie on it before heading to my room.

Today was fucking exhausting.

I spent the morning putting up handmade signs and cones throughout the farm to get ready for the customers who come next week.

I checked the pH balance of the soil near the trees ready for harvesting to ensure that they're in prime health.

I chopped down fifty trees with a chainsaw and bundled them up to throw on the tractor that Barney let me use to bring them to the warehouse.

And even though Bertha served me a delicious slice of warm fresh baked apple pie with a giant ball of homemade vanilla ice cream the second I got in, I'm spent.

All I want to do is head to my room and collapse on my bed with Tura Lura.

You're such a fucking liar.

That's not all you want to do and you know it.

I let out a groan as the truth of my statement smacks me over the head.

I've hauled my third leg around for the entire morning on account of the inescapable feelings I've had for Bentley.

It's only been a few days since our last conversation but I can't get Bentley out of my mind.

All week long, Bentley's walked Tura Lura around the Christmas tree farm with me to tell me about trees.

Bentley packed me a delicious turkey sandwich yesterday with kettle chips and a pumpkin spice cookie that Bertha made the previous night.

"I knew you'd agree to be my friend eventually," I growled jokingly, accepting the lunch.

"Don't get any ideas," Bentley snapped. "My grandparents don't want to interrupt your work schedule to drag you back to the house. You'll stay productive on the clock if you don't come back to the farmhouse to eat."

The sandwich was the most delicious I've ever tasted in my life.

The pumpkin spice cookie was even better.

And all night long, I could do nothing but think of Bentley.

He plagued my dreams like a character in a horror movie and didn't let me go.

"I'm such a monster," I groan, sauntering down the hallway as I adjust my aching cock through my work jeans. "I'm supposed to leave this boy alone. He's an anxious mess and I need to focus on the task at hand. This is a distraction. I need to focus on parole so I can take down the motherfucker who sabotaged my sentence."

But sometimes, focusing on what needs to be done is easier said than done.

My cock is already in my palm when I enter my bedroom and tear off my flannel shirt.

I collapse on my bed like a wild animal, deep groans escaping me as I hump the mattress with crazed abandon.

I smash my face in my pillow and pretend it's Bentley's thick ass, inhaling greedily as my cock oozes pre-come all over my clenched fingers.

But then I sniff the pillow again and everything whirrs to a halt.

"What the fuck?" I mutter, sniffing it one more time, scratching my temple.

The pillow smells... Like candy canes.

Like the most yummy Christmas tree candy canes I've ever dreamt of in my life.

My eyes dart to my bed and rake across my sheets.

They're crumpled and... Messy in all the wrong places.

I sleep on the *left* side of my bed... But the sheets are crumpled on the *right.*

It looks like someone's been sleeping in them, like Goldilocks wandered into my bedroom and had some naughty fun.

"Oh my God," I groan, my cock clawing at my hands, begging for release.

I sniff the air again and sure enough, the most angelic scent I've ever inhaled wafts into my nose.

It smells like butterflies and peppermint sweetness and all things that are holy in this world.

Lust assaults me from every angle when I realize that Bentley was in my room.

It's not just a conspiracy this time.

Bentley was here.

He did something to my pillow.

He left his beautiful scent on my sheets.

He probably rubbed his angel cock all over them while I was working and maybe he even had an orgasm.

A deep groan escapes me as I picture Bentley riding and

rubbing himself on my pillow, his thick curves moving to the beat of his heart as he cries out and trembles for release.

"Fuckfuckfuck," I groan.

I let my pillow drop to the mattress as my head spins with a million thoughts.

Bentley's supposed to be avoiding me.

This is dangerous on every level.

But something's obviously changed.

Bentley broke into my room and did exceedingly lewd things to my pillow.

There's only one option on the table for me.

I need to ask Bentley exactly what the H-E-Double-Hockey-sticks is going on so I can figure out what the fuck to do.

I need some private time with Bentley.

It's time to stop fucking around and admit that I want to make him mine.

14

BENTLEY

That afternoon

WHY IS it that having feelings for a man is so damn hard?

My heart is heavy when I step out of the taxi and onto the city streets in New York City.

My friends Macon, Christian, Lucas, Karter, Riley, and Rowan are trying on suits and picking out stuffed unicorns for Macon's engagement party next week.

We're at *Little Land*, the only full-service ABDL store in Manhattan, and we're getting ready to be spoiled and have the time of our lives.

But I can't focus on the festivities... My mind is only on one man.

Roman.

And the mysterious message on the teddy bear in his room.

A million emotions whirl through me as I follow my friends into *Little Land* and shut the door behind me.

What did Roman do all those years ago to help his sister?

Now I'm certain that I misjudged the hell out of him when he stepped on my grandparents's farm last week.

Roman did something brave and noble to land him behind bars.

Did he prevent his sister from getting hurt?

Did he attack someone who wanted to hurt his sister like my brother did?

I have zero clue what exactly he did.

All I know is that Roman's been through a lot — maybe as much as my brother — and that the message on the teddy changed my perspective of him.

Emotions wash over my body as I tighten the straps on my backpack.

One thing's certain.

The second I get home from the city today, I'm going to sit down with Roman and ask him exactly what's going on.

I need to hear it from the horse's mouth.

Macon and his friend Christian take my bag when we walk into *Little Land*. "Hey, Bentley," Christian says, nudging my ribs.

I turn to face Christian with a smile on my face. "Hi, Christian," I say, smiling as I slide out of my shoes. "It's nice to see you again."

Christian is a close friend who Macon met last September.

He's a twenty-year-old boy who attends the City University of New York with his friends Rowan and Karter but his true passion lies in running ice cream parlors.

Christian's the brilliant mind behind the *Dino Tracks* ice cream parlor chain and he's basically the best entrepreneur ever.

Christian kindly gave Macon a place to work when Macon wasn't making any money with his Fans4Camz business and believed in Macon.

Macon was a total asshole to Christian at first and always jerked off in Christian's workplace bathroom but Macon mellowed out and the two became friends.

Christian and I have seen each other a couple of times in the city before Macon and I left for my grandparents tree farm last week and we walked around Central Park and went to Christian's ice cream parlor to bond and we even went to *Little Land* once for a playdate and jumped in the stuffy pit together but it's been a while since I've seen him.

Christian claps my shoulder. "I'm glad you got here from your farm upstate, Bentley."

"Oh yeah?" I say.

"Yes." Christian nods. "I was just telling my husband Nikolai that I wanted to see you again before the holidays, but I was bummed you didn't invite me up to your farm. It's been a long time since I've seen a real Christmas tree."

"Really?" I ask, turning to face my friend, my eyebrows migrating to my forehead in confusion.

Wait... What?

I *definitely* invited Christian and his friends to my farm.

What's going on?

"Yes." Christian lets out a sigh. "Macon told me all about the fun you're having on that Christmas tree farm and I got quite jealous. It looks like you're living in a fairytale land."

Everything in me grinds to a halt.

Is this boy serious?

Christian didn't... Get my invitation to the farm?

"Oh sweetie," I snort, patting Christian's back. "I thought I invited you to the farm. I must've forgotten. You don't have to ask me to visit, especially during the holidays. *Mi finca es tu finca.* I'm sad to think that I forgot to give you an invitation."

"Hey, Bentley," a familiar voice says.

I glance up to see Rowan and Karter, Christian's two closest friends, waddle over from across the store.

"Hey, Rowan." I wrap Rowan in a hug and pat his shoulder. "Merry Christmas."

Rowan slides his day pack off of his shoulders and pulls a blue pacifier out of his coveralls. "Merry Christmas and Happy Holidays to all of our Kwanza-celebrating brothers and sisters."

"You and Macon sound like you're having so much fun on your Christmas tree farm," Rowan says at last, untangling his arms from my body.

I cock an eyebrow at him. "Yeah?"

"Yeah." Rowan nods. "Macon sends pictures of all the beautiful trees to us on Discord all the time. I was just telling my husband Igor the other day that I've never seen a real Christmas tree in person and that it would be lovely if Bentley decided to invite us all up, but you never did. I was so bummed."

I let out a groan.

Oh, for crying out loud.

I gave Macon an open invitation to give to all of his friends.

Did he seriously forget to pass it along?

I whip around to face Macon. "Seriously, dude?"

Macon's blue eyes are the spitting image of innocence as I confront him. "What did I do?"

I tap Macon's forehead with my index finger. "Before we left Manhattan last week, I told you that your friends could visit me whenever they wanted. I can't believe you didn't relay my message," I lament, shaking my head in disappointment as sadness washes over me.

For fuck's sake.

I told this boy that my grandparents had SO many extra rooms on the farm and that they'd be overjoyed if I brought friends up for Christmas.

Macon was specifically instructed to invite *anyone* he pleased so that we could have play dates together.

Really letting me down here, bud.

Macon's makin' it look like I don't have any Christmas spirit.

Macon rolls his eyes. "Sue me for forgetting to pass that along to my friends," he drawls, slipping out of his T-shirt.

"It's not that hard to remember things like that," I snap, unbuttoning my khaki pants.

"I'm a forgetful bitch." Macon twirls around fabulously. "Aleksei thinks I need to see a psychoanalyst for ADHD. Apparently, you're not the only one who thinks I exhibit symptoms."

I let out a groan.

Any other day, I'd press Macon for more details.

But for some reason, an ADHD diagnosis seems very fitting for Macon who doesn't seem like he remembers anything for longer than two seconds.

"This wouldn't be the first time I thought you'd do well on Adderall," Lucas drawls, shedding his briefs. "You're fabulous and sassy as hell, Macon, but you do tend to go overboard some-times. I think a small dose of prescription stimulants would do you wonders."

"I might have problems with time management and remem-bering things," Macon snaps, giving Lucas the finger, "but I don't need medication. And besides, my Daddy loves me just the way I am."

I can't help but snort a laugh.

Well, I think as I slip into my favorite onesie and slide Señor Antlers under my arms, *Macon has a point. Who cares if he's a little wilder than the rest of us? Aleksei doesn't care, and that's what matters in the end. His Daddy accepts him the way he is.*

And what's the deal with diagnosing everyone who's unique with a "disorder?"

Maçon can't help it that his brain travels at five-thousand miles a minute and that everyone around him can't keep up.

"Come on," Christian shouts, nudging Macon in the ribs. "I'll race you to the stuffy pit."

"That sounds amazing!" Macon smirks. "But you'd better not judge me if I get up to some naughty fun with the stuffies."

"I wouldn't dream of it."

The day passes quickly.

We paint beautiful princess pictures with diamonds and play to our heart's content in the stuffy pit.

We eat unlimited bowls of ice cream and try on princess dresses for Macon's engagement party.

When we strip out of our onesies to play in the hot tub, I get a little self-conscious of my belly and confess that I have problems with body positivity.

Rowan and Christian change my mood at once.

"Oh hell no." Rowan's jaw drops as he runs over to me. "We need a body positivity intervention!"

"*Wee ooh, wee ooh*," Christian hollers, making the sound of a siren as he sprints to my side. "*No negativity allowed in Little Land*," Christian shouts in a robot voice. "*Code red. Code red. Friend is feeling insecure so we must make him feel better.*"

Rowan and Christian pat my belly. "Bentley is beautiful just the way he is!"

I fight them at first but at last I accept their love.

It's so adorable and I definitely start to feel better.

Who knew that a dorky body positive intervention was just the thing I needed?

But everything changes when I confess that I have feelings for my houseguest.

Roman.

I tell my new friends that I have real feelings for Roman and that it scares me because I don't know if he has feelings for me.

"Open communication is the foundation of Daddy boy relationships," Karter explains, cuddling a rubber ducky. "That's the only way you'll know if Roman can be your Daddy too, Bentley. You need to talk to him in person."

That's why I'm overjoyed when I finally get the text later that afternoon.

Maw Maw: Hey, sweet cheeks. This is Roman. I'm still not allowed to buy a phone yet, hence why I'm using your grandmother's phone. Meet me in the woods at seven o'clock sharp if you want to hear something I have to say. I'll be waiting with a special surprise.

15

Saturday night

WORTH. The. Risk.

That's what I think as I stand right next to the horse drawn carriage I borrowed from Bentley's neighbor to surprise him tonight.

It's worth the risk.

The beautiful horse drawn carriage brimming with food and treats.

The bouquet of roses I have tucked under my arm that I ordered from the finest florist in Manhattan.

The reindeer stuffy that I had Aleksei bring me from New York City when he came up this afternoon to meet Macon.

Tonight's the night I finally take the next step with Bentley.

I've put it off for so long but I can't any longer.

Bentley broke into my bedroom and jerked off on my pillowcase this morning.

We're crossing boundaries that we have no business crossing and we need to have a direct conversation with each other to finally take the next step in our relationship.

"Hey, Felon," a voice says as two footsteps approach me from behind.

I turn around and a groan escapes me as I take in the beautiful twenty-year-old boy standing in front of me.

Bentley's floppy brown hair is neatly brushed to one side and his cheeks are bright and rosy.

He's wearing a sweater with a teddy bear stitched onto it and his skin glistens in the moonlight.

A beam of moonlight courses through the trees and illuminates Bentley's eyes like nothing I've ever seen before.

Oh. My. God.

It looks like somebody airbrushed the spot behind Bentley because his entire body is backlit like nothing I've ever seen.

He looks like an angel, a beautiful, curvy angel that fell down from the sky.

Bentley literally doesn't even need wings, because he's so perfect just the way he is.

Jesus. Fucking. Christ.

I've spent eight years fighting off ruthless criminals with my bare fists and shanking murderers in prison showers.

I nearly killed a man who hurt my sister and I've gone through countless hours in federal court.

Not once have I felt the slightest twinge of anxiety, not a droplet of fear coursing through my veins until tonight.

Not until this boy fell down from the sky and changed my entire life forever.

Bentley's the only person who's ever made me anxious in my life.

It's fated. Destined. Pre-ordained by the gods on Olympus.

The gods want me to make Bentley my boy tonight.

I know this is meant to be.

"Hi, boy." I shove my hands in my pocket as I walk over Bentley. "You look great tonight. I'm glad you came."

Bentley glances up at me. "What's this?" he asks, gesturing to the carriage. "This carriage belongs to Grandma Harmony, not my grandparents. I've seen it a million times in Preston's garage."

I sigh. "We... Need to talk."

Bentley shoots me a quizzical look. "Will you explain how you got the carriage first?"

I let out a sigh. "I got the carriage because we need to have a serious discussion tonight, Bentley. When I came back from work this morning, I discovered... Someone had been in my bedroom."

Bentley freezes on the spot. "What?"

"Look."

I reach into my suit coat pocket and pull out the pillowcase I found on my bed.

It's freshly washed and smells like flowers on account of the lovely detergent that Bentley's grandmother had in her laundry room.

Bentley turns pale when he sees the pillowcase.

His jaw drops to the forest floor.

"Oh my God!" Bentley shouts, pain and shame rippling across his features. "What the fuck? Why do you have a pillowcase with you?"

"It was on my bed, Bentley." I let out a sigh. "Right where you left it after you finished... Doing something to it this morning."

"You can't accuse me of that!" Bentley shouts, his eyes widening. "That's totally wrong, Roman! I'd never dream of doing something like that."

Uhhhm.

Well, you did it, so deal with it.

"You were in my bedroom this morning, Bentley," I say,

staring into Bentley's eyes. "When I came back from chopping down Christmas trees this morning," I explain, "my sheets were rumpled and my pillowcase smelled like candy canes. Tura Lura sure as hell didn't do that, and I highly doubt your grandparents broke into my bedroom either."

"It wasn't me," Bentley mutters, his cheeks tinging pink. "I promise, Roman. I'd *never* break into your room."

"The sheets were rumpled and smelled like candy canes, boy," I snap, rolling my eyes. "And lo and behold, when I followed the scent down the hallway, it was coming from your room."

"You can't do that to me." Bentley's eyes grow wide. "You had no right to barge into my room, Roman. I didn't break into your bedroom this morning. I didn't touch your pillowcase. You shouldn't have done that. I'm really, really upset."

"I'm like one hundred percent sure you jerked off on my pillow," I grunt, putting all my cards on the table. "Just be honest with me, Bentley. I won't judge you."

"I didn't do it."

"You're lying."

"I was *not* in your bedroom this morning."

I ball up the pillowcase in my hands. "I know you were in my room this morning, Bentley. You jerked off in my bed. It smelled like candy canes. Just admit that you did it, Bentley. Fess up so we can discuss this and figure out what to do."

"No I didn't." Bentley starts to tremble. "I promise."

"Don't lie to me, boy."

Bentley tears his eyes away from me. "Knock it off, Felon. This is totally unfair to accuse me of this."

"I know you were in there, boy. You took your pants off and rubbed your pretty dick on my bed. It is what it is. You're attracted to me. There's nothing wrong with needing to act out your attraction. I'm not mad and I don't blame you for it. But you need to admit it out loud."

Bentley slowly raises his eyes to me. "What if... I did do it?"

"That's what I'm trying to say, Bentley." I let out a sigh as I shake my head. "I think it's hot as fuck that you did that. You're such a sexy fuck. I don't care at all. We're getting closer faster than I ever imagined, and now we know that we both have feelings for each other. That's why I needed to have this conversation with you face-to-face. I liked it, Bentley. I liked the fact that you rubbed your cock all over my pillow. I jerked off in my pillowcase right before I threw it in the wash. It was so fucking hot. I came on every inch of that pillowcase. I couldn't control myself."

Bentley gasps. "So... You don't care that I rubbed my dick on your pillow? You're not mad that I shot my cummies where you sleep?"

"No, Bentley." A smirk forms on my face. "I knew you were a dirty little freak the first fucking second I saw your picture in Rikers Island. Your big blue eyes told me that you had a naughty side to you, and I liked it. I don't hold what you did this morning against you at all, Bentley. It's fine. But you needed to admit it out loud so we could take the next step tonight."

Bentley and I stare into each other's eyes.

A spark travels out of Bentley's eyes and drifts into mine.

My heart swells in my chest as I stare at this precious young man trembling before me.

He's so nervous that I'm going to yell at him or report him to his grandparents.

You know what to do, Roman.

Reel this boy in and become his Daddy.

Bentley clears his throat. "So... What do you want to do tonight? Why did you arrange this carriage?"

An invisible hook tugs my lips into a smirk. "I'm going to woo you, cutie. Pretty angel like you can't get away with doing what you did this morning without me sweeping you off your feet."

I don't say another word as I march over to Bentley and wrap my arms around his waist.

I swoop Bentley off his feet and heave him into my arms, pressing him against my chest.

Bentley lets out a yelp as I bring him to the carriage. "What are you doing, Felon?!" he shouts, pounding my chest with his fists. "Put me down, Roman! You're kidnapping me!"

"Stop hitting me, boy," I grunt, carrying Bentley to the carriage and lifting him inside. "I'm going to drop your ass on the ground if you don't stop smacking me."

Bentley hits my chest relentlessly. "Help!" he hollers into the woods. "I'm being kidnapped by a convict! Someone please rescue me!"

"Look at what I bought you inside the carriage, boy. Otherwise I'm going to haul you out and drop you on your ass."

Bentley sighs in defeat as he settles into the carriage seat.

A moment passes as Bentley registers the sight of the delicious treats surrounding him.

Then Bentley's jaw drops and his eyes burst wide open as he stares at me.

"Roman!" Bentley gasps, his voice barely audible in the night. "What are... These treats?"

"I flew these in from New York City for you, boy," I growl, climbing into the carriage next to Bentley and settling down on the seat beside him. "I got gold-dipped roses from the most expensive florist in Manhattan. I got an extra-large reindeer stuffy for you to hold while we tour your Christmas tree farm and so much more."

"And what are these?" Bentley gasps, pointing to a box of truffles on the far side of the carriage covered in silver.

"Silver-dusted truffles, boy," I grunt, heaving the box onto our shared leather seat. "I got milk and dark chocolate for you. And gingerbread cookies that are so thick they'll melt in your mouth. I flew everything in from New York City for you tonight."

Bentley can barely believe his eyes as he drinks in the sight of the treats surrounding us.

"Food," Bentley musters at last, barely able to speak. "You got me food. Truffles. Delicious things to eat. But why?"

"I wanted to, boy," I growl, picking up the box of truffles from the finest chocolate house in NYC and removing the lid for Bentley. "This is our first official date, Bentley. I couldn't live with myself if I let it pass without getting you the most delicious treats in the world."

"But Roman..." Bentley furrows his brow as he trembles next to me. "This isn't... Necessary. I know I'm a bigger guy, but I don't... Need to eat food on a date."

"That's not the point, boy. Look." I reach into the box of truffles and retrieve one.

Flakes of silver fall to the seat between us as I slide it into my mouth.

I let the chocolate melt in my mouth while staring into Bentley's eyes.

"I know you don't need food on a date, Bentley. I'd never insinuate that."

"But?" Bentley stares at me questioningly.

I smirk. "But I know you can't afford to eat like this while you're at Cornell, boy. Tonight, we can enjoy my money together. My billion-dollar bank account is still frozen but I secured a five-million-dollar advance from JP Morgan. I wanted to surprise you with all the finest things in NYC."

"Look," I say at last, brushing silver truffle dust off my fingers. "If it makes you uncomfortable, I can remove the sweets from the carriage. I'll eat them by myself later tonight. It's no problem if you'd prefer to ride around without food."

"No, no." Bentley shakes his head. "It's just that..." He blows out a breath. "I've never exactly had a guy tell me that I should... Eat more."

"What do you mean?" I ask, popping a raspberry tart into my mouth.

Mmm.

So damn good.

Bentley stares at the trays of pastries with hunger in his eyes. "Guys typically don't encourage me to put on more pounds, Roman. It's hard enough even getting a text back from guys at Cornell."

"I doubt that," I say.

"I'm serious." Bentley bites his lip. "I'm not really a hot commodity. Guys are pretty superficial in the gay community, and once they find out I have curves, they don't respond to me. I've never been on a date before."

Holy. Fucking. Shit.

I was right about Bentley.

He's faced discrimination for his body type.

I can barely believe it.

What kind of moron would reject Bentley because of his weight?

Don't they find his curves mouth-watering as hell?

I don't even pause, hesitate.

I tell Bentley the truth, bold and unfiltered, and raw as fuck.

"Those guys are fucking idiots, Bentley," I growl, eating another truffle and savoring every bite.

"No, no," Bentley says quickly, shaking his head. "They... Mean well. They're willing to give me a chance on the teddy bear stuff."

"But?" I snap, wanting to hunt down these men and snap their necks.

"But when I send them pictures of my body," Bentley

confesses, "they leave me on read. They don't want anything else to do with me."

I pop another tart into my mouth to let Bentley know that it's okay to eat the treats around us. "Those *boys* are fucking morons, Bentley. They're rude and nasty and bitchy as hell. They're not men. They don't know how to appreciate a curvy prince like you."

Bentley rolls his eyes. "That's not exactly the complement that you think it is."

"It's the truth," I say with a growl, brushing a strand of floppy dark hair from Bentley's forehead. "They don't know how to handle your curves. You're so fucking special, Bentley. I knew you were unique the second I saw you. Those *boys* at Cornell have no idea what they're talking about. They're whiny little brats who don't know how to treat you right."

"I..." Bentley lets out a breath. "I thought about reaching out to someone older than me this past semester. A man who was more mature than the college boys in my classes."

"Why didn't you?"

"I never had the courage. I downloaded dating apps but my friends always talked me out of following through. They said I just needed to see if any more of the students at Cornell wanted to date me. They said I should find someone my own age. But none of the students ever wanted to take me out."

I bring a tray of Nutella Danishes over to Bentley. "Take a Danish, boy. Your new Daddy loves your curves and your body. A yummy Danish treat is the best way to start this night off right."

Bentley gulps as he stares at the Danishes. "Did you just call yourself my Daddy?"

"Damn fucking right I did," I growl, setting the tray of Danishes on the seat next to my angel. "I'm your Daddy now, boy. Whether you like it or not."

"And are you sure I can eat a Danish?" Bentley asks. "I don't want to sound insecure and stupid, but I'm afraid I'll make a fool of myself if you give me permission to eat this tonight."

I roll my eyes. "I want to see you eat it, boy. Take that Nutella Danish and put it in your mouth."

Bentley clears his throat. "And you promise you're not mad about the... Thing this morning?" He gulps. "You're not going to hold it against me for the rest of the night?"

I nudge Bentley's fingers to the Danish. "It's water under the bridge, cutie. Now eat this damn Danish before I gobble up everything in sight."

"You're not the only one who likes to eat around here," I rasp, biting Bentley's earlobe and dragging my lips down his neck.

Bentley rams the Nutella Danish into his mouth and stuffs his cheeks like a chipmunk.

"No comment," he squeals, munching on the pastry as his cheeks turn bright pink.

He squeezes his thighs together to cover up his rock-hard dick.

I let out a laugh as I take his hand in mine.

"This is going to be fun, Bentley," I say as I instruct the driver — i.e. Macon, who volunteered for the role tonight — to take us off on our date. "Let's eat all we want and have a kickass time."

"And you're really my Daddy now?" Bentley gushes through a mouthful of Danish.

I squeeze his hand even tighter. "You bet your perfect ass I am."

16

HOLY. Fucking. Shit.

This date is freaking amazing.

Roman is my knight in flannel shirts and prison tattoos.

The man actually knows how to have a *really* good time.

I was shocked as hell when I saw Roman standing in the woods with the horse drawn carriage by his side.

I thought Roman was going to pull a prank on me or scare me or something.

I thought he was going to do something ridiculous to make me hate him.

But Roman didn't do that at all.

No — He actually gave me a really amazing time.

Not only did Roman arrange a carriage ride for me — which is freaking amazing on every level — but he made damn sure to make me feel comfortable in my skin.

He bought me food.

Delicious, amazing, taste bud-melting food.

Roman bought me yummy chocolates, boxes of truffles, raspberry tarts, and even adorable gingerbread cookies from the most fabulous baker in New York City.

He even brought a thermos of hot chocolate with Baileys in it for us to drink while our private driver — who I'm pretty sure is Macon — takes us around the Christmas tree farm.

I'm eating truffles and drinking alcoholic hot chocolate and losing myself in the magic of the night.

It's been so long since I've allowed myself to totally pig out like this.

Normally I get so ashamed by the time I'm on my fifth pastry that I force myself to put everything aside and stop eating altogether.

But tonight... Tonight is different.

Tonight is wonderful, unexpected, and oh-so-freaking perfect.

Roman doesn't give a shit if I lose myself in food.

He encourages me to enjoy the things I'm eating and to truly savor every bite.

Roman gives me a chance to stop feeling horrible about myself for overeating for once.

Roman's decision to surprise me with these yummy things that I've deprived myself of for so long shows me that he actually gives a shit about who I am.

He understand my needs.

Yes, Roman — i.e. my new Daddy — would probably be upset if he saw me eating like this every single night in my bedroom and yes, I understand that the food we're eating isn't healthy and that I shouldn't eat it on the regular.

But Roman's gesture isn't about healthy foods vs. unhealthy foods.

It's about Roman showing me that he accepts me for me, and that he doesn't judge me at all.

In fact, he seems to think my body type is sexy... At least according to what he said about my hijinks in his bedroom this morning.

I probably should've realized that Roman would notice I left his sheets all crumpled and messy.

It's a little hard to disappear inconspicuously when you've left a trail of candy cane scent in your wake.

But I'm not thinking about candy canes, pillowcases, or the fact that I nearly ruined everything by pleasuring myself in Roman's bed this morning.

I'm only thinking of one thing.

Roman.

Big, tattooed, sexy Roman, who accepts me for me.

I'm still insecure about my body — even after Christian and Rowan's body positivity intervention at *Little Land* — but I'm willing to put my worries aside for the night and focus on my new Daddy.

Roman's my Daddy now and I want to make sure I enjoy this date with everything I have.

My Daddy.

"Mmmm," I moan, taking a bite of a gingerbread cookie from the finest baker in New York City as I ogle Roman's bulging muscles in the moonlight. "This is so good."

Roman smirks. "The cookie or my muscles?"

I nearly choke on gingerbread. "The cookie, dumbass. Don't make comments like that or else you'll get a big head."

Roman lets out a laugh. "I'm glad you're enjoying the cookie, sweet cheeks."

"I'm enjoying it *soooo* much." I take another bite, then sip my alcoholic hot chocolate. "This is so good. I can't believe they actually make cookies like this."

"Me neither." Roman takes a sip from the thermos and swallows it down. "These bakers are nothing to scoff at."

"Oh yeah?" I say, my heart beating fast as I stare at Roman's chiseled jawline in the moonlight.

Jesus, the guy could cut steel with that jawline if he wanted to.

Everything about Roman is perfect.

"Yes," Roman grunts, popping a silver truffle in his mouth. "These bakers spend countless years honing their craft. I'm more than happy to pay for their years of labor."

My cheeks turn pink as the carriage takes us through the moonlit forest. "I actually have a question about that. Would you mind if I asked it?"

"Go for it." Roman issues me an encouraging nod.

I take a deep breath to give me the courage I need. "Did you ever get food like this in Rikers Island?"

"Why do you ask?"

"These cookies are amazing, and it'd be a shame to deprive prisoners like my brother of such yummy treats."

"I'm glad you asked that." Roman grins. "Do you want the long or short answer?"

I snicker. "Both."

Roman brings his fingers to my chin and nods. "We ate like this... Sometimes. We'd have professional bakers come in once in a while and teach us how to bake."

"Seriously?" I say, taking another sip of cocoa, savoring the delicious chocolatey alcoholic warmth on my tongue.

"Yes." Roman nods. "They came in occasionally on Saturday morning to work with prisoners who'd expressed interest in baking during the week. It didn't happen very often, but the prisoners were super grateful."

"That's amazing." I take another bite of my cookie. "And the short answer?"

Roman lets out a snort. "The short answer is that no, we didn't get food like this often."

"Why not?"

"Our volunteer cooks were great... But they couldn't exactly compare to the top bakers in New York City. These cookies are *way* better."

"That makes sense." I swallow my cookie and follow it up with another sip of hot chocolate. "It's hard to make cookies like this. I bet it takes years of training."

"I imagine it does." Roman directs his sexy brown eyes to mine, sending a flutter of lust coursing through my chest. "But I'll tell you something."

"Go for it." I stare into Roman's eyes, barely able to sit upright.

Wow.

This man is a work of art.

Roman smirks. "I imagine baking is just as hard as running a Christmas tree farm. Bakers and Christmas tree farmers are both masters of their craft. They're artists in their own way."

"Oh yeah?" I ask.

"Yes." Roman nods. "Both work for years while making very little money. Then one day, the talent they've worked so hard to build and the trees they planted suddenly begin to grow and they're able to actually make money from their craft. It snowballs from there. The farmers sell their trees and the bakers make money off their art. They both get the payoff they deserve."

Wow. Roman is spot on.

Never in a million years have I thought about it like that.

I finish my cookie and stare at the Christmas trees shrouded in moonlight before me.

"I'm wondering if I can ask you something else." I scoot closer to Roman on the leather seat. "You don't have to answer me if you don't want to."

"Ask away."

I turn my eyes up to Roman. "Do you think my brother ever volunteered in the kitchen at Rikers?"

Roman slowly places his hand over mine. "I don't know,

Bentley. I never ran into your brother when I was in Rikers. I looked him up in the online prisoner database last week after your grandparents told me about his situation but I never saw him inside. His name was Jericho, right?"

"Yes." I nod. "Jericho Johnson. He was the best older bother I could've ever had."

Roman gives my palm a little nudge with his knuckles. "That's incredible, Bentley. It's touching to hear that you and your brother were so close."

I let out a breath. "We spent so much time together when we were younger. We were best friends. But everything changed when Jericho went to prison."

Roman nods. "Why didn't you stay in contact with him?"

"We didn't know where he went after he aged out of juvie," I say with a shrug. "My grandparents asked Jericho's court-appointed lawyer but he said he didn't know. He gave us the runaround and never told us where Jericho was staying. It wasn't until three weeks ago that we discovered Jericho was in Rikers Island. I was pretty freaking devastated when I found out."

Roman lets out a breath. "I know how you feel, Bentley. I know how horrible the court system in this country is."

"You do?"

"Yes, Bentley. The system gives innocent families the run around and never gives them honest answers. The judges and lawyers are in cahoots and corrupt as fuck. There's something I need to tell you, boy. I haven't found the right time to say it yet. But it's time now. I've wanted to get this off my chest all night."

My breath hitches as I nod. "Go for it, Roman. I'm all ears."

Roman lets out a breath. "What happened to your brother was a travesty. We both know that. Your brother sacrificed so much to help your parents. He wasn't going to let the carjacker's actions go unchecked. Your brother did a very brave and honor-able thing. Not everyone would have the courage to do what he did. But Jericho did. He didn't care about social conventions. He acted from the bottom of his heart. He fought like hell to defend you and your parents that night. Unfortunately, the criminal justice system didn't see it that way."

"What are you trying to say, Roman?" I ask.

"I've decided to pay out of my own pocket for Jericho's new lawyer." Roman squeezes my hand and sends tingles down my spine. "The Russian authorities will unfreeze my billion-dollar bank account when I'm out on parole next month. I'm going to pay my attorney Antoine to take a look at your brother's case. Antoine's a powerful well-connected lawyer with relationships with lots of judges in New York. He's the best legal representation your brother could have. Your brother will have the best lawyer in the state. Jericho shouldn't have been locked up, Bentley. But I can make this right. I refuse to sleep another night while he's stuck in Rikers. Now is finally Jericho's chance to get the justice he deserves."

I can barely breathe as I stare into Roman's eyes.

Roman wants to... Pay for Jericho's new lawyer?

"You're... Joking," I muster, my jaw falling to the carriage floor.

Roman shakes his head. "No. I'm dead serious. I want to pay for Jericho's lawyer and get him out of prison."

I stare into Roman's eyes to see if he's lying.

But instantly I know he's telling the truth.

This man will fight for Jericho.

This man will get justice for my brother and get him out of prison.

Roman is a strong, brave man, and he's willing to do whatever it takes to bring what's left of my family back together.

"Oh, Roman." I let my cookie fall from my fingers. "You don't have to do this, Roman. I'll still be your boy even if you don't pay for Jericho's new lawyer. I'll still adore you with everything I have. You don't have to do this for me, Roman."

Roman stares straight into my eyes. "I'm doing it because I want to, Bentley. Your brother has suffered long enough. I know what it's like to have no one in your corner. It's time that Jericho finally gets out of Rikers once and for all."

Roman doesn't think, doesn't hesitate.

He sinks his fingers into my jaw and slams his lips on mine.

17

ROMAN

I CRUSH my lips against Bentley's and kiss him hard.

Oh. Sweet. Jesus.

This boy is perfect.

The boy's lips are plush and soft, and they taste exactly like what I imagined in my fantasies.

I fight a Herculean battle not to completely lose myself as I gorge on his mouth.

But it's so damn hard to hold off and think rationally anymore.

It's so damn hard to remember that I'm supposed to be avoiding this boy at all costs so I can finish my work release.

But can I ignore Bentley when he's submitting to me?

How can I ignore Bentley's beautiful curves, his perfect personality, and the way he melts in my arms when I say that I want to help his brother?

I groan as I thread my fingers through Bentley's hair, kissing him passionately, desperately, losing myself in his plush soft lips.

Bentley mewls as he kisses me hot and hard.

"Oh Daddy," he whimpers, his curvy hips grinding against my thighs, his body working up and down as he licks my lips into another kiss. "Giving me my first kiss, Daddy. Feels so good and perfect with you."

Oh sweet Jesus in Heaven.

There's no damn way in hell I can control myself around this boy.

A deep growl escapes me as Bentley's adorable words transport me to a superior plane of existence.

I've waited nearly a decade for a man like Bentley and Bentley's exactly what I've been missing out on my entire life.

But this moment is even more special for Bentley — This is Bentley's first kiss.

It's the first moment he's ever pressed his lips against another man's.

This is something Bentley's dreamt about for years and years and fantasized about for so long.

I bet he's even jerked off in his college dorm thinking about kisses.

Now it's finally happening.

Bentley's finally experiencing this incredible thing he's wanted for so long with *me*.

I'm the man kissing Bentley tonight, the first man to ever claim him in this beautiful horse drawn carriage.

I'm the man supporting Bentley's curvy body with my firm muscles, cupping his thick juicy ass as I prop him up on my thighs, holding him safe and sound.

I'm the man canting my hips against Bentley's, pressing my giant cock against Bentley's thighs as he loses himself in my mouth.

I'm the man who's so damn lucky to kiss this precious angel's lips for the very first time.

"Kiss me, boy," I growl into Bentley's lips, cupping his ass cheeks with my palms as I kiss him harder, rutting against him with everything I have. "You're my horny kissy boy tonight, aren't you, Bentley. You like when Daddy kisses you and holds you tight in his big strong arms. Tell Daddy this is what you want, sweet cheeks. Tell Daddy this is what you think about when you jerk your big cock off in your room. Tell Daddy that you think about him, Bentley. Tell Daddy that you think about him picking you up with his giant muscles and making you feel so safe and weightless in his arms."

Bentley doesn't say a word in response, but the sinewy moans that bubble out of his lips let me know I've hit the nail on the head.

This is something Bentley's dreamt about for years, possibly his entire life, kissing a man who doesn't judge him at all.

Bentley's response to my kisses tonight lets me know that I've tapped into his true fantasies more than I could've ever dreamt of and that I'm truly connecting with this angel on a deeper plane.

Bentley feels so safe and secure with me. Protected from all danger and harm.

I've given Bentley the gifts he needs to feel totally at peace with me, and now he's rewarding me by giving me the most scrumptious kisses I've ever experienced in my life.

He dips and dives into my mouth, whimpering as he bites my lips, rutting against me so tenderly.

Bentley rubs his sticky palms all over my suit coat and that's when I realize that he needs more.

My angel needs so much more.

Bentley needs me to remove his teddy bear sweater and truly show him that he's what I crave tonight.

He needs me to praise him, worship him, and give him every bit of goddamn devotion that I can.

The good news is that this should be easy, considering that Bentley's exactly what I've been craving for eight long years.

Bentley on my lap tonight is like a bucket of temptation poured all over me.

I want to be Bentley's everything and show him that I adore everything about him, from his pretty red lips to his sexy irresistible curves.

I'm going to make it happen.

Right. Fucking. Now.

"Such a perfect boy for Daddy," I growl, threading my fingers through Bentley's hair and hoisting him up on my lap. "Daddy's having a hard time controlling himself around you tonight, Bentley. He adores your precious kisses but he needs... More."

"More, Daddy?" Bentley gyrates on my lap, kissing me hard.

"Yes," I rasp, running my big hands up and down Bentley's innocent back. "Daddy's going to tear those pretty khakis off and see what you're wearing underneath. Don't be afraid. Daddy's going to give you everything you desire, sweet cheeks. Daddy didn't touch one inmate in Rikers Island the entire time he was locked up and he was such a good man who kept his hands off of everyone. But Daddy can't take it any longer. Tonight you're finally going to be the cure for Daddy's incessant erection."

Bentley pries himself off my lips and stares into my eyes.

His floppy brown curls bounce around his eyes as he touches himself between his legs.

"Here, Daddy?" Bentley stares into my eyes, rubbing his bulge between his legs. "You want... Here tonight?"

Oh sweet Jesus in heaven.

Bentley's being naughty as fuck.

He's speaking in a way that deserves a spanking.

"Are you teasing Daddy, boy?" I growl, raising my palm and bringing it down hard on Bentley's thick juicy ass cheeks with a *smack*. "Are you trying to get a rise out of me tonight?"

Bentley bats his eyelashes as he spreads his thighs even

further, pressing his bulge against me. "I want what Daddy wants. Anything Daddy wants is good for me."

A deep groan escapes me as my eyes roll back to the whites.

This young man is so innocent and inexperienced in every way but he's also a fiery male Siren.

He picked this up from some novel somewhere but I'm not complaining.

Bentley knows exactly what he's doing, and he's turning me into the raging Hulk that I am inside.

The possessed convict.

The lusty felon.

I heave Bentley into my arms and slam him against my chest.

A deep growl tears out of me as I claw at Bentley's zipper and pop the button off his pants.

Bentley moans when I yank his khakis down and throws his head back when I drink in the sight of his hard cock.

My vision blurs when I touch Bentley's dick for the first time.

I'm in shock and I refuse to believe it.

Bentley's dick is... Seven inches long.

It's hard and achy and it springs forth from a tuft of hair between Bentley's thighs.

It sticks straight up and presses against his belly.

The skin surrounding his dick is white and soft and it almost looks like fresh fallen snow in a meadow.

So curvy. So perfect.

Droplets of pre-come ooze out of the tip and drip down his quivering shaft.

It's crazy to think that I didn't even realize that Bentley had such a perfect shaft.

I stare into Bentley's eyes. "Boy," I grunt sternly, forcing myself not to betray the lust welling up inside me. "You're keeping secrets from me."

Bentley bites his lower lip. "Did I do something wrong, Daddy?"

I let out a groan as I bring my palm to Bentley's shaft and wrap my fingers around his hardness.

His dick is fleshy and soft beneath my grip and I can barely believe that I'm actually touching it.

It's so big and beautiful and I can't believe that Bentley kept this from me.

Why didn't he tell me he had such an enormous shaft?

Why did he keep this secret from me?

I stare into Bentley's eyes. "You did something very wrong, Bentley."

"How so, Daddy?"

"I've been around you for an entire week and not once did you hint that you had a perfect dick," I growl, pumping Bentley's shaft. "You didn't even hint that you're packing. For fuck's sake, I beat off thinking about you every single night and not once did I imagine that you had such a beautiful cock between your legs. You made your Daddy think you were average. How dare you, boy? How dare you let Daddy believe such lies?"

Bentley bucks into my palm, throwing his head back and moaning.

"Nervous, Daddy." Bentley trembles in my palm and gyrates in my firm grip. "Didn't know I had anything special. Would've told you if I'd known."

My head explodes as Bentley's words smack into me.

I can't even believe that Bentley had no idea he's packing.

But deep down I know it must be true.

I'm the first man Bentley's ever been with in his life.

How can I blame Bentley for not knowing that he's Heavenly perfection on Earth?

I can't, I groan to myself as I palm Bentley's hardness, jerking it as I keep Bentley safe in my arms. *Bentley's not responsible for any of this. I should've guessed that Bentley was perfect in every way. It's my failure that I didn't realize that every part of my boy was perfect. He's nothing but a virgin. How would* HE *know he's walking perfection?*

"You know what this means, boy." I stare into Bentley's eyes.

Bentley gulps. "W-What's that, Daddy?"

I lay Bentley down on the seat of the carriage.

"Daddy's waited far too long to meet a boy like you in his life," I rasp, climbing on top of Bentley and running my hands up and down his thighs. "He has no choice but to suck this pretty cock tonight."

I dip my head down and take Bentley's cock in my mouth.

18

MY ENTIRE UNIVERSE detaches from its freaking orbit when Roman takes my cock in his mouth.

I let out a gasp and sink my fingernails into his back, thrusting upward into the hot wet hole that opens up around my dick.

My cheeks burn and I can barely comprehend the sensations taking control of my insides.

Holy. Fucking. Shit.

It feels like I'm penetrating a cloud with my cock.

Or like I'm thrusting my dick into five thousand pillows.

"Oh Daddy," I moan, scrunching my eyes tight as I push my hardness inside Roman's throat.

I've heard of blowjobs before. I've even fantasized about blowjobs from guys at Cornell.

But never in a million years did I think a blowjob would feel so good on my dick.

For crying out loud, I'm a damn virgin who's been with exactly zero guys until tonight.

I've seen blowjobs in porn but I didn't actually think anyone would want to perform one on me.

But this... This blows even my most wild expectations out of the water.

It feels like I've lost control but also stumbled upon the most amazing sensations I've ever felt in my life.

But I know it's only because of Roman.

Roman's the only reason I'm receiving any pleasure at all.

Roman worked so hard to make me feel comfortable and at peace with myself earlier.

When I was nervous, Roman comforted me and let me know that I had nothing to fear.

"I don't judge you, Bentley."

"I've been waiting so long for a boy like you."

And then Roman even complemented my dick.

Gah.

That was something I didn't see coming.

I definitely compared myself to boys in high school and knew that I was slightly above average.

But not once did I actually think that I was well endowed.

I figured I had an average sized cock, nothing to write home about.

But Roman told me that I had a perfect dick and that he was furious that I kept it from him for so long.

I'm so lucky Roman's my Daddy.

Roman teaches me things about my body and makes me feel so proud about who I am.

Roman buries my dick even further in his throat.

He flattens his tongue and draws a line up the underbelly of my shaft, stimulating my crown with quick flitting motions.

I cry out when Roman licks a path to my full balls, before he wraps his lips around them, swirling his tongue around the tender flesh.

Roman spits on my cock and pumps my aching shaft with

one hand while he sucks my balls, groaning and grunting as he suckles me.

Roman turns up to face me. "Let me at that asshole, sweet cheeks. Daddy's begging to taste the inside."

I whine and moan. "Yes, Daddy. Please."

I see stars when Roman nestles his nose between my cheeks.

He drags his lips up to my crack, then plunges his tongue deep into my hole and pushes past my walls.

I whimper as Roman laps at my virgin insides with his tongue, flattening it and flicking it back and forth in fast swirling motions.

Oh. Sweet. Jesus.

I've read about this act online before.

This is a rim job.

It's when one man eats out another man's ass during sex.

I've seen men do it in videos but I never dreamt it would happen to me.

I think I like it even better than the blowjob.

It feels so damn good and I can barely stay in control of my body.

"Look at that puckering hole, boy." Roman spits on my opening and wriggles his tongue back and forth, burrowing deep into my passage as I let out a moan. "So tight and clean for Daddy. You knew Daddy wanted to do something to that tight hole before you came here tonight, didn't you, boy. You knew Daddy's been dreaming about a sexy tight hole like that for eight long years when he was locked up in Rikers Island and that he wouldn't be able to control himself the second that he tore those pants off you tonight. You're a naughty man tempting Daddy tonight, boy. You knew Daddy was in need of a curvy prince and that he dreamt about men like you every night locked up in federal prison. He didn't have access to curvy hunks like you inside of Rikers. That's why Daddy went crazy when he saw your hole tonight."

I spread my legs wider for Roman.

Roman groans against my hole, flitting his tongue around my insides as he plunges it deep into my passage, stimulating me like nothing else ever has.

He spits on his thumb then stabs that deep into my channel, ramming it deep into my body as he laps at my quivering flesh.

Unexpected sensations send jolts of sheer electricity through me.

I mewl and hug the enormous reindeer stuffy Roman bought me as I buck hard against Roman's massive thumb.

"That's it, boy," Roman growls, staring into my eyes as he finger fucks my ass. "Hug that precious stuffy, sweet cheeks. You're Daddy's reindeer tonight. You're a precious elf and Santa's going to give you the pleasure that you need."

My cock twitches between my legs as pre-come starts to gush out of the tip.

"It's going to happen, Daddy!" I cry out as my orgasm bubbles up. "I feel it in my balls, Daddy! I'm going to go boom!"

Tendrils of pleasure snake through me as fire rips down my shaft.

The freight train of my orgasm slams into me and I explode and squirt all over my belly.

"Oh Daddy!" I cant hard against Roman's calloused thumb in my asshole, trembling and moaning. "It feels so good, Daddy. Had a big orgasm with you tonight."

Roman laps up every droplet of come from my tummy and thighs like a caveman.

He ravenously bites my belly and pants as he swallows every drop.

"Such a perfect boy." Roman kisses my groin and balls before sucking the last of my nectar out of my cock head. "Such a great curvy boy for Daddy. Spasming and crying out for your big Daddy. That's what you were born to do, isn't it, Bentley. That's why the gods sent you to me. To give you pleasure you could only dream of."

I whimper when Roman heaves me into his mammoth arms and presses me against his body.

I can barely believe it as Roman kisses me in the moonlight with clouds floating above us as he holds me in his arms.

Holy. Freaking. Shit.

Roman's *carrying* me like I weigh nothing.

"Daddy's going to take you back to the farmhouse," Roman rasps into my lips, palming my cheeks with tenderness and devotion, causing me to soar. "He's going to kiss every inch of that perfect body and give you the most amazing massage. Don't you think you can get out of precious aftercare tonight, sweet angel. Your new Daddy's going to give you the gentle cuddles and warm bear hugs you deserve."

Oh sweet mercy me.

Roman cares about giving me *aftercare* too?!

"Thank you, Daddy." I feather my lips against Roman's, kissing him softly but with so much heart. "I'd like that so much."

19

Later that night

I'M FINALLY BACK in the farmhouse with Roman after the most amazing night ever.

It's so freaking crazy that I actually had such an incredible time.

I never thought Roman would work so hard to take my needs into consideration.

But he gave me things I didn't even think I needed and proved to me that he accepted me just the way I am.

It's amazing and beautiful but to be honest, I shouldn't be surprised.

Roman's shown nothing but patience the entire time he's been at the Christmas tree farm.

I was the one who was sassy and rude AF to *him*.

But Roman looked past my bad attitude and pushed through my barriers.

In Roman's eyes tonight, I'm desirable, wanted, a man to be loved.

I'm not just the chubby kid who jerks off in his room alone and fantasizes about men way out of his league.

I transformed into a prince for Roman tonight and he was so freaking crazy for me he couldn't control himself around me.

Roman desired me in the depths of his soul when he slammed his lips on mine and his heart lit up when he took my khakis off.

Roman is crazy for me.

How special is that?

How freaking amazing is it that I finally met a man who adores me for who I am?

"And the sweetness he showed me didn't stop there," I mutter under my breath, snuggling against Roman's muscular chest in the moonlit bed.

When we got back from the carriage ride earlier, Roman carried me into the house in his giant arms and took me to his bedroom.

My grandparents were up and they didn't even try to stop us, instead they laughed and gave us their blessing.

"We don't mind, Bentley."

"We're so happy you finally found the Daddy of your dreams."

It's amazing to have a family that accepts me for me and doesn't try to lecture me or stop me from following my dreams.

Roman took me into his bedroom and pulled out massage oils and worked his giant manly hands — the same beautiful hands that I noticed the very first day he arrived at the farm-house — all over my body.

He kneaded the stress knots out of my back and paid special attention to my curves.

And when Roman finished giving me my fourth orgasm of

the night, he wrapped me in his big strong arms and took me to bed.

Gah.

It was simply amazing.

I've met the man of my dreams who's strong enough to carry me into my house while still treating me like I'm as light as a feather.

The boys at Cornell simply weren't equipped to be with a man like me.

I needed Roman, someone strong and muscular who knows what to do with my type of body.

Roman knows how to please a big boy like me.

Roman is my diamond in the rough and I'm so damn lucky he's mine.

"Hey, sweet cheeks." A growly murmur distracts me from my thoughts as a firm finger trails across my neck.

I snuggle even deeper into Roman's chest. "Hi, Daddy. I didn't realize you were awake."

A deep chuckle escapes Roman's lips. "I'm definitely awake, baby boy. I'm watching the way your big beautiful body rises and falls on my chest."

"Really, Daddy?" I plant my chin on Roman's pecs and stare into his brown eyes.

A smirk creases Roman's mouth. "Yes, angel. The way you sleep is better than any movie or TV show I've ever seen in my life. You're my big, beautiful angel with the most perfect body I've ever run across. I'm a greedy bastard and I'm so lucky you're mine."

"Hey, Roman?" I ask after a pause, planting a kiss on Roman's tattooed chest. "Can I ask you a question?"

Roman drapes his big arm across my shoulder. "Ask away, sweet cheeks."

I blow out a breath.

Roman's already shown that he desires me physically tonight.

But I need to know if Roman accepts my little side.

It's one thing to have sex with a man — and it was amazing to receive a rim job and a blowjob in *one night* — but Roman must show me that he accepts that I play with stuffed animals too.

Being a sexy alpha male in the bedroom is only one of the requirements for being a good Daddy.

I clear my throat. "You were amazing in the carriage today, Daddy. You treated me with so much respect and paid attention to every inch of my body."

"It was an honor, boy."

I stare into Roman's eyes. "But I must know if you're okay with the fact that I'm a little too." I blow out a breath. "We went over this briefly the other day after I sent you that picture of my reindeer stuffy at Preston's house. But I need to hear you say it out loud, Daddy. I need to know you actually like my little side and don't just tolerate it."

Roman tilts my chin up. "I love that you're a little, Bentley. I figured there was something special about you when I saw your picture in Rikers Island."

"Really?" I peep.

Roman nods. "Yes, baby boy. You had the most beautiful blue eyes and chubby cheeks I've ever seen with a hint of brattiness lurking beneath the surface. I thought to myself, *Now there's a boy who needs a Daddy.* You were so sweet and innocent but you had a naughty side underneath your sweetness. My suspicions that you were a little with a dash of brat in you were confirmed when you opened up to me about your reindeer stuffy."

"Are you serious?" I gasp.

"Yes, angel." Roman kisses my shoulder blade. "A good Daddy should always be able to intuit who his boy truly is inside. I think that I did that with you. I'm a ruthless man who's spent nearly a decade in prison, but I was able to tell that you were a beautiful boy who just needed a good Daddy to push past his walls."

I melt in Roman's arms. "Have you had experience being a Daddy before?"

"Yes, angel." Roman brushes a strand of dark hair from my forehead. "I dabbled in the scene before I went to prison."

"What did you do?" I ask.

"My brother Sasha and I used to frequent a BDSM club in New York City where we learned all about the lifestyle," Roman explains, cradling my shoulder. "I loved playing with chubby guys in their late twenties and Sasha was partial to hairy bears. We attended fantastic workshops that taught us about limits and consent and how to treat our boys the right way. The instructors in the workshops taught us that being a true Daddy is so much more than saying sexy things in bed."

"Really?" I ask.

Roman grunts in the affirmative. "The Daddy boy lifestyle encompasses protection, nurture, and caring in a relationship inside and outside of the bedroom. Being a Daddy to a sweet boy means that you support your partner at all costs. When they have a tough day at work, you stick up for them and stand by their side. When they're feeling sad, you wrap them in a big hug and make them feel like they have nothing to ever fear again. When they have financial trouble, you pay their bills and make their worries go away. It doesn't matter if your partner is a forty-year-old man or a twenty-year-old college student who likes to wear diapers and suck on pacifiers before going to bed at night. Good Daddies support their partners no matter their age and nurture them at all costs."

"Is that what you want to do with me, Daddy?" I whisper.

Roman nods. "Yes, boy. I was so excited when you confessed

that you had an age play kink. The feelings I had for you were so much more than sex alone. I wanted to support you and learn your needs, protect you from harm, and cherish you in every way. My last boy broke up with me when I went to Rikers Island and he took my ability to be a Daddy away with him. I didn't sleep with a single man in eight long years because I was so heartbroken. But you reawakened those protective instincts in me, Bentley. You helped me realize that it wasn't too late to be a Daddy again."

"Do you mind that I'm probably a little younger than the guys you usually go after?" I hedge, nervousness raking down my spine. "You said that you typically played with men in their late twenties when you were involved in the scene. Am I too young for you, Daddy?"

"No, sweet boy." Roman lets out a snort of amused laughter. "I don't mind that you're younger at all. It's true that I usually go for guys older than you — I always picked men in their late twenties with meat on their bones in the club— but you have a strong will and you know what you want inside. You've tried to date before without success and you know that you need a man with life experience to treat you the way you deserve. We're a match for each other, Bentley. If my age isn't a problem for you, then your age isn't a problem for me."

"Okay..." I pick up Señor Antlers and place him on Roman's chest. "I want you to officially meet my stuffy Señor Antlers. He's my comfort companion and I want him to say hi to you."

A smirk tugs at Roman's lips. "Hi, Señor Antlers. It's nice to meet you."

My insides start to get warm and fuzzy.

I start to regress as I stare into Roman's eyes.

"You're so big and muscular, Roman," I sing-song, speaking in a silly voice to give life to my stuffy. "You're tall and covered in menacing tattoos. But Bentley thinks you're sweet inside. He talks about you quite often to his friend Macon and he knows that you're a true protector."

Roman lets out a gruff laugh. "You're very sweet, Señor Antlers. Bentley's the sweetest little I've ever met in my life — far sweeter than my good-for-nothing ex — and he's truly my dream partner in every way. I've spent a long time dreaming about someone like Bentley and I'm so lucky he's in my life. He's my everything and I can't wait to truly be his protector in every way."

Oh. My. Gosh.

Roman's actually playing with my stuffy with me.

He's helping me regress into little mode.

Isn't this what I've truly wanted for so long?

To feel so safe and secure that I feel like nothing could ever harm me again?

I press my nose against Roman's chest. "Señor Antlers says that you didn't deserve to be in Rikers," I mumble into Roman's tattoos, not caring that my voice is muffled by his strong pecs. "Señor Antlers says that he doesn't know exactly what landed you in Rikers, but you didn't deserve it. You're far too caring and nice to ever be in a place like that. You accepted Bentley even when he was a brat to you and pushed past his walls and defenses. You showed him true acceptance and helped him become the sweet boy he was meant to me."

"Bentley is such a sweetheart, Señor Antlers." Roman kisses Señor Antlers and strokes my curly hair. "He's the boy I've dreamt about for so long. I'm so lucky fate brought us together and did something right for once in my life."

Roman pulls something out of his bedside table.

It's the stuffy I saw earlier this morning when I broke into Roman's room.

I gasp when I recognize it.

"I know that stuffy, Daddy," I say, kissing Roman's chest. "I saw it on your bed when I did things to your pillow."

"This is the stuffy that my sister Anastasia gave me before I went to prison," Roman says in a soft voice, brushing hair from my temple. "I kept it in a secret hole in the wall in Rikers Island to protect it at all times. It was the only thing that kept me going on the inside and it reminded me of my real life. My home. The family that I sacrificed so much to protect. This stuffy gave me the courage to keep going, sweet cheeks. I'd never judge you for playing with stuffed animals because I know how much they mean to me."

Roman makes our two stuffed animals hug and dance together on his chest.

I make mine *ROAR* and Roman chuckles and tells me that silly reindeer can't roar, only dinosaurs can.

"Well, mine can," I retort sassily, burying my nose in Roman's muscles. "Mine's a special reindeer that Santa says can say whatever he wants."

"Well, I'll have a chat with Santa later tonight," Roman grunts, tapping my nose, "but I'll let it slide for tonight."

My head spins with so many beautiful emotions as we continue playing.

Maybe this is exactly what I needed.

Maybe this is why none of the boys at Cornell were good for me.

I needed a man who also had a special stuffy he cared for to truly understand me.

I needed a man who's known pain and hurt in his life so that he knows exactly how to comfort me and take away my sads.

My breath hitches as I stare into Roman's eyes. "So you accept that... I'm a little inside, Daddy?" I whisper. "You don't care that I need lots of playtime?"

Roman lets out a laugh. "I accept you, sweet cheeks. I know

that you're a little and I love it so much. I want to be your Daddy with everything I have."

My heart fills with so much warmth as I stare into Roman's eyes.

It's the most precious thing in the world when I tilt my head up and plant a soft kiss on Roman's lips.

It's a sweet, innocent kiss, and we barely dust our lips together, but it means so much to me.

Roman holds me close and we fall asleep in the bed with moonlight trickling in through the window.

Roman accepts that I'm a little.

He adores me for me.

My Daddy is the best Daddy IN THE WORLD!

20

"Wow," I grunt, cupping my angel's ass in the sunlight as I wake up the following morning.

Holy. Freaking. Shit.

Last night was amazing in every way.

Bentley and I had so much sexy fun in the carriage and we drank delicious hot chocolate and ate so many forbidden sweets.

And Bentley's naked body was the sexiest sight I've ever seen.

His cock was so big and perfect, and his curvy ass was so delicious it drove me into a fucking frenzy.

Bentley's body was like candy canes and rainbows and every-thing sweet in this world, and he was so much sexier than I ever could have anticipated.

But the sexy fun was only part of the night.

The best part was when Bentley accepted me as his Daddy in bed.

Bentley was precious and unbelievably sweet, and I melted when he regressed into little mode with me.

Bentley's the one for me.

Bentley yawns as I kiss his cheek to wake him up. "Good morning, sweet cheeks."

Bentley stretches his arms out in the bed and beams at me. "Good morning, Daddy. Did you have a good sleep?"

I press the pad of my thumb against Bentley's cheek and drag it across his skin. "Yes, baby boy. Daddy had the best sleep he's had in nearly a decade."

"Why, Daddy?"

"You were so precious and adorable next to him," I say, nuzzling Bentley's cheeks. "It's what Daddy dreamed about for so long in Rikers Island. He's so fortunate you gave your gift of snuggles to him."

Bentley blushes like a baby rose. "I'm soooo happy to hear that, Daddy. I was nervous that you'd have a bad dream after our snuggle session because we talked about your incarceration in Rikers Island. I feared that our discussion about Anastasia's teddy bear would bring you back to that scary place in your life. But I'm relieved to hear that it didn't."

"It was because of your cuddles, little prince," I say, letting my fingers glide down Bentley's back and smack his thick perfect curves. "Your cuddles warded off the bad dreams and kept them at bay. You're like the Big Friendly Giant who gives good dreams to the people he visits at night. I dreamt of rainbows and sunshine and everything that is beautiful."

Bentley snorts. "You're silly, Daddy. *You're* the Big Friendly Giant to me, not the other way around."

"Oh yeah?"

"I'm so little and small compared to you," Bentley whispers, kissing my pecs. "I could never be the one to give other people good dreams. You're my Daddy. You give good dreams to me."

A groan escapes me as I run my hands over Bentley's gorgeous body. "Someone's being humble with Daddy this morning," I drawl, planting a kiss on Bentley's cheek as I drag my palm down his back. "Good boys must always listen to their Daddies. Their Daddies will never tell them lies."

"I'm not disagreeing with you, Daddy." Bentley giggles when I slide my palm into his pajamas. "I'm merely saying that you're the Big Friendly Giant to me. I'm the boy you blow dream bubbles to through the window and you make me so happy while I sleep. You're the sweetest giant in the world to me."

It's clear that Bentley woke up in little mode.

I let out a gruff laugh. "Someone needs a tummy kiss to start the morning."

I tug back Bentley's pajamas and blow a big juicy raspberry on Bentley's belly.

BRRRRRRRRRRRRPPPPP.

"No, Daddy!" Bentley screams, batting my head away with his fingers. "No belly kisses for Bentley! It's too early in the morning!"

Yeah, too late for that.

I do it again and blow another giant raspberry on Bentley's tummy to make him giggle.

Bentley pushes me away as he laughs hysterically. "Too much silliness, Daddy! I didn't agree to all these tickles! You're going to make me pee my pants this morning!"

I stare into Bentley's eyes. "Nothing wrong with a little accident in your pajamas, boy. Daddy would never judge you for your kinks."

Bentley groans as he pushes me away and pulls his pajamas back on. "That's not my kink, Daddy. I have friends at the Age Play club at Cornell who are into wetting but it's not something that interests me. I like other types of fun."

I growl playfully as I attempt to peel Bentley's pajamas back one more time. "Take your pajamas off, boy. Daddy wants to give you another silly kiss on your belly."

Bentley keeps his top on. "No, Daddy. I don't want that this morning."

I sense a change in Bentley's mood so I stop joking with him at once.

I flit my gaze up to Bentley's eyes. "What's wrong, boy? Daddy sensed something changed in the atmosphere just now. Tell me what it is so I can make adjustments."

Bentley bites his lower lip. "I don't want to tell you."

"What is it, Bentley?" I lean back on the bed and take my angel's hand. "Was the belly kiss too ticklish for you, sweet boy? Is that something that you don't want Daddy to do anymore?"

"No, Daddy." Bentley blinks hard at the mattress. "I... Like the belly kisses. But I'm afraid."

I furrow my brow. "Tell me what it is, pretty angel. Use your words to express your limits with me. Speak your fears into existence so Daddy can swat them down."

Bentley takes a sharp breath. "I'm a big twenty-year-old, Daddy. My weight and curves are my biggest insecurity."

"Go on, little prince." I hold Bentley's hand tight. "I'm listening."

Bentley blows out a breath. "My weight is... The reason I couldn't get dates for many years. I'd match with a guy online and I'd tell him all about my little side and the fact that I liked to play with toys and teddy bears. He'd accept me at first. But when he wanted sexy pictures, he'd stop talking to me. This happened so many times I lost track. I'd send the guy a picture of myself naked in one of the university bathrooms and they'd never respond to me. They'd take one glance at my tummy and never speak to me again."

I shake my head in disgust. "Those guys are children, Bentley." My voice is stern as I stare into my angel's eyes. "They're boys, not men. They're losers who don't know how to deal with a curvy prince like you."

"They're not losers, Daddy," Bentley confesses. "They were successful students and very open-minded. But none of them ever spoke to me after I sent them naughty pictures. They left me on read. It's the reason why I stopped trying to find a beautiful relationship."

A deep growl escapes me. "If I could, I'd find every one of those boys and teach them an unforgettable lesson. They made you feel insecure about your body. I'd beat them senseless for making my sweet angel feel bad about his beautiful curves."

Bentley shakes his head. "No."

I sternly grip Bentley's hand. "You're such a special young man and you have every right to be pissed at those boys, Bentley. They don't have what it takes to be with a boy like you."

"Don't say that, Daddy."

"I bet they couldn't even pick you up and carry you down from a horse-drawn carriage," I snap. "They don't even deserve a text back from you. You should never be with a man who can't carry you for miles and then make passionate love to you over and over again. These boys are disgusting. I want to murder them with my bare hands. I will always do this for you."

"Bentley." I stare into my angel's eyes. "I love your body. I didn't sleep with a single man in Rikers Island because none of them were shaped like you. I love your delicious curves. My cock needs them. My soul needs them. I'm so fucking attracted to you."

Bentley scrunches his eyes tight then nods. "Then there's something I need to tell you."

My eyebrows knit together. "What do you mean, boy?"

A beat passes before Bentley points to his tummy. "I... Have a belly praise kink."

I stare into Bentley's eyes. "A belly praise kink?"

"Yes." Bentley nods. "It's something I discovered earlier this year. I'd just come back from an afternoon in Central Park where

I was supposed to meet up with a boy from my Greek Mythology course. I was supposed to read books with him next to the Bethesda Fountain. But he stood me up and texted me that he wasn't going to come. I left the park and headed back to my dorm at Cornell, super upset with myself. I kept thinking that I was too big to love and that my weight was the reason he didn't go on the date with me. I went online to PornWorld to see if there were people who enjoyed bigger guys as boyfriends. I wasn't expecting to find much, honestly, because my experiences thus far had fucking sucked. But what I found on PornWorld shocked me."

I rub Bentley's wrist. "Tell me, baby boy. I won't judge."

Bentley inhales a sharp breath of air. "I found... An entire section of the site devoted to men with belly praise kinks. They weren't ashamed of their curves or their unique bodies. They wanted their partners to... Worship them in unique ways. Some of the partners used their rolls for pleasure. Some of the men wanted to put their dick in their belly. I thought it was bizarre at first but the more I watched the more I realized that we bigger boys go through so much in this world, so why is it so wrong to just want to lay back and have someone worship our belly? I think it's beautiful to show your partner you're truly attracted to them in bed. You're not just paying lip service to body positivity. You're actually using their body for pleasure. You're praising and worshiping and loving your partner for the same thing that so many people have rejected them for. I got so hard watching those videos and I really wanted a partner to try it with me. A partner who could use my belly for their pleasure. That's why I was so nervous when you blew raspberries on my belly a moment ago, Daddy. I started to feel like I wanted you to worship me."

"That's incredible, baby boy. I had no idea you felt this way."

Bentley nods. "There are a few limits associated with the

kink that I'm probably not comfortable with, but the rest is something I've wanted to try with the right partner for a very long time."

"Tell me your limits, boy. I want to make sure we don't cross any lines."

Bentley inhales a sharp breath. "No degradation. A lot of the men in the videos online liked it when their partners called them *slut* or *whore*. I don't want any of that. I just want you to worship me."

"I love that, Bentley. That sounds like a perfect limit to me."

Bentley stares into my eyes. "I'm ready for you to prove it now, Daddy. Prove you're attracted to me. Prove that my belly doesn't make you want to leave this farmhouse forever like the students I talked to online."

I squeeze Bentley's palm. "Tell me one more time what you want, boy. I refuse to have any misunderstandings between us."

It's so important to discuss things like limits when engaging in a new kink with your partner.

Situations like this have the potential to veer off course and I want to make sure that Bentley and I stay within his limits.

"I want you to use me, Daddy." Bentley's blue eyes blaze a path into mine. "I want you to put your dick in my tummy and go crazy with me. Show me your primal side and prove to me that you love my body."

"And what about this delicious chest, boy?" I grunt, running my thumb over Bentley's nipples. "Will you let Daddy put his dick in there too?"

Bentley's cheeks turn pink. "Yes, Daddy. You can put your dick between my mitties. That's what I call them. Maybe show me you can't control yourself a second longer around me. Show me this is something you *must do or else you'll fucking die* and that you've wanted to do this for all the time you've been in Rikers Island. I'd love that so much."

My jaw drops.

Bentley must be joking.

He's actually... Giving me permission to worship his perfect body?

Oh sweet Jesus Christ.

This is all I've wanted for the past eight years.

A sexy curvy man who I can show just how much I love him.

A man who won't be offended or weirded out when I express my love to him in unique ways.

A man who lets me worship him.

"Say it one more time, angel." My voice is a low growl as I press two fingers against Bentley's wrist. "Give Daddy permission to do what he wants."

Bentley nods. "I give you permission, Daddy. Make me feel like the most desired boy on Earth."

Bentley's words tear the cap off the lust that I've been keeping locked up inside of me for nearly a decade.

I can barely believe my ears but I know it's true.

Bentley wants me to worship him.

He wants me to show him my wild side, the raw side of me that desires to shoot my spend all over his delicious curves.

Bentley wants me to get fucking crazy and adore him, just like what I've wanted to do to a man for so long.

I can barely control myself as I tug my dick out of my pajama bottoms and grip it in my hand.

I peel back Bentley's pajamas and nearly gasp when I see his beautiful belly underneath.

It's thick and white, like a can of buttermilk biscuits that I want to scarf down with a giant knob of butter.

I bury my face in Bentley's tummy and growl like I'm praising a deity.

BRRRRRRRPH.

Bentley giggles as I blow raspberries into his delectable curves, stroking myself with wild abandon.

I flatten my tongue against his sexy belly, then tunnel it into his belly button and lose myself in lust.

"Bentley..." I groan, tentatively brushing my aching dick against Bentley's flesh, unable to stop myself. "Such a... Thick boy. Giving Daddy the permission he wants to... Do anything he wants to his sexy tummy."

"Yes, Daddy!" Bentley giggles.

"Daddy wants to... He wants to put his dick... Daddy's going to..."

I can't control myself a second longer.

A groan escapes me as I plunge my cock into Bentley's tummy, burying it in his gorgeous mounds.

I fold my cock deeper and deeper into his sexy flesh, settling it between his delicious rolls as my balls throb with need.

A cry of desire tumbles out of me as I sync my thrusts with Bentley's moans, spearing him harder and harder like a warrior in battle, determined to win this war.

Bentley trembles and cries out but I focus on the task at hand, which is completely losing myself in Bentley, and pleasuring myself with his body.

This is the command Bentley gave me.

He wants me to lose control like a beast in his belly, to prove that I'm attracted to him in every way.

"So perfect..." My eyes roll back to the whites as I rut my cock against Bentley's sexy chest, plunging my engorged mushroom head deep between his mitties and wiggling it around. "So perfect, Bentley. You're what Daddy's been craving for eight long years. A perfect curvy boy with such a delicious body. Must... Go... Harder..."

My soul shakes as I press my dick even harder into Bentley's chest.

Bentley whimpers as I growl like a caveman, using his rolls for pleasure, masturbating furiously and pumping as hard as I can.

I pant and sweat as I hungrily spear Bentley's mitties with my ten-inch dick, feeling the way his sexy chest parts for me.

Then I do something totally crazy.

I glance down and focus my attention on the beautiful sight of my uncut dick grazing Bentley's puckered belly button, smearing pre-come on his untouched flesh.

A growl clings to my mouth as I circle my foreskin around Bentley's virgin button, mapping a path to his sensitive tummy, testing his entrance before gently nudging myself inside.

My foreskin ripples across Bentley's flesh as I squeeze my veiny head into Bentley's belly hole, my dick throbbing in antici- pation of the pleasure gardens that await me.

I don't hesitate, don't hold back.

I fuck Bentley's virgin belly button with caveman abandon.

This is the time to show Bentley that I can't go another fucking day without his sexy body in my life.

This is the time to capture his insecurities in a Mason jar and then blow that Mason jar to smithereens.

I must worship Bentley, show him that I'm attracted to him, and prove that I can't go another day without his perfect body in my life.

It's what Bentley needs to see that I'm truly attracted to him today.

When I finish pumping in Bentley's belly button, I clasp Bentley's hair in my right palm and drag my aching shaft up to Bentley's gaping mouth.

I plunge myself deep inside his mouth, and Bentley moans as he sucks my hardness.

"That's right, beautiful boy." I fuck Bentley's tight virgin throat as my eyes roll back. "Daddy waited so long to meet a boy like you. You're everything Daddy's been dreaming about. Such a perfect boy with such voluptuous curves. I'm so goddamn attracted to you."

Spit trickles out of Bentley's lips as I plunge myself into his mouth over and over again.

A gasp gurgles in the back of Bentley's throat and I burrow myself deeper and deeper, relishing the sounds of Bentley's pleasure around me.

My engorged balls smack into Bentley's chin and send spit into the air.

Bentley's eyes turn moist as I impale him with my cock over and over and his floppy brown curls shake with delight.

I let out a primal roar as fire licks the inside of my gut.

It's time to prove to Bentley once and for all that I'm absolutely crazy about him.

It's time to show him that he's so much more to me than a twenty-year-old boy who cuddles with stuffies.

He's my passion, my life, my everything.

He's the principle object of my desire come to life and I won't let him down.

With a roar, I yank my dick out of Bentley's throat and point it at his chest.

The sound of a fighter jet fills the room when my cock sprays thick hoses of semen all over Bentley's belly, shooting out so much spunk it seems like I haven't had an orgasm in a decade.

Bentley's sexy curves drip with my seed, and come sprays all over the mattress.

Bentley lets out a laugh. "So sexy, Daddy! You got cummies everywhere! You really are attracted to me!"

"You're so perfect, Bentley," I groan, as I squeeze my come onto Bentley's belly. "I haven't had a curvy boy by my side in so long. I love your body, sweet angel. You're everything I need."

"This is amazing, Daddy." Bentley grins devilishly. "This is just like what I dreamt about in my fantasies. I love it so much."

I let out a moan as I scoop the come up from Bentley's tummy and rub it all over his sexy chest.

"You're covered in Daddy's come now, sweet cheeks," I groan, rubbing my seed all over Bentley's stomach, fingering his thick curves as I smear my seed into them. "Daddy adores your precious body in every way. Daddy's never going to let you go."

It's the sweetest thing ever when Bentley thrusts his come-soaked fingers through my hair and steals a kiss from my lips.

He buries his tongue in my mouth and then collapses on the mattress, allowing me to massage him using my come as massage oil, kneading it into every inch of his belly.

This is my dream partner come to life.

How did I get so damn lucky?

21

I'M FLOATING on cloud nine when Roman leads me out of the farmhouse.

We're lucky that it's a Sunday morning so Paw Paw doesn't have any work for Roman to do on the farm so we can have a breakfast picnic together.

We have our stuffed animals with us and a special blanket covered in teddies.

But I'm not thinking of the wonderful breakfast we're going to have or the memories we'll make.

I'm thinking of Roman.

Sexy, strong, possessive Roman, who couldn't keep his hands off me in bed this morning.

"Oh sweet Jesus," I groan, squeezing Roman's hand even tighter as I press my cheek against his muscular arm.

This morning was the best freaking morning of my life.

I woke up nestled snug in Roman's firm arms and I seriously felt like I slept on a cloud.

This morning, Roman showed me that I had nothing to be afraid of about my body.

He adored every inch of me, my curves and my tummy, even more than I could imagine.

And Roman didn't just pay lip service to body positivity like so many other people do in this day and age.

Roman proved he was fucking attracted to me, foaming at the mouth to treat my curves right and come on my stomach.

Roman wanted to rip my PJs off and coat my sexy curves with his come like only a man who's attracted to a guy like me could do.

I was on freaking cloud nine when Roman used me like a sex doll and didn't relent because it showed me that he truly wanted to be with me.

He didn't tiptoe around my weight nor did he use kid gloves with me.

Roman was brutal, ruthless, and rough, which is exactly what I needed deep down in my heart to know that Roman accepts me.

Every memory of every student at Cornell rejecting me for my weight flashed back in my mind this morning but Roman pushed straight past that.

He proved that he was unlike every other man in the world when he accepted me for me.

And when Roman finished coming on my tummy, he brought me into the shower and gave me the most beautiful aftercare I could've ever imagined.

He shampooed my hair and soaped up every inch of my body, paying special attention to the curves that he loves so much.

He ate me out in the shower and gave me three more orgasms with the hot water flowing down on us, and I left the bathroom breathless as he carried me in his big strong arms.

I guess what I've been missing my entire life was a growly Russian man.

A man who's caring, devoted and a true animal in bed.

Could I get any luckier than that?

"Hey, sweet boy." Roman's deep baritone awakens me from my musings. "We found your special spot."

I glance at the clearing in front of me. "Daddy!" I gasp breathlessly, wrapping my arms around Roman's chest. "How did you know this is my special place?"

Roman lets out a gruff laugh. "You mentioned it last night on our carriage ride."

A snort escapes me.

Damn. I must've had way too much Baileys infused hot chocolate.

"I don't even remember that," I say with a giggle.

"Yes, angel." Roman's heart beats loud as he nuzzles our noses together. "You like to come up here to eat cookies while watching the trees grow. It's one of your favorite places in the world."

My heart fills with so much warmth as Roman nuzzles my nose.

I think back to last night and realize that I did confess that this was my special reading place where I come with my Kindle Oasis.

I let out a snort. "You put way too much Baileys in that hot chocolate, Daddy. I don't even remember that I told you this."

Roman sits on the ground and lays me on the grass next to him. "It wasn't the Baileys, baby boy."

"No?" I coo, rubbing my forehead against Roman's shoulder. "Then what was it?"

"You had way too much fun eating and spending time with me in a beautiful carriage in the moonlight. You were too focused on the yummy treats to remember what you said."

I roll my eyes. "No, Daddy." My cheeks turn bright pink as I stare into Roman's eyes. "I forgot what I said because of you. I was so focused on being close to you that I didn't remember anything I said. You took over my memories."

Roman brushes a strand of hair from my temple and plants a chaste kiss on my cheek. "You're such a sweetie pie, Bentley. You brought me back to life. I don't know how I survived without your cuteness."

I'm blushing like a strawberry when I pull our picnic breakfast out of my backpack and set it on the ground.

"Breakfast time, Daddy." I point to the container, so relieved that I can finally drop my bratty act around Roman and be the sweet boy I am inside. "Your boy is feeling hungry. He needs his big strong protector to feed him."

"You're the silliest boy in the world, you know that, Bentley?" Roman barks out a laugh.

"I know you are but what am I?"

Roman smirks. "I know you didn't really just say that to me, boy. You're being immature."

I stick my tongue out at Roman. "Maybe that's just who I am inside, Daddy. Maybe I pretended to be mature this entire time so you'd talk to me. But you're stuck with me now, Mister. So I'm going to let my little flag fly."

Roman leans across the grass and pecks my lips.

He runs the pad of his thumb across my trembling cheek and then kisses me again.

"No more silliness this morning." Roman unpacks the breakfast from the Tupperware containers. "We have a big day ahead of us."

"Nooooo, Daddy. You can't eat yet." I let out a wail as I pull Roman's fingers away from the Tupperware.

Roman furrows his brow. "Did I do something wrong?"

"Yes, Daddy." I sniffle. "Humans never eat before our stuffed animals do. You must feed Señor Antlers first before we can have anything."

A beat passes before Roman rolls his eyes and lets out a groan. "Damnit, Bentley. I'm starving."

I cross my arms over my chest. "You must, Daddy. Those are the rules of the stuffy kingdom. Our stuffies eat before we eat otherwise our food is cursed."

"Our food isn't cursed, boy." Roman rolls his eyes. "Keep this up, and I'll eat everything."

I shake my head. "The rules are the rules, Daddy. I didn't make them up but you can't break them. I'll be very cross with you if you eat before our stuffies and I'll never speak to you again."

Roman picks Señor Antlers up and lets out a sigh. "Fine," Roman says, pulling out a piece of bacon from the Tupperware container and bringing it to my stuffy. "You're going to be the death of me."

My heart turns warm and fuzzy when Roman feeds Señor Antlers and his teddy the bacon.

Holy. Freaking. Guacamole.

Roman actually wants to feed my stuffies.

He realizes that this is serious to me and he's not just paying lip service to my kink.

Roman actually wants to play pretend with me and it's seriously the best thing ever.

"Thank you, Daddy." I nuzzle Roman's cheek with my nose. "Señor Antlers is a happy boy now."

"I'm glad I could be of service."

When Roman and I finish eating, we pack up our Tupperware and walk around the tree farm.

Roman holds my hand and asks me to tell him about my life growing up.

I tell Roman about my adventures with my brother and what it was like to spend the holidays on a Christmas tree farm.

Roman listens to everything and internalizes every word.

I also tell Roman about this amazing new author discovered on my Kindle last week.

There's this author named Aster Rae who writes the most adorable books with loving boys and their protective Daddies.

At last, Roman leads me underneath a beautiful oak tree and sets me on his lap.

He strokes my hair and holds me close as we listen to the sounds of the forest.

And that's when I realize that it's time.

Here. Now. Right this second.

It's time... To confess my deepest reality to Roman.

There's no more time for half truths or incomplete pictures now.

Roman needs to know exactly what happened with my brother that fateful night eight years ago.

We're Daddy and boy now, and he deserves to know everything about me.

"It's time to tell you something, Daddy," I say at last.

Roman's lips graze my cheek. "Go ahead, boy. I'm listening."

"It's about what happened... Eight years ago." I press my cheek against Roman's chest. "The night the carjacker changed everything."

"Tell me."

I close my eyes tight as the memories come back to me. "My family and I were coming back from a performance of Tchaikovsky's *The Nutcracker*. We had the most amazing time at the New York Ballet and the dancers in the show were amazing.

I loved watching the sugarplum fairy prance around the stage in a silly dress."

"Let it all out, sweet boy." Roman massages my back.

"We were sitting in our Toyota in traffic at a red light. We talked about the performance and about how much fun we all had. Jericho made a joke that someday I should be the sugarplum fairy and dance around in a dress on a stage. He said that I'd be perfect in the role and that everybody would cheer for me. I was thinking about how sweet my brother was and how much I wanted to give him a big hug.

"That's when the man burst out of the alley in all black." My breath hitches. "He had a knife in his hand and ordered my parents to get out of the car. My parents said that they weren't getting out of the car because it was Christmas Eve. The carjacker didn't like that my parents talked back to him. He pulled a giant gun out of his back pocket and fired into the car. He killed my parents instantly."

"Oh my God." Roman holds me tight. "That's horrible, Bentley."

"My brother tried to protect me," I continue, holding back tears. "He yanked me out of the backseat of the car and brought me into an alley. He gave me an X-Acto knife that he found in the backseat and told me to hold it close. I was supposed to use it if anyone came for me. My brother kissed my forehead and told me he'd be right back. He said he needed to do something fast and that I shouldn't be around to see it.

"He ordered me to put my fingers in my ears and then he left the alley and went back to the carjacker. He didn't know that I tiptoed out of my hiding spot to watch the entire thing. He found the carjacker moving my parents's bodies out of the front seat and he charged the carjacker and threw him on the ground. He kicked in the carjacker's face. The carjacker nearly died. But a police car pulled up from around the block at the wrong moment and pulled Jericho off of him. They arrested my brother and brought the carjacker to the hospital. My brother was supposed to get off but the judge didn't acknowledge the facts of the case. The judge sentenced him to twenty-five years in Rikers Island for attempted homicide without the possibility of parole. Jericho wasn't acting in self-defense, the judge said. He deemed Jericho a threat to society and took away his rights. Jericho had a court-appointed lawyer — we couldn't afford anything more — but the court-appointed lawyer didn't do shit for him. He let Jericho suffer in Rikers Island and and didn't even try to negotiate a plea bargain. It was the worst thing that could've happened and it crushed my family. That's why Jericho's been locked up in prison ever since."

Roman blows out a breath. "I'm so sorry to hear that, Bentley. You don't know how upset and angry that story makes me."

"I know, Daddy. It makes me so mad too."

"You went through so much at such a young age," Roman whispers tenderly, running his fingers through my hair. "Your brother saved your life. He saw your parents die and didn't know if the carjacker would come after you. He knew he had to act. The court may not think he's a hero but he took on the carjacker and beat his fucking ass. Jericho protected you and avenged his parents's death that night, Bentley. And the courts fucked Jericho over by locking him in prison. It's wrong and disgusting on every level and he deserves to be set free."

I nod. "I'm ready to hear your story now too, Daddy. Tell me."

A deep breath escapes Roman. "My story is very similar to yours. Just like Jericho, I was involved in a situation where I had to protect someone close to me. It was my sister Anastasia."

"I know," I say, burrowing into Roman's chest. "I saw that on your teddy."

Roman blows out a breath. "My sister Anastasia was involved with a very bad man. His name was Alphonso and he was a

member of a rival Mafia family that were vicious human traf-
fickers in Manhattan. He commanded an empire of fifty men
and he was under constant scrutiny from the NYPD. My sister
met Alphonso on a one-month vacation to New York City from
Russia. They met on an online app for billionaires and he told
her that his family owned mines in Africa and that they sold
diamonds to jewelers like Cartier and Tiffany at full price. My
sister didn't know this was a lie and she went out on a few dates
with him and they started dating seriously. She also didn't
realize how unethical the blood diamond trade in Africa was
otherwise she'd never have gone out with him in the first place
because that's wrong. Alphonso became Anastasia's boyfriend
and they moved in together after only three weeks.

"One night I walked into Anastasia's hotel suite to deliver her
an ethically sourced diamond bracelet for her twenty-second
birthday. I was there to surprise her and take her on a helicopter
ride over New York City to check out the Statue of Liberty. She
was a big fan of the Statue of Liberty. She also loved Frédéric
Auguste Bartholdi's work and also the sonnet the French poet
Emma Lazarus wrote in 1883 to raise money for the statue at a
charity art auction in France. *If only Anastasia was as avid a
student of human character as she was of history*, I would later
think ruefully from behind the bars of my cell, *then none of this
would've happened.* I only wanted to give Anastasia her first tour
of *La Liberté éclairant le monde* because I knew she cared about it
so much.

"So I knocked on Anastasia's door. She didn't answer. I
furrowed my brow and knocked even louder. I didn't know if she
was listening to music or reading a copy of Chekhov's short
stories but I needed to get her attention. But Anastasia didn't
come to the door. Eventually concern consumed me and I
slammed the door in with my huge muscular shoulder that can
break through anything. The door didn't stand a chance against

my strong Hulk-like body. I marched into the hotel suite to see if Anastasia was all right and that's when I saw Alphonso standing over Anastasia in the living room with a knife in his hand. Anastasia was bound in rope with blood dripping out of her mouth. She had a black eye and Alphonso was standing over her with a pair of brass knuckles and screaming at her to give him information about our family. Anastasia couldn't tell him anything because truthfully she didn't even know what we did for a living. She knew that we were one of the most powerful families in Russia but she had no idea that we were involved in the mob. She was an innocent angel who browsed turn-of-the-century French designs and read highbrow literature in her suite in Moscow who'd never stepped foot in the real world. She lived in the *monde de l'art* where the worst that can happen is a critic you love writes a rave review about a piece you find overrated. I barged into the room and grabbed Alphonso by the throat because I lived in the real world, not the world of books and design, and I knew how to deal with monsters. I tugged Alphonso off my sister and slammed his face into the wall, causing him to scream. I'll spare you the details, Bentley, but let's just say that I beat him within an inch of his life. I only spared him because Anastasia figured out a way to free herself from her ropes and begged me to stop. I argued with Anastasia to convince her to let me kill Alphonso but she wouldn't let me. She said that Alphonso was taking her to Paris in a week and that they were going to drink hot chocolate at *Les Deux Magots*. Alphonso escaped during that time that she was pleading with me. He ran away into the night and left me with Anastasia alone."

"How did you get put into Rikers Island for that?" My voice is a gasp.

"Alphonso's attorney filed criminal charges against me two hours later. He had contacts inside the Department of Justice in

New York City. They filed federal level criminal attempted homicide charges against me and argued that Alphonso and Anastasia were engaged in consensual role-play that night which is why I was in the wrong to beat him. They argued that I was trying to kill my sister's boyfriend because I was jealous of him. They said I was attracted to my sister and wanted to make love to her. They were so wrong. I was gayer than a Lady Gaga backup dancer at a Pride parade and never wanted my sister. The entire night was a miscarriage of justice in every way.

"I had no recourse," Roman continues. "My extended family wasn't established in America yet so they didn't have connections with upper levels of government like Alphonso's family did. The feds threw me into Rikers Island. It was horrible every step of the way. And I just found out this week that Alphonso's attorneys paid off the judge in my case to send me to prison. My brother Sasha discovered that when he was digging around my old case files. So there's a corruption element as well that I can prove in court. It was so gross in every way."

Wow.

I can barely believe it as Roman's story washes over me.

Both of our siblings were attacked on Christmas Eve.

Both Jericho and Roman were imprisoned in Rikers Island for crimes that weren't justified.

We've both been through trauma. Raw, unadulterated trauma.

We have a connection that binds us on such a deep level.

I misjudged Roman horribly when he first came here but now I know that he's brave and strong.

He defended his little sister after a vicious mobster attacked her in her hotel suite.

Roman beat him senseless to protect Anastasia's honor.

I can't help but wonder if Roman and Jericho's cases are

connected in a different way but now is not the time to ponder that.

All I know is that Roman is going to help Jericho get out of Rikers.

He's going to help my brother be free.

It's the best thing in the world and I'm so damn lucky Roman's in my life.

"You're so brave." I thrust my arms around Roman's neck. "You did the right thing, Roman. I'm so sorry your judge didn't see your side of the story."

"I'm going to fight like hell to prove my innocence." Roman's voice is firm and growly. "I'm going to get this conviction over-turned. And then I'm going to sue the state of New York to make sure this never happens to anyone else again."

22

One week later

"Merry Christmas."

I accept the one-hundred-dollar bill from the man in the down jacket in front of me and wrap my arms tight around Bentley.

One week has passed since Bentley and I confessed our feelings to each other and my life has only improved since.

Bentley and I have gotten closer every day and we spend every moment that we can together.

When I come in after a long day of chopping down Christmas trees, Bentley's always there with a steaming mug of hot cocoa and a grin on his face to take my stress away.

He gives me lots of hugs and angel kisses and tells me that I'm the best Daddy in the whole wide world.

When the Christmas tree season started this past week, Barney and Bertha tasked me with being the primary salesperson of the residence and I'm selling more trees than I can count.

People are coming up from the city to buy trees and I'm selling a ton.

We're all anxiously watching the sky to see if snow will finally come, and that's definitely a central talking point with the customers, but we haven't had luck on that front yet.

But I don't need snow to receive my gift from Santa this year.

I already have my present in my arms.

Sweet, beautiful Bentley, the sassiest and most bashful boy I've ever met in my life.

"Merry Christmas to you too, Sir." The man in the down jacket issues me a curt nod as Bentley and I hand him his change.

"That's a beautiful tree you've got there," Bentley sing-songs, swooning into me and winking at the customer.

"It sure is." The customer pockets the change and smiles at Bentley. "My family and I are going to decorate it later tonight when I get back to the city."

"I'm so glad to hear that," Bentley says with a grin. "It's great to keep traditions alive."

"You can say that again," the customer says with a gruff laugh. "Last year we tried to decorate a plastic tree that we bought from an infomercial on TV. It was trash. The holidays just aren't the same without a real tree in your living room."

"You can say that again," I growl, nudging Bentley's ribs. "There's nothing like a real Christmas tree to brighten up the season."

Bentley and I head to the man's car and tie the giant tree on his roof.

The customer thanks us as he drives off with Christmas music blasting from his speakers.

Bentley snorts as he turns to me. "Well, that was easy."

I let out a grunt. "That man wasn't even here for ten minutes. How can you decide on a quality tree when you haven't even looked around the lot?"

Bentley rolls his eyes. "My grandparents have the best Christmas trees in the state, Daddy."

"And?" I say gruffly, wrapping my arms around Bentley's waist.

Bentley winks at me. "The customer doesn't need to spend any time looking for trees because they know that every tree here is amazing. My grandparents would never let them down."

I'm opening my mouth to respond but before I can get a word out the familiar sound of laughter fills the air.

I glance up to see a giant black limousine pull up at the end of the driveway.

Two young men hop out with each other and two bigger men lumber out of the limousine behind them.

I immediately recognize the older men as my American cousins Nikolai and Igor who I haven't seen in eight long years.

"Daddy," one of the young blond men whines, putting his hands on his hips as he turns around to face my cousin Nikolai. *That must be Nikolai's husband Christian.* "You didn't load the refrigerator with fresh ice cream bars in the limousine for my snacks. I'm huuungry."

Nikolai lets out a grunt. "Sorry, baby boy. You know that you're on an ice cream free diet for the next three weeks."

Christian's other friend, who I immediately guess is Igor's husband Rowan, lets out a snort. "You need to quit being such a brat, Christian. We're lucky to spend any time in a limousine at all and we should thank our Daddies for hooking us up with this cool ride to Bentley's farm."

Christian rolls his eyes up to the sky. "It's not my fault that I get hungry, Rowan. It was a long ride, and we only stopped at

McDonalds to get chicken nuggets and fries twice. A boy can only starve to death for so long."

Bentley claps his hands together. "Christian," Bentley gushes, rushing across the driveway to meet his friend. "I'm so glad you made it."

"Hey, Bentley." Christian hugs his friend. "This farm is absolutely gorgeous. Rowan and I were taking pictures for Instagram when we pulled up because we can't believe how pretty it is."

"It *is* pretty." Rowan wraps Bentley in a hug. "I was telling Christian that I want to bring a Christmas tree back to Igor's penthouse in New York when we leave. It's the perfect thing to bring some holiday cheer into our lives and we could decorate it with silly teddy bears and beautiful strings of light to brighten our days wherever we go."

Bentley chuckles to himself. "We do have plenty of trees here... You could definitely take one home if you wanted."

"Really?" Christian's eyebrows migrate to his forehead.

"Yes." Bentley nods. "We just have to figure out how to tie it to the roof of your limousine first, but once we get those logistics out of the way, the transportation should be a piece of cake."

Rowan lets out a groan. "Don't say cake, Bentley. Christian and I are starving and we're going to lose it if you talk about sweets."

Christian rubs his belly. "My tummy's grumbling, so I think it's time for Nikolai to feed me."

Christian turns around to face Nikolai. "Did you hear that, Daddy? I'm getting the hungries and you need to give me a snack break."

Nikolai's face is dark and unwavering as he glares at his angel.

"Hell no," Nikolai barks, a vein bulging in his forehead. "You were an incorrigible brat the entire ride up here so you're going to learn what it feels like to starve until dinner time. That's what you get for being a brat."

Christian sticks his tongue out. "Bentley and I are heading inside to get some unicorn cupcakes. We'll see you when it's dinner time."

Nikolai lets out a groan. "I need to take off my belt and whip that boy into submission. He's going to be the death of me."

Uhhhm.

Holy shit.

My cousins and their partners are basically the funniest people I've ever seen.

Christian and Rowan could have their own reality show if they wanted.

They could call the show *The Real Housetwinks of New York City.*

"*Rad videt' tebya, kuzen.*" I walk over to Nikolai and take his bag. It's nice to see you, cousin.

"*My davno ne videlis', Roman,*" Nikolai growls. It's been a long time since we've seen each other, Roman.

"*Vse normal'no,*" I say. It's fine.

"*Prinosim svoi izvineniya za to, chto ne naveshchayem vas v tyur'me chashche,*" Igor says with a grunt, staring at me. "*Bylo nepravil'no ne videt' tebya na ostrove Raykers vse eti gody. Nadeyem-sya, vy nas prostite.*" We apologize for not visiting you in prison more often. It was wrong to not visit you in Rikers Island all of these years. We hope you'll forgive us.

I let out a grunt. "Don't even worry about it, *zhopa*. The past is in the past. I understand that the NYPD will put you under surveillance if you visit someone in Rikers Island. I'm going to be out in less than two weeks so we can put all this behind us very soon."

Igor raises an eyebrow. "We have news that you might find interesting."

My eyebrows rise. "*Deystvitel'no?*" Really?

Igor nods. "*Da.* Apparently Sasha's men found evidence that a secret powerful family interfered in Jericho's case at the same time as yours. No one ever caught it because Jericho's court-appointed lawyer didn't bother to look into it. He figured that Jericho was just another run-of-the-mill teenager who got over-invested in his parents's murder and took matters into his own hands. Well, Sasha discovered that there were powerful forces bribing Jericho's judge to keep him locked up in Rikers. Antoine is getting the evidence to help us with the case."

My head spins as I process my cousin's words.

What the fuck?

Powerful forces tampered with Jericho's case just like they did with mine?

I already knew that my enemies bribed my judge to keep me in Rikers Island but I had no idea that Jericho went through the same thing.

It's disgusting how much happens under the table in this country but that's how the system works for the rich and powerful.

Someone used their privilege and connections to put me and Jericho behind bars.

But now I can use my power and privilege for good to free Jericho and help change the system.

It's the best gift I could ever give Bentley and it will truly help me become his forever Daddy in his eyes.

I'm opening my mouth to respond to Igor when a blur of light bursts out of the farmhouse and rushes across the driveway straight into my arms.

Bentley moans as he thrusts his arms around me and gives me a big hug.

"Daddy's so good at helping customers with their trees and welcoming new friends into the farmhouse," Bentley murmurs as he sinks his teeth into my chest. "Bentley appreciates every-thing Daddy's done for him so much."

I grunt and brush a strand of curly hair from Bentley's fore-head. "Well, this is sweet, baby boy. I wonder why you're giving me this big hug."

"I saw how Christian was acting toward Nikolai when he got out of the limousine," Bentley says, staring up into my eyes. "I wanted to make sure you know that I'm not like that and that I adore and cherish you with everything I have."

Nikolai lets out a laugh. "That's sweet, Bentley. But you should know that Christian is only feeling cranky because he's on a new ice cream-free diet."

"An ice cream free diet?" Bentley turns around to look at Nikolai.

Nikolai nods. "Christian's sugar levels were too high at his last medical checkup. He hasn't had ice cream in three whole days and he's going through major withdrawals."

Bentley shakes his head. "Okay, well, I'll go a little easier on Christian then. It must be hard giving up ice cream."

"I bet it is, boy," I growl, wrapping my arms tight around Bentley's waist. "Luckily your blood sugar levels are just fine so you don't have to give up sweets anytime soon."

Fuck.

I don't know what I'd do if Bentley had to give up sweets.

He's the type of young man who needs unicorn cupcakes and delicious baked goods every second of the day because they give him so many happies.

Bentley's so much fluffier and more adorable because of it.

Bentley kisses my chest. "Thank you for understanding me, Daddy."

"You still have to eat your vegetables, though," I bark, nuzzling Bentley's nose. "A good Daddy always makes sure that his boy gets his nutrients."

"I will, Daddy," Bentley says. "I promise."

Bentley clears his throat. "Can we go inside and eat some ice cream in front of Christian to tease him?"

I let out a laugh. "That's my boy."

23

Later that day

WHAT. A. Freaking. Success.

My heart is warm and fuzzy as I take Roman's hand and lead him into my heated barn.

Today was so amazing in every way and I seriously can't believe it actually happened.

I bonded so well with Christian and Rowan and we played a silly game with dinosaur stuffies in my bedroom.

Roman and I helped so many people pick out Christmas trees and Roman cut them all down like a boss.

He was the most perfect salesperson Paw Paw's ever had and he exceeded my expectations in every way.

But the day is finally over and now it's time to spend some one-on-one time with my sexy ex-convict Daddy.

It's time to play in my barn.

Specifically, in the loft where my brother and I used to play all the time growing up.

"Up here, Daddy." I wrap my fingers around Roman's and lead him into the barn.

Roman lets out a grunt. "It's hard to see in here, angel. I think you need to pull back the blinds."

A chuckle escapes me as I realize that Roman has a point.

It's dark AF in the barn.

I turn on the switch to light the barn up. "I turned the light on, Daddy. Now you'll be able to see when we head up the ladder into the loft where we're going to play all afternoon."

Roman smirks. "Now I see what you're talking about, baby boy. This is a beautiful barn and it really seems like a sanctuary for you. I'm lucky you're taking me here today."

My cheeks turn pink. "I'm the lucky one, Daddy. This is where Jericho and I came all the time to play growing up. Sometimes we'd sneak up here in the middle of the night and have special bonding time together. I'm lucky you came here with me."

I lock the door of the barn and lead Roman to the loft.

I climb up the ladder and plop down on a bale of hay when I reach the top as Roman climbs up after me.

Roman kisses me when he reaches the loft and rearranges some yummy smelling wreaths my grandparents moved up here for storage to sit down next to me.

I pull my favorite onesie out of a backpack and show it to Roman. "Look at this, Daddy."

"Wow." Roman runs his fingers over the fabric, feeling the softness of the PJs. "This is such nice fabric, Bentley. I love this onesie."

My heart turns warm and happy. "You mean it, Daddy?"

Roman nods. "I love the reindeer and elves on the side. It looks like Christmas came early this year and blessed you with these beautiful pajamas. I bet wearing this onesie makes you feel so safe and happy inside."

Wow. Just wow.

Roman seriously understands the best parts of my regression kink.

He gets that I don't wear these types of clothes because I'm a freak or anything.

I wear onesies because they make me feel so safe inside.

"Yes, Daddy." I scoot next to Roman and put my chin on his shoulder. "This is my favorite onesie I've ever owned. I feel like the littlest elf in the universe when I put it on."

An invisible hook tugs Roman's lips into a smirk. "Let Daddy help you put it on, boy. Daddy wants to see what you look like in your onesie."

My jaw drops. "You mean it?"

Roman nods. "Yes, boy. You must remember that I spent eight long years of my life surrounded by savages and sheer brutality. I was a Daddy long before I went to Rikers Island and I had to bury those parts of myself when I was locked up behind bars to stay safe. I'd feel honored if you let me put this on you today. It'll help me get in touch with who I am."

I can barely believe my ears as Roman's words wash over me.

He doesn't think I'm a freak.

He doesn't think I'm a weirdo for wanting to wear little kid clothes in my loft.

He knows this is my kink and he still wants to experience this with me.

How. Freaking. Lucky. Am. I?

"I'd love if you helped me put it on." My cheeks flush. "I'd feel so protected and safe."

"Great, boy." Roman brushes a strand of hair from my forehead. "Tell me what to do."

I shake my head. "That's not how it works, Daddy."

"No?" Roman says with a smirk. *He's teasing me.*

I nod. "I did my research beforehand, Daddy. In a Dom and sub relationship like ours, the Daddy Dom should always be in charge. That's the role I want you to take with me. You're my Daddy so I want you to make these decisions for me. I don't want to wear any clothes or eat anything that you don't want me to eat. I want you to be in control at all times and help me make decisions that I'm struggling with on my own. This is a perfect space to practice just between us. No one's around to see you make decisions for me."

Roman smirks. "You're so fucking special, Bentley. That's exactly what I hoped you'd say."

"Really?"

"Yes, boy. It's important to discuss things like roles and consent in a relationship. A clear discussion of roles is the foundation for relationships like ours and it's so necessary to go over these things before engaging in activity together. Serious miscommunication can occur if two parties in a relationship don't hash things out beforehand. Negotiation in any kink activity — even helping a partner change into a onesie — is a must. I'm proud and happy that you brought this up to me, Bentley. This is exactly the role I want to take with you. I want to guide you and help you be the best boy you can be. But I'd never do that without your permission. I needed you to give me your full consent and you did that just now. Thank you so much for this gift."

"You're so good with words, Daddy." I blush as I bite Roman's shoulder. "That's exactly what I want too. I want you to guide me through these decisions."

"Stand up, boy," Roman commands. "Daddy's going to help you change into your onesie now."

My insides are so full of warm fuzzies as I stand up in front of Roman.

I close my eyes tight as Roman helps me remove my big boy clothes.

I have a big boner as I strip down but Roman doesn't care.

"Lift your left leg, Bentley," Roman commands, his lips feathering over mine.

I force myself to stay in the present moment as I obey Roman's commands and not melt into a giant puddle of warm fuzzies.

But it's so freaking hard.

This is something I've dreamt about forever.

A firm Daddy helping me make decisions in life.

A firm Daddy doing what's best for me and guiding me through choices.

A firm Daddy who's willing to help me with anything no matter how big or small.

Roman takes my hand in his when we sit back down on the floor. "Tell me what you used to do in this loft, Bentley. You brought me up here for a reason."

"I want to play the games I used to play with my big brother, Daddy." I squeeze Roman's hand.

Roman nods. "What sort of games did you play?"

"We played a little game with toy soldiers because Jericho had dreams of going into the military when he was younger," I say, grinning at Roman. "It's because Paw Paw was in the Armed Forces before he met Maw Maw and flew helicopters over the ocean. Jericho and I pretended we were opposing countries in war and shot bullets at each other. It was a silly game because both of us were really against war but it was still fun to play. Our parents probably would've flipped out at Jericho if they knew that he was still playing with soldiers with me so late at night but that's why Jericho was so awesome. He never judged me for playing with toys in middle school. He never made me feel silly or dumb because I was playing with stuffed animals past the age where it's normal or because I wasn't like the rest of the kids in my class. He accepted who I was unconditionally. There was never anything I could do that was too much or too weird for Jericho. He didn't care if I slept in a onesie or played with toy soldiers up here while hugging my reindeer stuffy. He loved me regardless. He was the best older brother I could've ever had."

"These are the soldiers we used to play with." I tug a basket of toy soldiers out of a cubby in the loft and place them in front of Roman, removing the lid and setting the toys on the floor.

Roman places his hand on mine. "Tell me what soldiers I should take, Bentley. Red or blue."

"You can take blue," I say, regressing into little headspace as warm fuzzies fill my chest. "That was Jericho's favorite color."

"Oh yeah?" Roman asks.

"Yeah." I nod. "Jericho always liked to make jokes that they were the same color as my beautiful eyes but I never believed him. I thought he was full of it but brothers always love to tease you and provoke you so I didn't mind. I just liked playing with him."

Roman lines the blue soldiers up in front of him and begins the game.

He takes his soldiers and makes them shoot bullets into mine.

I make my toy soldiers shoot and blast Roman's soldiers to smithereens.

It's like something switches inside of me as we play.

I've finally been given permission to tap into a part of myself I buried eight long years ago.

I feel like the little kid I was with Jericho again, so dumb and naive about the cruelty of the world.

I don't know that my parents aren't going to live much longer.

I don't know that Jericho will go to prison.

All that matters as I play is that I'm safe, and that I can completely lose myself in the game without feeling worried at all.

I'm safe in this little loft space and Daddy is protecting me, he's being my true protector and playing a game to help me feel safe and small.

I glance up and Roman becomes Jericho for a moment, and for the briefest wrinkle in time, I see my brother next to me, the same brother from all those years ago, the brother I adored who loved me, never hurt me, the brother who accepted me and never judged me for being who I was.

When the play session winds down, I press the soldiers to my heart.

"Thank you, Daddy." My voice is a whisper as I stay in my headspace.

A firm arm wraps around my shoulder. "Did you have a good play session, Bentley?"

"Yes." I rest my forehead on Roman's shoulder. "I got into my little headspace so good and played with soldiers just like I used to when I was a boy."

"I miss my brother so much, Daddy." I rest my nose on Roman's chest.

"Oh sweet boy." Roman runs his fingers over my cheek, giving me the protection I need. "These past eight years must've been so hard for you. But I'm going to fight like hell to get Jericho out of prison, Bentley. I spoke with my cousins Nikolai and Igor in the driveway today and they let me know that my lawyer Antoine is pairing up with the top prosecutor in the city to look over Jericho's case. Antoine will make it happen, Bentley. Mark my damn words. I won't rest or sleep until your brother is out of Rikers forever."

"And then Jericho can come up to this loft and have a big play session with me," I continue, blinking hard as I wrap myself in Roman's arms. "Nothing will have changed, Daddy. He'll come up to the loft and we'll play together for hours just like we used to when we were boys. He'll still be the best brother to me and I'll be his little brother who loves toys."

Roman's jaw flexes against my cheek.

He says nothing and he remains silent as he leads me back to the farmhouse.

24

BENTLEY. Sweet, precious Bentley.

I bring the chainsaw blade through the trunk of the Christmas tree and let it fall.

The tree smacks onto the ground and sends detritus and wood chips into the air.

As I heave the tree onto Barney's tractor and bring it back to the farmhouse, I can only think of one thing.

Sweet, beautiful Bentley.

My heart aches to be back with Bentley after cutting down so many trees today.

I've worked since four-thirty in the morning and my muscles are screaming for a break.

I helped so many people and I even brought a freshly cut tree across the road to Grandma Harmony to brighten her day.

Grandma Harmony treated Tura Lura and me to hot cocoa and a date with Preston's pet monkey because he was busy hanging out with Bentley, Christian, Rowan, Karter, Lucas, and Riley.

But the day is over now and I just want to see my boy.

My precious, precious boy, who opened up so honestly to me

about his brother the other day when we played toy soldiers in his loft.

With the Christmas tree tied to the back of the tractor, I drive to the farmhouse and head in through the garage door.

I walk to my bedroom and fumble around for the light switch.

But I've barely stepped inside the room when a soft hand places itself on mine and stops me from me turning on the lights.

A curvy angel's body presses against me.

"No lights, Daddy." A pair of soft lips kiss my chest. "Just darkness tonight."

I drop my gaze down and see my beautiful boy hugging me.

"Bentley?" I trail two fingers across Bentley's cheek, caressing his skin. "What are you doing up, Bentley? You should be asleep."

Bentley smiles. "No. I couldn't fall asleep, Daddy."

"Why not?" I grunt.

Bentley clears his throat. "You worked so hard chopping down Christmas trees today, Daddy. You were so big and strong when you helped my grandparents out and I wanted to surprise you tonight."

Bentley takes a step back into a beam of moonlight that shines in through the bedroom window.

He spreads his palms over his shirt.

I gasp when I see the message on his T-shirt.

It says *SANTA'S FAVORITE HO* and it has pictures of a cartoon elf on it.

And Bentley's wearing a candy cane knit over his cock.

Lust assaults me from every direction when I realize that Bentley's rock hard beneath the cozy.

Bentley's been trembling and miserable in his bedroom and he's been waiting for this exact moment so he could surprise me.

My hands rake through my hair. "What are you doing, sweet boy? Why are you wearing that beautiful outfit tonight?"

Bentley's blue eyes lock on mine. "It's time to lose my virginity, Daddy. I want to role-play Santa and elf."

Oh my God.

I didn't think a T-shirt that said *SANTA'S FAVORITE HO* would look so sexy on Bentley.

But holy shit.

Bentley looks like he just walked off the cover of *Daddy Kink* magazine.

He looks like an absolute angel who got into some kink clothes and is trying them on to surprise his partner in bed.

My cock twitches in my work jeans and I let out a groan as I drink in the sight of Bentley in his slutty shirt.

"You're such a naughty little ho tonight, Bentley." My voice is a growl as I thread my fingers through my shirt, undoing the buttons. "I worked long and hard today and you decided to wear *this* to surprise me?"

Bentley blushes innocently. "It's what I wanted, Daddy. You're taking my biggest gift tonight and it needs to be exciting for both of us. I've never had a man inside me before and I want to make sure that we both remember it always. I want to be your elf."

"And that's why you wore the dirty T-shirt?" A deep breath escapes me as my fingers unbutton my work jeans, thrusting them to my feet, and my cock springs to an erection in my briefs and mashes hard against the fabric. "You wore that to tease me? To make me lose control and go fucking crazy?"

Bentley moves his hips back and forth and shakes his candy cane between his hips. "No, Daddy." Bentley's voice is as innocent as fresh fallen snow in December as he pokes his cock with his index finger. "I wanted to be your elf tonight and to give you a night you'd never forget. If you don't want to make love tonight, that's okay. I can take off the T-shirt and we can play with each other the normal way. I don't need to be kinky. Normal is fine with me."

Oh sweet Jesus.

Do it... The normal way?

Any other man, I'd say yes.

I'd say *Let's not get too damn kinky because then we can't go back to simple kissing.*

But there's nothing normal about Bentley.

Bentley is exceptional, perfect, an outlier in every freaking way.

Bentley is a shining diamond in a sea full of dollar store crystals, and no man I've ever met in my life holds a candle to his flame.

His body is a perfect vanilla sundae and his personality is the cherry on top.

Bentley wants me to take his virginity tonight in a slutty t-shirt with a candy cane knit cozy on his cock.

There's no way in hell I'd do it any other way.

Desire beats a war drum in my chest as I cross the bedroom floor to Bentley's side.

I heave Bentley into my arms and press him against my hard chest, supporting every inch of his body.

My lips feather against Bentley's neck as I rub the cock cozy on his penis, squeezing his shaft in my firm fingers and then fondling the knit with my thumb.

Bentley lets out a moan as he grinds himself against my hard abs, rubbing his quivering cock against my muscles to give himself the friction he so desperately needs.

A groan tears out of me as I smash my lips against Bentley's, kissing him passionately, with everything I have.

I savagely lay Bentley down on the bed and shove my tongue

even deeper into his mouth, swirling it over his teeth and forcing it deep into his throat to claim him as my own.

Our mouths mate in a fusion of primal need, and a deep moan ushers out of my lips as my hand slides down to Bentley's voluptuous curves, grazing his thick beautiful belly as I make my way to his taint.

My vision blurs when I turn Bentley around on the bed, pushing him face down into the mattress.

Bentley hunches up on his knees, sinking his teeth into my pillow as he sticks his ass out for me.

It's time.

Time to become one with my boy.

Time to pry my heart out of my chest and give it to Bentley.

Bentley's fantasized about this moment his entire life and dreamed about losing his virginity to a man who adores him for so long.

I'm Bentley's fantasy come to life.

It's a fucking honor and a goddamn obligation and I will exceed his wildest expectations tonight.

Pre-come oozes out of the tip of my ten-inch cock as I skim the edges of Bentley's curves with my palms, positioning myself at the entrance of his perfect hole.

From the top drawer of my dresser, I retrieve a bottle of lube and squeeze it onto my palm, spreading it over Bentley's virgin hole.

I work my fingers deep into Bentley's channel, taking my time to slide my digits in and out to prepare him for my entrance.

At last, Bentley's ready for me, and his hole starts to pucker and tremble around my fingertips.

A fissure of desire opens in me as I run my cock head up and down Bentley's opening, testing the waters to prepare Bentley for what's in store.

I work the tip of my cock into Bentley's ass, wriggling it in slow so I don't hurt my boy.

Bentley's tight channel clamps down around my length, and I instinctively stop because I don't want to hurt him.

But a moan flutters out of Bentley's lips and his hole loosens around my shaft.

"It's okay, Santa," Bentley whispers. "My little workshop is open for you now."

Oh sweet fucking Jesus.

Did Bentley just... Say that out loud?

Don't think.

My beautiful elf's words are all I need to proceed.

I push my dick even deeper into Bentley's ass, and a whine escapes Bentley as I give him the sensation he needs.

I press down on Bentley's back and enter Bentley all the way, penetrating his thick ass with everything I have and burrowing myself balls deep.

I let spit drool down from my mouth as I flatten myself against Bentley's back, stabbing Bentley over and over again in the most sensitive part of his body.

Bentley's perfect body melts beneath me as his channel gives way to my cock, and he grips the bedsheets as I enter him fully, grinding hard against my length.

My eyes roll back and my jaw falls open as I tunnel myself hungrily into Bentley.

It's like I've rammed my dick into everything that is pure and holy in this life, so fresh and untouched in every way.

I've never met a boy like Bentley, someone who pushes me to my limits but who's so sweet inside.

And Bentley's freaking body. Holy fucking shit.

Bentley's curves are the sexiest goddamn things I've ever seen.

Bentley is the man I dreamt about for years and years locked up in Rikers Island, the man who only visited me in my fantasies late at night.

He's the type of man who was off limits to me in prison because there were just no men with his body type behind bars.

There were only muscle heads and bears and skinny twinks but none had beautiful curves like Bentley.

None of them could grip my dick like Bentley.

None of them *were* Bentley.

That's it, I think as a desperate groan escapes me, my synapses firing like a machine gun as I plunge even deeper into Bentley's channel. *The men in Rikers weren't Bentley. Bentley is my dream man come to life. He's everything I've wanted and he makes me feel like a steed. He doesn't just want sex from me or to use me like my ex did before abandoning me. He wants me to be his true Daddy in every way.*

"Santa's little elf." I crush my lips against Bentley's neck as I grind against him harder and harder, rolling my hips against his thick juicy ass until my balls heave with tightness. "That's what you are, Bentley. You're Santa's elf tonight. Santa doesn't care if he has to chop down one hundred million Christmas trees to keep you by his side. Santa loves every inch of your curves and every part of who you are. You may not know it, but you're everything Santa's been looking for his entire life."

"Yours." Bentley's voice is a whine as he ruts and ruts. "Your elf, Santa. And you're mine."

The world falls away as it's just me and Bentley in this bedroom.

I make love to him with my entire heart, pouring every bit of my soul into my thrusts and grinds.

This time, Bentley and I truly make love and reach another plane of existence.

Unlike the ravenous rim job I gave Bentley in the back of Grandma Harmony's carriage, this time my heart is overflowing with pure unadulterated love for this boy as I make sweet sweet amor to his curvy ass.

Bentley's everything I've ever wanted and more, and I know in my heart of hearts that I'm the luckiest man in the world tonight.

"It's happening, Santa," Bentley cries out, cinching his hole as he shakes beneath me. "Elf is going to have his first orgasm ever. T-That's what he gets for sneaking into Santa's workshop to play with *tooooys*."

I see two Bentleys on the bed beneath me, each as diaphanous as the moonlight through the window.

I thread my massive Russian palm through Bentley's hair and tilt his head up, bucking into him wildly as I grip his curly locks.

"Spread those sexy curvy cheeks for Daddy, boy." My voice is a growl as I pump into Bentley's hot warm hole. "That's what elves like you deserve as punishment. Santa's going to put a present in your stocking tonight. A big Daddy present in your elf stocking. Clap those cheeks around Santa's big uncut dick and say my fucking name. Santa fucking owns you tonight."

Bentley claps his cheeks against my dick as hard as he can.

He cries out as his cock shoots out shot after shot of hot white come into his cock cozy.

I let out a primal roar as I bulldoze my seed deep in Bentley's hole.

I roll my hips and deliver as much passion as I can to Bentley, giving him every bit of my seed.

When I finish squirting, I sear Bentley's lips in a kiss.

It's just me and Bentley.

I take him into the shower and soap up every inch of his body.

Bentley is my elf. My lover. My boy.

25

MY HEART IS full of the most amazing sensations when I wake up the following morning in Roman's bed.

I take a sniff of his pillowcase and groan.

I had the *best* freaking night ever last night.

Christian and Rowan lent me an extra-large slutty T-shirt and a candy cane cock cozy that Rowan brought from his kink shop in upstate New York and told me to wear it for Roman.

I laughed at Rowan's suggestion at first and said he was full of it.

Who would really want to role-play Santa and elf in bed?

But then I thought about it.

I decided to wear it and pray that Roman would love it.

And OMG.

Roman loved it too.

Roman accepted me despite my kinks and really got into the role-playing with me.

I never thought I'd have a partner who was totally cool with role-playing Santa in bed, but Roman was.

I felt like the most pampered little ho ho on this planet when

Roman took my virginity last night, and I knew in my heart of hearts that my Santa Daddy loved me so much.

Roman made sweet sweet love to me all night long and treasured every inch of my curves.

And Roman took me into his shower when we finished making love and scrubbed every inch of my body to give me the amazing aftercare I needed.

I latched onto Roman's nipples and let him wash my worries away.

Ugh.

Talk about the best Daddy ever.

"Morning, Daddy." I yawn and stretch in the bed.

I'm eager to spread my legs out and touch my Daddy's tattooed chest.

But there's no one there.

I prop myself up on my elbow and turn to the spot where I thought Roman was laying.

There's no one in the bed.

"Daddy?" I shove the blankets off my body and glance around the room. "Where are you, Daddy? We have a big day of activities planned and we need to talk about it ASAP."

Nothing.

I clear my throat and try again. "Where are you, Daddy? Christian, Rowan, Karter, Lucas, Macon, and Riley went to Preston's farmhouse today to see his monkey. We have the whole house to ourselves."

No answer.

Hmmmm.

If Roman isn't in the bedroom, I'll just have to go out and find him myself.

I step into my reindeer slippers and stand up on the hardwood floor.

But I've barely exited my room when I bump into Roman in the hall.

"We need to have a discussion in the kitchen, Bentley."

FUCK. Double fuck.

Double fuck with a shot of espresso.

This isn't what I wanted at all this morning.

This morning was supposed to be easy, breezy, and beautiful with my boy.

Bentley and I had a perfect night last night and he was so perfect and amazing in bed.

I've never fantasized about Santa role-play before but Bentley made it work.

He was the most adorable, cutest elf in bed and he seriously made me rethink all of my kinks.

When Bentley and I finished making love, I took him into the shower and scrubbed every inch of his precious body.

Bentley got on his knees and sucked my dick in the shower and told me to deliver my presents straight into his tummy.

I let out a groan and came all over Bentley's face three times.

Bentley's the kinkiest angel ever and he's so perfect for me.

But I'd barely woken up when the landline rang and I got the voice message that changed everything.

Sasha: Call me right away, brother. Antoine stumbled across something that you need to hear ASAP

I borrowed Bertha's phone so I didn't have to wake Bentley in the bedroom and learned something horrendous.

Jericho's case is connected to mine in more ways than I thought.

Someone wired one million dollars to both of our judges that fateful night eight years ago from the same offshore account.

And Alphonso and the Riccis were involved in both of our fateful events.

I must tell Bentley this ASAP.

Bentley bites his lip. "You have something to talk over with me, Daddy? Did I do something wrong?"

"No, boy." I take Bentley's hand in mine. "You didn't do anything wrong, precious boy. You could never do something to upset Daddy. Follow me to the kitchen and I'll explain everything."

My stride is deadly as I take Bentley's hand in mine and lead him to the kitchen.

I pick up a mug of hot chocolate and slide it across the table to Bentley when we sit down at the table.

Bentley takes a big sip of his hot cocoa and wipes a marshmallow mustache from his upper lip. "I'm not good with long silences, Daddy. You're going to make me think I messed up by wearing that t-shirt in bed last night. What do you have to discuss with me?"

The information that I have can't wait a second longer.

I blow out a breath and squeeze Bentley's hand. "Antoine discovered something last night about Jericho's case that throws everything I've thought for the past eight years into doubt."

Bentley furrows his brow and sets his mug of cocoa on the

table. "What did he discover, Daddy? Is it something that will help Jericho be free?"

"Yes." I hold Bentley's hand. "It'll help your brother go free. It's evidence of systemic corruption and bribery. It'll help both Jericho and me get out of Rikers forever."

Bentley nods. "Tell me, Daddy. I want Jericho to be free. I'll put on my big boy pants and listen now."

I let out a breath. It's now or never.

The opportunity to tell Bentley won't come again.

I blow out a breath. "My lawyer discovered someone meddled in your brother's case eight years ago. It was buried in encrypted court records which is why no one found it."

"What was it, Daddy?"

"A receipt for a wire transfer to Jericho's judge that arrived on Christmas Eve night."

"Antoine also found something else," I continue, barely able to get the truth out. Why do I have to be the one to tell Bentley this? It's so fucking unfair.

But deep down, I know I must do it.

Even if it's hard as fuck, I'm Bentley's Daddy now and I must tell him the truth.

It's up to me to get the job done.

"What did he discover, Daddy?" Bentley trembles.

"The wire transfer came from the same institution that wired money to *my* judge on Christmas Eve," I say, forcing myself to spit out the words. "Antoine and Sasha started mapping things together and he slowly discovered something."

Bentley starts to shake. "W-What is it, Daddy? You're scaring me."

I stare into Bentley's eyes. "The man who jumped out at your family all those years ago is the same man I chased away from my sister on Christmas Eve. Alphonso Ricci."

Bentley can't speak.

His eyes widen like saucers and I can see a million thoughts race across his mind.

He tries to gulp down air and fails miserably.

Finally, Bentley tilts his head up to me. "I don't understand, Daddy. How is that possible?"

"Alphonso left Anastasia's hotel suite and ran through a hidden network of alleys that night. He ended up at a cross street in Midtown. Alphonso was panicking because he thought I was coming after him. He decided to carjack the first car he saw to get away. It was your parents's car. That's why everything happened the way that it did."

Bentley quivers in his seat.

A tear slips out of his eye and falls into his hot cocoa.

I squeeze Bentley's hand. "I'm at fault here, boy. If I hadn't beaten Alphonso up that night, he never would've hurt your parents. They'd still be alive if it weren't for me."

"No, Daddy." Bentley shakes his head as his beautiful tear-stained eyes blur. "I-It's not your fault. You were protecting your sister."

"Yes it is," I growl, unwilling to back down. "I should fucking pay restitution to you and your grandparents because of what I did. Alphonso never would've hurt your family if I hadn't beaten him up that night. It's my fault for beating him. If I hadn't done it, he never would've tried to carjack your parents's car. I did this, Bentley."

"No." Bentley shakes his head again. "You couldn't have known what would happen, Daddy. You couldn't have known that Alphonso would run out of Anastasia's hotel suite and attack a family on the street. You're innocent."

"I could've let him go earlier," I rasp. "I could've told Alphonso to get the fuck out of Anastasia's hotel suite but not beaten him. Then he wouldn't have needed to find a car that night. He wouldn't have thought that I was coming after him and he wouldn't have tried to carjack your parents's vehicle."

Bentley drives his fingers into my palm. "It's not your fault, Roman. What Alphonso did that night is his responsibility. He chose to threaten your sister and use brass knuckles to beat her up. He chose to treat her like garbage to try to find out information about your family."

"I could've stopped it. I could've let him go."

Bentley grinds his teeth together. "There's nothing you could've done that would've changed anything, Roman. Alphonso was a sick, sick bastard and he was going to murder someone that night no matter what. If it wasn't my parents, then it would've been another innocent person who got in his way. There's nothing you could've done to change the outcome of that night, just like my brother couldn't. Everything that happened after Alphonso left Anastasia's hotel suite is Alphonso's responsibility. I'm sorry that Alphonso beat up your sister, and I'm pissed as hell that I'll never get my parents back, but it's not your fault. You were merely trying to protect your baby sister from harm. What happened that night eight years ago isn't your fault and I refuse to let you think that it is. I refuse to let you shut me out because of this. You *couldn't* have caused my parents's death. Alphonso chose that path for himself and he's going to pay the price. I'll make sure of that. But you didn't do it, Daddy. You're innocent."

I stare into Bentley's eyes. "I did this to you, Bentley. You have to accept that."

Bentley kisses my hand. "You couldn't have done this if you wanted to, Roman. Nothing that happened that night was your fault. I won't let you think that you could have done anything differently because that's impossible. And I won't let you go to the dark place where you were inside of Rikers Island to try to take responsibility for this. Not when we've finally gotten together. Not when I've finally found the protector I've dreamt about my entire life who loves and adores me and who'll fight for me until the bitter end. You protected your sister and Alphonso chose to kill my parents out of his own free will. Those are the facts."

I let out a breath. "What can I do to make this right?"

Bentley's eyes flicker with life. "You're going to be very disturbed when I tell you what I want."

"Tell me." I slam my fucking fist on the table. "I have the connections to do anything you want, Bentley. The criminal justice system failed both of us in this regard and I'm going to make this right. I don't care who I have to kill to make this up to you."

Bentley stares dead into my eyes. "I need you to lure that bastard here this afternoon."

27

Maw Maw

"DEAR," I say, pulling the fresh-baked chocolate chip cookies out of the oven and turning around to face my husband, even though I know he's not here. "I made the Christmas cookies, dear. Come and try one to see if I put enough vanilla in."

But I know my husband Barney isn't sitting at the kitchen table.

He's deep in the Christmas tree forest preparing the helicopter he's going to ride with my grandson's partner's cousin Nikolai.

Roman's target is standing behind me.

I've lived here for fifty years and I know every creak of these floorboards like the back of my hand.

This is the man.

This is the man Roman lured here.

This is the man who killed my son and his family and sent my grandson to prison.

"Set the fucking cookies on the counter, Grandma," a low voice says. "Where's the girl?"

I turn around to stare my son's attacker straight in the eye. "She's in a parked car in the driveway. She wants to meet with you."

28

MY HEART IS SO nervous as I wait in the trunk of Anastasia's Ferrari for Alphonso to arrive.

My palms are sweaty and I can barely breathe.

But I know this is the right decision.

This is the plan I proposed to Roman at the table this morning.

Anastasia was in Manhattan and Roman summoned her to the Christmas tree farm to lure Alphonso up here.

We're using Anastasia as bait to bring Alphonso to our tree farm so Roman can take him out in a helicopter with Barney.

I'm scared AF.

This is the man I've seen in my nightmares when I've closed my eyes for the past eight years.

This is the man who put my brother in prison and killed my fucking parents.

But I will be strong.

Roman will protect me.

Roman will do fucking anything to keep me safe and secure in his arms.

My Daddy won't let me down.

I blow out a breath as I turn to face Anastasia in the back seat. "Are you ready?"

A glistening lock of blonde hair falls across Anastasia's porcelain cheek as she nods.

"Yes." Anastasia's accent is thick. "I'm ready to take Alphonso down."

A tiny booklet with a drawing of the Statue of Liberty sits in her left hand and a keychain with a cup of hot chocolate from *Les Deux Magots* in Paris dangles off her right.

Everything is just as Roman and I planned this morning.

"You sure about that?" I hedge, taking a breath.

I want to make damn sure Anastasia's on board with this plan and that she's not going to back out at the last second.

The last time Roman tried to murder Alphonso, Anastasia stopped him and begged him to spare Alphonso's life.

I'll be damned to hell if Anastasia prevents Roman from murdering Alphonso again.

Anastasia directs her crystal blue eyes to me. "Yes, Bentley. I've been waiting for this moment every fucking day for the past eight years. It's time to make this man pay for what he did to my brother."

My balls clench as I face the farmhouse.

I take in a breath of air as I rub my palms on my khakis to stay in control.

Alphonso will walk out any minute and I must remain cool around him.

It's so scary because this is the man I've been scared of my entire life.

But I can't think about that now.

Roman and my grandfather are firing up the military grade helicopters that will blow this Ferrari to smithereens.

I refuse to let my fear win.

I glance up at the sky through the tiny window Roman installed in the Ferrari's trunk and see the first snowflakes of the season drift down from the clouds.

That's when the man of my nightmares walks out of the farmhouse.

"You've got this."

My voice is black as I cross the clearing in the Christmas tree farm and lead Barney to Nikolai's helicopter.

I couldn't believe my ears when Bentley told me that Barney is a former military pilot in the Armed Forces who knows how to fly.

Barney turns to face me. "Thanks for letting me do this, Roman. I won't let you down."

I blow out a breath and load fresh bullets into my G43. "You'd better not, Barney. This is a big responsibility and you should let my cousin Nikolai fly if you're not up to the task. We can't afford to fuck this up."

Barney puts his hand on my shoulder. "Alphonso destroyed my family eight years ago, son. He attacked my son and his wife and his children. He forced my grandson into a brutal prison and he bribed the judge to keep him locked up. I want to murder this man with my bare hands, Roman. I know that's impossible so I'll follow our plan. But I won't let you complete this mission without me."

"I get that, Barney," I say. "But you must let Nikolai fly the helicopter if you have second thoughts. That's the only way to ensure that we take Alphonso out once and for all."

Barney stares me dead in my eyes. "I trained for years flying Armed Forces helicopters across the Atlantic and taking out Nazi submarines in war zones. I won't fucking let you down."

Barney removes his hand from my shoulder and climbs into Nikolai's helicopter.

Nikolai lets out a grunt and guides Barney into the front seat where he straps Barney into a seatbelt.

Nikolai shoots me a glance before he and Barney take off.

"*Etot ublyudok chertovski sumasshedshiy,*" Nikolai shouts. This bastard is fucking crazy.

I walk over to Nikolai and stare him straight in the eye. "*Yesli Dzhon ne mozhet upravlyat' vertoletom, kogda vy nakhodites' v vozdukhe, vy dolzhny vzyat' na sebya upravleniye. Eto slishkom opasno dlya Dzhona, chtoby oblazhat'sya v posledniy moment. Vam pryamo prikazali vzyat' na sebya upravleniye, yesli Dzhonu nuzhno budet postuchat'.*" If Barney can't fly the helicopter when you're up in the air, you must take control. This is too dangerous for Barney to fuck up at the last moment. You're under a direct order to take control if Barney needs to tap out.

Nikolai nods. "*U menya yest' ty, kuzen. Ya tebya ne podvedu.*" I've got you, cousin. I won't let you down.

Nikolai slams the door to the helicopter shut and Barney pulls back the throttle and sends the helicopter into the air.

I leap into my own helicopter and check the rocket launchers to ensure they're ready to blast the Ferrari Alphonso will be driving to pieces.

I yank back the throttle and soar into the air.

It's time to take this motherfucker out.

30

Alphonso wastes no time marching out of the farmhouse and making a beeline straight to Anastasia.

His eyes are burning embers and his jaw is taut.

"Little fucking bitch," Alphonso spits out, unleashing a bundle of metal cords from his trench coat pocket.

Anastasia lets out a cry as Alphonso grabs her wrists and slams them together. "W-What are you doing?"

Alphonso throws Anastasia into the back seat as hard as he can. "You're going to get what's fucking coming to you today, bitch. I should have murdered you that fucking night, you dumb little slut. I've waited long enough for my revenge."

Alphonso violently lashes Anastasia's wrists together.

She screams but Alphonso smacks her cheek to prevent her from speaking.

He ties her to the back seat of the Ferrari and climbs into the front seat.

"You had eight long years to stay out of my fucking business," Alphonso says as he presses the buttons to start the luxury car. "I should've murdered you that night in Manhattan, Anastasia. You knew exactly what your family and brothers were up to in

Russia and you didn't tell me. You lied and then you sicced your brother on me."

"I didn't know anything." Anastasia's blonde hair cascades all over the backseat as Alphonso ferociously speeds down the dirt driveway. "I didn't know that my brothers were the most powerful Mafia family in Russia. I swear, Alphonso. I didn't know. I would've told you if I did."

Alphonso spits out the window, attesting to the type of man he truly is. "Well, now you know, bitch. I bet you fucking thought I'd come up here and sweep you off your feet again like I did eight years ago and pretend like everything's the same."

Anastasia coughs violently. "I don't know what you're talking about."

"You probably wanted this Italian dick in that tight Russian pussy again, right, Anastasia? You wanted me to bend you over your sofa and be your Daddy? Too fucking bad, slut. You had your chance and you fucking blew it by unleashing your psycho brother on me. I know you two were fucking, Anastasia. You probably took his cock up your ass in Russia in that billion-dollar mansion you grew up in, sheltered little whore. I'm not going to treat you kindly today, bitch. I'm going to murder both of you like I should've done eight years ago."

I stay calm inside.

I'm ready to viciously murder this man for killing my family and putting my brother in prison but I don't flinch in the trunk of the vehicle.

I don't even look at Alphonso as I watch the first snowflakes of the season fall outside the trunk window.

Out of the corner of my eye, I spot two black blobs flying fast over the horizon, and I know that Alphonso's time on this planet has come to an end.

I fear nothing.

Roman and my Paw Paw are right behind me in military

grade helicopters with enough ammo to take out the state of New York.

I clear my throat and poke my head into the backseat of the car. "Alphonso?"

Alphonso's face twists as he spins around to face me. "Who the fuck are you?"

"I'm the boy whose parents you murdered eight years ago in Midtown."

SOMETIMES IN LIFE, a man is inclined to show mercy.

He's inclined to take the high road and forgive his enemies for fucking with him.

He chooses forgiveness over vengeance, patience over impulsivity, and peace instead of rage.

If Alphonso had only fucked with me and forced me into prison for eight years, I'd be inclined to negotiate with my dark side and let the legal system deal with him.

But Alphonso fucked with Bentley.

He fucked with my sweet baby boy.

Alphonso took Bentley's parents life on Christmas Eve night while attempting to carjack them after they were coming back from *The Nutcracker* in Manhattan.

He put Bentley's brother into prison and took away the only person Bentley was close to growing up.

He fucked with my sister and threatened to beat her into a pulp when he tied her up with cord in her Manhattan hotel suite.

If I was the only one Alphonso had fucked with a long years ago, I'd be satisfied with merely kidnapping him and locking him in a room to torture the ever-loving hell out of him for the rest of his goddamn life.

Mahatma Gandhi might be able to take the high road in this case, but I'm not fucking Gandhi.

I'm a brutal Russian mobster who solves issues with my bare fucking hands.

The sand of Alphonso's life has run out and it's time to shoot him dead today.

Right. Fucking. Now.

I raise my radio transmitter to my mouth. "*Gotov kogda ty, Nikolay.*" Ready when you are, Nikolai.

Nikolai's voice crackles. "Ready. Aim. Fire."

I don't pause, don't hesitate.

I'm fucking Rambo when I press the button to initiate the sequence of military grade weapons and shoot the first rocket straight into the gravel road next to the Ferrari.

"Dumb little bastard." I reposition my helicopter. "You're going to get what's coming to you, motherfucker."

I fire another rocket into the road.

The explosive hits the gravel with a sonic boom and sends shards of rock and detritus into the air.

Boom.

I switch on the secret camera Barney and I installed in the back of the Ferrari to see Bentley.

My precious angel is helping Anastasia with her bonds.

I placed a secret knife in the trunk of the car that can cut through anything.

"Bentley." Pride fills my chest as I watch my baby boy helping my sister. "Daddy's so proud of you, angel. You got this. You won't let him down."

Bentley turns his beautiful blue eyes to face the camera and I swear to God I nearly faint in my helicopter.

How is it even possible for a normal boy like Bentley to be so brave?

Bentley's just a regular college student who does regular student things and cuddles with stuffed animals when he's not in class.

He doesn't have experience in the Mafia or assisting in high intensity secret missions like this one.

But he's fucking doing it.

Bentley isn't chickening out like so many other boys would in his position.

Bentley's confidence shines like a beacon and it encapsulates his persona as he frees Anastasia from her bonds.

Bentley's everything that is pure and righteous in this life rolled into one person but he's helping me like a boss.

He cares about helping sweet old ladies like Mrs. Harmony get their Christmas trees.

He cares about doing what's right instead of what's easy.

And lastly, Bentley cares about helping his Daddy seek justice against an evil man who tried to destroy all of us.

He's the sweetest, bravest angel in the world, but he's also a young man who's willing to do whatever it takes to win a war.

"You can do it, Bentley," I urge through the secret camera, initiating the final sequence of the rocket launcher. "I believe in you. You won't let me down."

I glue my eyes to the camera as Bentley tosses Anastasia's cords out of the window of the Ferrari.

He stares into Anastasia's eyes and slides her parachute on.

It's time.

With only a second to spare, Bentley presses the secret button I installed this afternoon in the back of the Ferrari to expel both passengers out of the backseat of the car.

The top of the car blows off and Bentley and Anastasia fly up into the air together.

A flurry of relief cascades over me as I watch my sister and my precious boy twirl in the clouds and deploy their parachutes.

"Bentley's safe," I rasp, blinking sweat out of my eyes. "Bentley's not in danger. I can blow up this car and I won't hurt a hair on his head."

Bentley and Anastasia are free.

The launching device I installed with Igor in the back of the Ferrari this afternoon worked like a charm.

Bentley and Anastasia are floating in the clouds with their parachutes spread out above them and high-fiving each other for a job well done.

Adrenaline thrums as I redirect my helicopter over the Ferrari to end this motherfucker's life.

Alphonso's eyes rake up to mine when he sees my helicopter racing down to his car.

He snarls at me through the windshield and mouths one phrase.

"You think this is over, you piece of shit. My cousin Giuseppe Ricci will give you what you deserve."

Too late, motherfucker.

You had many chances to do the right thing and you blew it.

"Three, two, one."

I lock my eyes on my target and press the button.

The rocket launcher doesn't even hesitate as it roars with life.

Anastasia's Ferrari explodes into a million pieces and sends shards of burning metal and detritus soaring through the air.

BOOM.

I leap out of the chopper, jumping onto the ground with my steel-toed boots

My boots race across the barren farmland covered in snow as I hurry to catch Bentley's fall.

Bentley collapses in my arms and lands safely and snugly in my big tattooed muscles.

"Daddy!" Bentley nuzzles my chest and turns his beautiful blue eyes up to me. "You did it, Daddy. You completed your mission."

My heart pounds in my chest as I check every inch of Bentley's skin for marks.

Did anything happen to his forearm? Did a shard of burning metal singe the end of his curly hair?

No. Not a damn thing harmed Bentley.

Emotion pummels me as I feather my lips across Bentley's mouth, kissing him as hard as I can. "Oh sweet boy. Please tell me you're not hurt, baby boy. I couldn't live with myself if that explosion did so much as hurt a hair on your head. Please tell me you're okay."

"I'm not hurt, Daddy." Bentley grins. "We took out an evil man together and I won't have nightmares anymore. We did our job and now we're going to be safe forever."

I crush my lips against Bentley's and kiss him hard.

Time stops and for the first time in so long, it's only Bentley and me in the world.

The singing of angels that I first heard when I saw Bentley's picture in Rikers Island returns with a vengeance.

"I'm so proud of you, boy," I murmur into Bentley's lips as we make love with our mouths. "You faced your fears and helped me take out this bad man. I couldn't have done it without you. I love you, angel."

"I love you too, Daddy." Bentley kisses me even harder, swooning into my body. "You're my sun and my moon and my life. Thank you for helping me take out that evil man."

The Ferrari burns behind us in an inferno of Dante-esque proportions but I don't give a fuck.

Let it burn down, let the entire world burn for all I care.

All that matters is that my angel is safe in my arms.

I glance around to see if anyone's watching.

If anyone — including my sister — is close enough to hear what I want to say, I'm never going to live it down.

But I don't see anyone, so I press my lips against Bentley's ear and tell him what I need.

"Daddy could barely control himself watching you help his sister in the back of that Ferrari," I whisper, rubbing my lips against Bentley's earlobe. "Adrenaline is a potent aphrodisiac and Daddy needs to take you back to the farmhouse right now."

Bentley giggles. "You're crazy, Daddy. But I feel the exact same way."

I heave Bentley into my mammoth arms. "It's time to make love."

I'm. So. Proud. Of. Him.

Seriously.

I take one look at Bentley when we get back to the farm-house and nearly freaking melt.

How is it possible that my boy is so brave and so strong?

Bentley is seriously the sweetest, savviest, and most adorable little Mafia co-assassin I've ever met in my life.

He saved my sister.

He told Alphonso off to his face in the back of Anastasia's Ferrari and let him know that I was going to take him out.

And Bentley twirled like a ballerina in the air as he swooshed down in his parachute straight into my arms.

Bentley is the best of both worlds, combining bubbly adorableness with a fierce determination to make sure the right thing is always done.

I've never been prouder of him in my life.

I let out a groan as I hold Bentley in my firm arms, my cock clawing hard at my zipper as I lead Bentley through the farm-house door, warmth flooding my insides.

"Daddy's so proud of you, angel," I groan, taking Bentley into the living room and dusting my lips across his cheek as I sink into the sofa, cupping his ass. "You did such an amazing job today. You were so stealthy and fucking brave and strong. I've never been prouder of you in my life."

Bentley grins. "Thank you, Daddy. It's all because of you."

"Bentley?" a familiar voice calls out, as soft as the fresh snowflakes falling outside.

Bentley and I turn our gazes toward the voice and see Grandma Johnson walk into the room.

She's wearing a lovely checkered apron and cuddling Tura Lura in her hands.

"Hi, Maw Maw." Bentley's lips widen into a smile. "I'm so glad to see you. I'm sorry we had to put you in our plan this afternoon. Did Alphonso hurt you at all? Do I have to kill him again for putting his hands on you?"

"I'm perfectly fine, Bentley." Bertha lets out a laugh. "That bastard didn't mess with me."

"I'm glad to hear that, ma'am," I grunt, trying to put aside the fact that Bertha's grandson is straddling me in the middle of the living room and that we're both hard as rocks.

"Do you need something, Maw Maw?" Bentley asks, his brows stitching together. "Is there a reason you're here?"

Bertha smiles. "I wanted to get you both fresh chocolate chip cookies and special Yum Yum Cocoa. You went through such a stressful time this afternoon and I want to make sure you're all right."

Bentley drapes his arms around my neck and ruts hard against my lap.

He presses his lips to my ear. "Do you want some Yum Yum Cocoa while we fuck, Daddy? It could be... *Yummy* while your big hard dick is in my ass."

My eyes roll to the whites as I try with everything I have to stay in control of my body.

"We'll pass on the hot cocoa for now, Mrs. Johnson," I warble, repositioning Bentley on my lap to cover up my aching erection, desperately trying to shield my ten-inch cock from Bentley's grandmother's eyes.

"Are you sure, dear?" Bertha coos, taking a bite of a chocolate chip cookie. "It could be a great way to warm up after everything you went through this afternoon. It's so chilly outside so the Yum Yum Cocoa would do you some good."

"Maw Maw," Bentley groans, throwing his head back and making a pleading face at his grandmother. "Could you give us a minute? We had a near death experience this afternoon and we need to... *Bond*."

Bertha can't help but laugh. "Yes, sweetie pie. I'll let you and Roman bond in peace."

Bertha waddles out of the living room with the tray of chocolate chip cookies in her hands and shuts the door behind her.

I let out a groan and raise my hands to Bentley's shirt when she leaves.

"I don't want to be rude," I hedge, staring into Bentley's eyes as I place my greedy hands on his sexy curves, "but your grandmother *really* needs to learn to take a hint."

Bentley laughs. "She's fine, Daddy. We are trying to *bond* the middle of her living room, after all. We could be civilized people and go back to my bedroom in peace."

"Not a goddamn chance," I groan into Bentley's neck, lapping at his flesh. "We'll be back in Manhattan next week. We have to make the most of this farmhouse while we can."

"I agree, Daddy." Bentley breathes hotly on my ear. "What are you gonna do to me?"

My dick springs up between my legs and quivers with anticipation.

I can barely control myself as I pull Bentley's jeans off,

delirious pants escaping me as I trace the outline of his puckered hole with my calloused thumb.

This is my chance to make Bentley happy.

This is my chance to give Bentley the antidote to the poison
we both swallowed this afternoon.

I'm going to make sweet love to him and take away all his
scaries.

I jam a lubricating liquibead up Bentley's ass and smear the
KY Jelly around.

"Tell Daddy one more time that you want this, sweet boy," I
say as I brush his cheek with my fingers. "You went through so
much this afternoon, baby boy. Tell Daddy if you'd prefer a
sweet massage with lots of oil instead of sex tonight. That's no
problem at all for me, sweet prince. I'll put my dick away and
spend hours upon hours massaging you if that's what you want.
If you need Daddy to take it slow, he will absolutely do that for
you."

Bentley sniffles. "No, Daddy." Bentley brings his left hand
to my cheek and rubs my skin, moaning. "I went through a
very scary time this afternoon. I had to confront the man who
haunted my nightmares for the past eight years. Alphonso
stole so much of my life eight years ago. It was traumatic AF
seeing him again today and I'm really shook up over it. I don't
want your cuddles now, Daddy. A massage sounds nice but it's
not what my soul craves. No, I need you to fuck me tonight,
Daddy. My whole body is fucking aching for you. I need your
cock in my ass. Your big Daddy dick to make me whole. I need
to feel you inside me, working your thick shaft into my hole,
grinding hard to make me feel right. I'm still shaking with
anxicty over what happened this afternoon, and I need you to
fuck me. Raw and dirty and unprotected. Like a fucking little
dog on this couch. Like I'm your pet tonight. Fuck me on the
same couch where I used to watch TV with my big brother. I

need you to come inside me and love me passionately tonight. It's the only thing to help me forget about what happened today, Daddy."

Emotion seizes me as I stare into Bentley's beautiful blue eyes.

The "right" thing to do — the conventional thing to do — is to slow down and give Bentley the slow massages and gentle kisses he needs.

Cuddles. Passion. So much love.

But that's not what Bentley craves.

No, Bentley needs it rough, raw, savage tonight.

Bentley needs me to ram my fucking cock in his ass to expel the bad memories of this afternoon from his head.

He needs my thick Daddy cock in his ass, bucking and grinding in his perfect cheeks as I pound into him like a dog, wild and animalistic and brutal.

"Say it again, precious boy." I tilt Bentley's chin up, my heart pounding as I stare into his eyes. "Tell me the words I need to hear."

Bentley lets out a shuddering breath. "I went through so much trauma this afternoon, Daddy. I need you to fuck me raw to make it better."

I let out a groan as I yank down my zipper.

My enormous member springs up from between my legs and smacks into my muscular abs, dripping pre-come all over the sofa.

I grip my shaft with my right hand and guide my engorged crown to Bentley's hole, tracing the outline of his bud with my foreskin.

He lets out a gasp as his channel widens and accepts my raw cock.

I take his hand in my own and bury myself in his hole, gliding my dick into his channel walls.

I bulldoze my way past his resistance, pinning him down against my hips.

Bentley whimpers as I thrust powerfully into his body, a shudder coursing through him.

Bentley plunges his tongue deep into my mouth, and mewls as he shakes on my thighs, rolling his hips back and forth to extract the thing that will take his scaries away.

I glide my dick in and out of his ass, ravishing my boy with everything I have.

My own pleasure sits on the back burner as I focus all my attention on Bentley, dicking him hard and deep, so full of passion and love.

I squeeze Bentley's nipples and bear down even harder on his ass, and Bentley cries out as I pinch his buds, trembling like a daisy.

"Daddy," Bentley whimpers, throwing his head back and shaking his ass on my rod. "Big strong Daddy in my butt. Helped me take out the man of my nightmares today. Making me whole."

I can barely control myself. "That's right, angel." Sweat drips down my forehead as my hands rake over Bentley's sexy chest and lock on his hard nipples. "Daddy's giving you everything you need tonight, angel. Keep grinding those hips against Daddy's massive rod, Bentley. Fuck those tight hips on Daddy's dick. Wiggle your butt. Daddy won't let you down."

A whine flutters out of Bentley's lips as he cants his hips hard against me, rolling his precious ass around my cock.

"S-So big and hard in my channel, Daddy," Bentley gasps, clapping his cheeks around my ravenous shaft. "Going to make me cooooome. Right where my big brother and I used to play video games growing up."

The gasp that twists out of Bentley's mouth is too much to bear.

I let out a roar as Bentley arches his back and screams hard, my hands transforming into nipple clamps on his buds.

Bentley's cheeks clap and clap around my dick, and he bellows out a scream as his hole flexes on my member.

I jerk Bentley off. "That's right, baby boy," I growl, pumping his perfect shaft slow and steady. "Use Daddy to make you come tonight. God didn't give you those sweet cheeks to touch yourself in your room, sweet boy. God made you for Daddy's dick. Daddy's the only man in the world who can give you the pleasure that you need."

"Yes, Daddy!" Pink enflames Bentley's cheeks, turning him into a living strawberry. "I'm getting fucked by my big strong Daddy! Only my Daddy can give me the orgasm that I need!"

Bentley's orgasm slams into him like a fucking freight train.

He moans as his cock juts out shot after shot of hot white come onto my tattooed chest.

His hole cinches tight around my cock and spasms as he squirts.

I moan and grope Bentley's genitals as I grind into him.

"Here comes the explosion, Bentley," I groan, my eyes rolling back as I fuck his pulsating channel. "You're Daddy's tonight, boy. Daddy's to fuck. Daddy's to claim."

My cock squirts deep in Bentley's ass.

I let out a primal roar as I pump five hot shots deep into his channel, each more ferocious than the last.

A prayer of benediction to the gods torpedoes out of my heart as Bentley's quivering walls give me the pleasure that I need.

How is it even... Possible to have a hole this tight?

Bentley is perfect in every way, his bravery, his smile, his thick ass that pulsates around my ten-inch dick.

I'm still dribbling in Bentley's ass when he rushes toward me and thrusts his lips on mine.

"You did it, Daddy." Bentley drags his tongue into my mouth. "You did a big one in me tonight. I forgot all my scaries."

My heart is soaring through the mountains of Olympus as I heave Bentley into my giant arms and kiss him with everything I have.

So fucking perfect, I think desperately as I carry Bentley into my bathroom, where I run him a bubble bath with lavender and candles. *Bentley overcame his fears big time and helped me with my mission. And he's the sexiest boy in the world to me.*

There's only two things left to do.

Take Bentley to meet his brother.

And buy him a ring.

33

One week later

OKKKAYYYYYY.

So *this* is actually happening.

I blow out a breath as I sit in the yacht in the harbor with Roman.

My legs are shaking and my heart is racing out of my chest.

But I force myself to keep my emotions in check.

Today's the day Roman and I will finally visit Jericho in Rikers Island.

Roman finalized the plans last week.

I didn't actually think Roman would pull through when he promised that he had a secret way to see my brother but he did.

Three days ago, Roman told me everything.

"I found a way to get inside Rikers Island to see Jericho."

"There's a guard that Aleksei used to bribe to visit me and he's going to sneak us in through the back door."

So. Freaking. Amazing.

But I can't deny that there a bazillion ways this could go wrong and that scares the hell out of me.

How do I know that a guard won't stop us and demand our IDs?

How do I know that Jericho will even *remember* me?

"I'm scared, Daddy." I take a sip of hot cocoa from my sippy cup and sink my nose into Roman's chest. "It's been eight long years since I've seen my brother. I was twelve when I saw Jericho last and I bet he won't even remember who I am."

Roman pats my head and wraps me in a bear hug. "There's no need to be nervous, baby boy. I guarantee that Jericho remembers you and that he's excited to see you again."

I squeeze Señor Antlers and bite Roman's chest. "I don't know about that, Daddy. The last time Jericho saw me, I didn't even have facial hair yet. I was a twelve-year-old boy who knew nothing about life. If Jericho doesn't remember that I'm still his little brother, I'm going to be very sad."

Roman strokes my hair and kisses my forehead. "I'm going to tell you something personal, baby boy."

I nod. "You can tell me, Daddy. I won't interrupt."

Roman tilts my chin up and stares into my eyes. "I know what I'm talking about, Bentley." Roman hugs me tight. "Jericho didn't forget you. When you're locked up behind bars... You tend to spend a lot of time in your head. You think about your past and the people you love most. When I was in Rikers, I thought about my childhood growing up in Russia and the fun times I used to have with my brothers Aleksei, Demetri, Sasha, Maxim, and Vladmir X. We used to ride horses together and hunt foxes in the woods and visit our friends Ada and Van. Oftentimes when prisoners are behind bars, the only outlet that they have is their memories. We can't have new experiences so our past experiences become our most treasured possessions to us and the only things that get us through. We start to imagine that the people we used to know are still real and present with us, accompanying us throughout every facet of prison life. They're in the library with us, the meal hall, and by our side when we go meet our lawyers. We obsess over our past memories because we have nothing else going for us. Even strangers we only knew in passing become our most cherished friends simply because they become even more real in our minds. Prison is a horrible, horrible place, and every memory that you have turns to liquid gold. I'd bet Jericho remembers you even more vividly now than when he knew you. And I'd bet the last dollar in my bank account that Jericho is ecstatic to see you again."

I get chills as Roman's beautiful words wash over me.

Wow. Holy smokes.

I had no idea that Roman was this deep.

It's seriously like Roman got an entire university education from the books he read inside Rikers Island or read a lot of André Aciman essays on memory and time.

I nod. "You're right, Daddy. I was just nervous because I haven't seen Jericho in so long. I'd be so heartbroken if he forgot me."

"Jericho remembers everything, precious angel." Roman runs his thumb across my cheekbone and gives me so much comfort and warmth. "The only reason you and Jericho lost contact was because his court-appointed lawyer didn't tell your grandparents where he was. The judicial system prevented you both from meeting. Jericho doesn't hold that against you. Those are failures of the legal system and nothing that either you or Jericho did. I spoke to Jericho three days ago on the phone and he's just as excited to see you again as he was when he went inside. You're still the little brother he loves and adores with all his heart. Nothing has changed."

A lump forms in my throat as Roman heaves me into his big firm arms.

"Okay, Daddy." I force myself to be brave as Roman leads me off the yacht and takes me onto a dock. "I'm ready to see Jericho now."

"That's my little angel."

***

"Are you ready, baby boy?" Roman places his hand on my shoulder when we arrive in Rikers Island.

My head is spinning and my heart is beating fast.

It was so scary sneaking in here through the side entrance in the prison yard.

The evil prisoners stared at Roman and me as two guards led us into the grey building.

Their eyes were dark and menacing and their bodies were covered in dark black tattoos.

I knew that if Roman weren't with me, the prisoners would jump the guards and do something to me in front of everyone.

They wouldn't hesitate to tear my clothes off or violently fuck me on the prison yard.

I was a syringe of liquid heroin to these men because they haven't seen a sexy boy in so long.

But Roman slipped his arm over my shoulder to let everyone in the prison yard know that I was taken.

Roman didn't let a goddamn thing happen to me, so there's no point in thinking about what might have been.

"Yes, Daddy." I stare into Roman's eyes as I squeeze Señor Antlers tight. "I'm ready."

"Are you sure, sweet angel?" Roman feathers his index finger across my cheekbone, taking away my scaries. "We can do this another day if you'd like, baby boy. I'd never want to force you to do something you're uncomfortable with."

Uhh. I don't think so.

I've waited *eight years* to see my brother again.

Yes, I'm scared of the inmates here, and yes, this entire prison is terrifying as fuck, but I refuse to let this opportunity pass me by.

I stretch out my arm and take Roman's hand in mine. "Yes, Daddy. I'm ready. I've been dreaming of this moment for eight long years. When my brother went to prison, I had no one and nothing in this world. My parents were dead. The criminal justice system didn't give a shit. I only had my grandparents. They locked my sweet brother up and took away my last remaining immediate family member."

"I know, baby boy."

"The lawyer they gave Jericho didn't even tell me where he was," I continue, tears threatening behind my eyes. "Who knows what would've happened if Jericho's lawyer told us he was in Rikers? I could've sent Jericho candy canes and Christmas cards to make sure that he never felt alone during his time here. I could've visited him on his birthday and baked him Christmas tree cupcakes to show him that I missed him so much. But the court system prevented me from doing those things, Daddy. It's time to leave that in the dust. I want to see my brother today. This is my time."

Roman wraps his firm arms around my waist and pulls me flush with his body. "I hear you, baby boy. Oh God, I hear you. Oh poor Bentley. You've gone through so much in your life. You're the bravest, sweetest young man who's ever existed on this Earth. This is going to be the most wonderful day for both you and Jericho, sweet blessing. There's nothing more beautiful than seeing two brothers reunite. It wasn't your fault that you and Jericho were separated all those years ago. But now is your chance to see Jericho again and be the little brother that you've always wanted to be to him. You'll be so precious in his arms. I'll stand guard in the room and keep you safe if anyone tries to interrupt your meeting. Daddy's got you, sweet Bentley. You're safe with me."

My knees shake as I stare into Roman's eyes. "Thank you, Daddy. That means the world to me. I'm ready to see my brother now."

Roman grunts. "Let's go."

Roman places his palm on the small of my back and leads me to the door of the storage closet.

The guard opens the door... And that's when I see him.

Holy. Fucking. Shit.

My brother.

The same older brother I loved so much for all of those years.

Every freaking memory from when I was a child comes crashing back into me like a hurricane.

The times Jericho and I played together late into the night.

Our snuggle forts when December snowstorms raged outside.

The acceptance Jericho showed me when I played with my stuffed animals while we waited for Santa on Christmas Eve.

Jericho is exactly the same, from his firm jaw and chiseled cheekbones, to his blue eyes that glisten like diamonds, his penetrating gaze full of warmth.

The only difference is that Jericho's muscles are ten times bigger and he has tattoos on his arms.

"Hey, Bentley." Jericho smiles and clips out a nod from across the room. "Nice to see you again."

I let out a cry and drop Señor Antlers on the floor.

I rush across the room and throw myself in Jericho's arms.

"Oh my God," I cry, burying my nose in Jericho's chest. "It's been so long, Jericho. I'm so sorry that I didn't come to visit you earlier."

"No." Jericho untangles me from his arms. He sets me down on the coffee table next to him. "I've missed you so damn much, Bentley. I asked my attorney to tell Maw Maw and Paw Paw where I was so many times, but he wouldn't cooperate. I even asked a guard to send a secret letter up to the Christmas tree farm. But it was too dangerous, Bentley. He couldn't risk helping a prisoner break the law. No one could help me get back in touch with you."

I let out a sob. "I should've fought harder to come and see you, Jericho. I should've petitioned the judge to get you a better lawyer. They have these things called online petitions now, and I could've started one and made a super compelling YouTube video for people to like so your judge would set you free. I failed you as a younger brother, Jericho. It's my fault that we didn't see each other sooner. You didn't have the resources in here to even reach out to me. It's my freaking fault and I hurt you so much."

"No." Jericho's voice is firm and strong. "You were just a kid, Bentley. A child. You couldn't have done anything differently. You were traumatized from that night eight years ago, and don't lie to me by telling me you weren't. We all deal with horrible trauma in different ways, and you did the best you could given the chaos that went on. You helped Paw Paw and Maw Maw so much as they were dealing with the loss of their daughter, Bentley. That's not something a twelve-year-old who just lost a parent should ever have to do. I'm so sorry that I wasn't there to give you the comfort and warmth that you needed. It's my fault. You were just a kid and I was the older brother in the situation who should've fought like hell to find a way to see you. I should never have attacked that man that night. I'm so sorry that I failed you and I hope you can forgive me."

My heart trembles as I stare into Jericho's eyes. "I learned so much about Rikers Island from my Daddy Roman over the past couple of weeks, Jericho."

"Did you now?" Jericho's voice is soft.

I nod. "I found out that prisoners in Rikers occasionally get bakers from the city to teach them how to bake treats. I wondered if you ever got that opportunity to help bake yummy treats for people."

Jericho smirks. "I did bake in the kitchen, Bentley. Hell," Jericho says, letting out a laugh. "I was always in there with a couple of my friends from my cell block and we made delicious truffles and cupcakes for bakeries here in New York all the time. That program is seriously the best prison program ever because you get to learn new skills and put yourself to work. You're not just cooped up in your cell all the time reading awful early twenty-first century translations of Marcel Proust. You actually get to live in the real world."

My heart swells with warm fuzzies. "Gosh, that sounds amazing, Jericho. It's so nice that you actually got to learn how to bake something instead of reading bad translations of French literature in your bed all the time. I'd love to bake something with you when you're out on parole. You could teach me."

"I'd love that too, Bentley." Jericho rubs my wrist.

A beat passes as I stare into Jericho's eyes.

A million sensations crash through me as I look up at my brother.

Jesus. Fucking. Christ.

Not a damn thing has changed between us.

Our bond is stronger than ever and Jericho is still the same brother that I was close to all those years ago.

"There's something I must tell you, Bentley," Jericho confesses, staring into my eyes.

"Sure, Jericho." I suck in my cheeks. "Tell me."

Jericho blows out a breath. "I thought about you... A lot on the inside, Bentley. I'd think about... The amazing times we had together as boys."

I gasp. "You... Thought about me?" My heart triples its pace. My brother who I used to freaking *adore*... Thought about *me*?

Jericho brushes a strand of hair from my cheek. "Yes, Bentley. When I'd fall asleep, I'd think about hanging out with you on the Christmas tree farm. I'd picture us walking around the Christmas trees and sipping hot chocolate together as we laughed and watched the first snowflakes come down. I'd think about playing toy soldiers in the loft and having so much fun always picking the blue soldiers because they reminded me of your eyes. I'd think about snuggling together in my bed on Christmas Eve as we waited for Santa Claus to fill our stockings and how you always liked making me check your stuffy Señor Antlers to see if it could talk when the clock struck midnight. It was those memories, Bentley, those beautiful memories that got me through. They only grew more powerful inside. They compounded and grew as real as diamonds. You were the best little brother I could've ever asked for and it was because of you and you alone that I even made it through Rikers Island."

Tears well up in my eyes. "I thought about those things too, Jericho. I was crushed when you went away to prison all those years ago. The state painted you out to be a bad guy, but in my heart I knew you were the sweet brother who loved me, never hurt me, never let me even feel sad for a moment on Christmas Eve. I'd think about those wonderful things and the times where we talked through that little hole in the wall in the shower where we used to have conversations after we were supposed to be in bed. I pictured you holding me and kissing away my tears while I cried over what happened to Mom and Dad. In my fantasies, you always held me close, never judged me, never hurt me at all. You bought me the copies of *La Chartreuse de Parme* that I adored and read to me and always took time to explain the big words to me. You were the reason why I majored in English at Cornell and studied Latin and Greek. You were the best brother I could've asked for and I was so fucking lucky you were in my life."

Jericho grins at Roman. "Are you going to tell him, Roman, or should I?"

Roman walks over and places his manly palms on my back. "Jericho's coming home with us for the next week while he awaits his parole date. I bribed a guard to sneak him out. He's going to sleep in his old bedroom and spend Christmas with us."

I can barely breathe as I look up at Roman.

Oh sweet Jesus in the sky.

I'm staring up at a benevolent deity, a freaking god who answers my prayers.

I let out a cry as I rush toward Roman and wrap myself in his arms. "I'd love that, Daddy. Thank you so much for using your resources to help my brother get out of prison. We're going to have so much fun and Maw Maw and Paw Paw are going to be so happy to see him again. Thank you so much."

"A good Daddy will always do anything he can to help his baby boy," Roman grunts, wrapping his arms around my waist and rubbing my lower back. "I love you so much, angel."

"I love you too, Daddy."

"Let's head home and have a play session with Jericho." Roman massages my curves. "You'd like that, Bentley."

My head nearly explodes as I register Roman's words.

I slowly pivot to face Jericho. "You'd... Want to play with me again?"

Jericho laughs. "Hell yes, Bentley. It's all I've been able to think about for eight long years."

I'm no longer in control of my senses as I tear myself away from Roman and throw myself back into Jericho's arms.

I hug Jericho as the eight long years that have separated us fall to the wayside and disappear like they never happened at all.

Jericho's coming back for Christmas.

My Daddy figured out how to make it happen so Jericho and I can bond with each other just like old times.

How amazing is that?

"Bentley." Jericho's voice is gruff. "I only want to play with you if I can use the blue soldiers. Just like how we used to do."

My cheeks are on fire as I stare into my brother's eyes. "Yes, Jericho."

34

MY BROTHER IS BACK.

My amazing, sweetheart brother who was locked up for such a long time for a crime he shouldn't have been punished for.

"Jericho." My breath is fast and my cheeks are bright pink as I pull out my bin of toys when we get back to the barn at the Christmas tree farm. "Are you ready to play with me?"

In my heart of hearts, I'm still nervous that Jericho will laugh at me and tell me to buzz off.

After all, eight years is a long time to still have the same interests as when you were a teenager.

Jericho's had to fight for his life and fend off brutal men in Rikers Island who probably wanted to do horrible things to him.

Jericho's a good-looking guy, and I bet the men in Rikers constantly tried to make him drop the soap in the showers.

Would he even still be interested in playing with me?

Jericho winks at me. "Hell yes, Bentley. I already told you I was ready in Rikers."

I blush hard. "I know, Jericho. I just thought you might've been saying that to be nice. It's one thing to say that to make me feel happy but it's another to actually do it."

Jericho holds my hand tight. "I'm going to be honest, Bentley. And I don't want you to laugh at me."

I shake my head. "I won't laugh."

Jericho stares into my eyes. "These play sessions… Were the only things that got me through Rikers Island. It was so fucking hard being locked up without having anyone come to visit me. I dreamt about playing soldiers with you and winning these pretend wars. I was lucky as hell that I had these memories. Lots of prisoners don't have close bonds with anyone before they go to Rikers and they get into trouble behind bars. I escaped my own mind by thinking about you, Bentley."

I blow out a breath. "I'm so happy to hear that, Jericho. It's all I've been able to think about too."

Roman takes my hand and Jericho's. "This is therapy for both of you, boys. You were both so young when everything happened eight years ago."

"I know, Daddy."

"This play sessions will help you both overcome your trauma." Roman squeezes our hands. "Just focus on the game. Take it one step at a time. Let it be natural. There's no rush whatsoever to go right back to where you were eight years ago. Jericho's back now and that's what matters most. Are you up to that task, sweet boy?"

My heart fills with so much warmth. "Yes, Daddy. My brother needs lots of patience after everything that happened in Rikers Island. He needs me to go slow to bring back those good memories from when we were younger. I can do it."

Roman rubs my shoulder. "You have such a good heart, Bentley. You're so empathetic and sensitive to others' needs. I'm so proud of you."

My heart tumbles to my feet as I remove the plastic tub of toy soldiers from the secret nook. "These are our soldiers, Jericho. They're what will help you remember our special times."

Jericho smiles. "I know. They're the toys I thought about while locked up."

My cheeks are bright red as I tug the lid off the tub and set it aside. "Pick whichever ones you want, Jericho. Red or blue. I won't judge."

"I'll only ever pick blue, Bentley."

"I'm going to line them up right in front of you," I say, making sure that I stand the toy soldiers in a straight line on Jericho's side of the battlefield. "That's just how we used to do it. It'll be like old times."

Jericho nods. "That's exactly how I want it too."

I arrange our soldiers on the battlefield and set up my red soldiers across from Jericho's and then arrange his blue ones.

"Boom," I shout, starting the game off by firing an invisible bullet into Jericho's fleet.

Jericho chuckles as the invisible bullet sends his blue soldiers scattering in every direction and collapsing onto the floor.

"You think you're smart, don't you, Bentley," Jericho says, a glint in his eyes.

"I know you are but what am I?" I stick out my tongue.

Jericho smirks. "Just wait."

Jericho picks up a handful of hay from the side of the loft.

He raises it high in the air and then sprinkles it all over the battlefield, dropping it on top of my army.

"Hey!" My jaw drops to my feet as Jericho does this move. "What are you thinking? That's cheating!"

Jericho laughs. "Your soldiers ran into an unfortunate accident in battle, Bentley. They stumbled across fog and now they can't see anything. Unfortunately, all of the bullets and cannon balls they shoot out are going to go in the wrong direction from now on."

I let out a gasp as I try to make my toy soldiers fire at Jericho's.

But to my surprise, Jericho's scheme works.

My soldiers try to shoot at Jericho's but their invisible bullets don't go anywhere near Jericho's soldiers.

The cannonballs and bullets smack into the floorboards and bales of hay and wreaths but they don't hit Jericho's army.

Jericho seizes the opportunity to attack my fleet from behind.

I glance up into Jericho's eyes, and all of a sudden, it's like everything moves in slow motion once again.

A time warp envelops us.

We're the same people we used to be before he went to prison.

My parents are still alive, probably telling jokes with my grandparents in the farmhouse right now and drinking wine in front of the fire.

My life is still normal, not disrupted by the horrible carjacker that ruined everything one night in New York City.

And Jericho is still mine, my amazing brother who's always cared about me and doesn't judge me at all.

Nothing has changed.

I'm still the boy I was when I used to play with Jericho all those years ago and Jericho is my brother who loves me with all his heart.

We're two best friends, Jericho's never hurt me or been mean to me, and nothing has ruined our bond.

"I'm having so much fun, Jericho," I muster as we duke it out on the battlefield. "Thank you."

Jericho turns his blue eyes up to me and for a second, for a measly second, I swear to God not a fucking thing has changed. "I'm so freaking proud of you, Bentley. I'll always be your big bro who cares about you more than you could ever know. I love you so much."

Roman chuckles as he wraps his arms around me. "There's nothing like brotherly love."

I blush. "Yes, Daddy. Jericho's my big brother and I love him with all my heart."

I hug my brother so tight.

This is my brother who loves me unconditionally.

No time has passed between us at all.

Everything is the way it used to be.

Me, my brother... And the beautiful new addition of Roman who arranged *everything* for me.

Just like in my wildest hopes and dreams.

35

Four hours later

JERICHO, Roman, and I had the most amazing bonding experience in the loft of the barn.

We played toy soldiers and showed Jericho my stuffed animals to help him back into real life.

Jericho and I hugged for a long time and we both cried endlessly as we started to feel at home again.

It was angsty as fuck but it was worth it after so long apart.

Jericho's my older brother and he's back in my life.

And when Jericho, Roman, and I exited the barn to meet Maw Maw and Paw Paw, Jericho hugged them as tight as he could.

We all cried when Maw Maw made a special batch of Yum Yum Cocoa to celebrate Jericho's homecoming.

Jericho will go back to Rikers at the end of this week to get his parole the right way but it's so special spending Christmas with him.

And after eight long years, I think a little week-long break that the wardens don't know about is justified.

I'm so happy Jericho's back in the farmhouse where he belongs.

"Hey, sweet boy," a deep voice rumbles as two firm fingers trail down my backside and cup my ass through my pajama bottoms.

I turn over on the bed and see my perfect Daddy staring at me, studying me in the darkness.

"Hi, Daddy." My cheeks burn as I stare at my beautiful protector, who's done so much for me over the past three weeks. "Thank you for arranging that play date this afternoon. I had so much fun with Jericho."

Roman smiles. "It was nothing, Bentley. You and Jericho have been apart for so long. You needed time together to regain those memories."

"I know." I nod in agreement. "Jericho and I reconnected this afternoon and we got our bond back. It's because of you, Daddy. Thank you."

Roman stares into my eyes and trails his fingers across my hips.

His breath hitches and a spark travels out of his eyes and into mine.

Roman puts his thumb on my jaw. "Can I kiss you, Bentley? You can tell me if you don't want to. I just think you're the most special partner a man could ever wish for in his life who's so caring and affectionate with others. I'd love to kiss you tonight."

My cheeks burn bright. "Yes, Daddy. I'd love to kiss you too."

Roman bridges the gap between us and dusts his lips against mine.

A breath flutters out of his mouth as I rub my lips against Roman's.

Moonlight drifts through the window and bathes the bed in silver, and I scoot close to Roman and press my elbows on his chest.

"I want to go on top of you, Roman." My voice is soft as I kiss my amazing partner. "It'd make me feel better."

"Okay, sweet cheeks." Roman threads his fingers through my hair as he pulls me onto his chest.

I climb on top of Roman and spread myself against his rock hard chest.

I kiss Roman passionately, wiggling my hips seductively as our mouths mate in the moonlight.

I lean backward and feel Roman's member between my thighs, which is hard and stiff in his briefs.

"Fuck." My voice is a whisper as I rut my ass cheeks against Roman's cock, feeling his aching hardness press up between my legs. "You're so hard."

Roman places his palm on my chest. "I know you are but what am I."

"I..." My head spins as I stare into Roman's eyes. "I felt so *in my headspace* in the barn today. I was playing with toys and I couldn't help but think how special you were for setting up that reunion for me. You helped me see my brother again."

"It was nothing."

"No." I shake my head. "It was something."

"No."

"Yes." A breath escapes me. "You gave me the biggest gift in the universe, Daddy. I loved playing with Jericho in the barn and it made me feel like everything was going to be okay again for the first time in so long. It was like no time had passed at all. I was still the same boy that I was before my parents died. My family was intact. Nothing could hurt me. We played just like we used to all those years ago when we were young. And it's all because of you. You let me have that special moment with my brother. You made me feel loved for the first time in so long."

"Bentley..." Roman's palm finds my ass cheeks and squeezes them through my pajama bottoms. "I appreciate everything you're telling me, Bentley. But you need to roll off of me."

"Why?"

Roman breathes hard. "Your brother... Is in the room next to us, Bentley. He hasn't had a good night's sleep in eight long years. You're going to wake him up."

"But I need you, Daddy," I whisper, rutting against Roman's cock and kissing him with everything I have. "You gave me the most special gift of my entire life today. I have so much love for you. You must let me show you."

Roman's eyes roll back. "Get off of me, Bentley. I don't want to wake your brother up."

I moan as I drape myself across Roman's body all the way. "No, Daddy. I need you in me tonight. I don't care that my brother is in the room next to us. He's a heavy sleeper. He'll never know. Please. I need you inside me tonight."

I pull a bottle of lube out of Roman's dresser and pour some onto Roman's cock.

I slide my pajama bottoms down and cant my hips above Roman's dick.

The world stops spinning as I stare into Roman's eyes.

"It's almost in, Daddy." My voice is a whisper. "It's poking me. Please. Just one love session tonight."

"Once it goes inside, there's no going back," Roman rasps, his voice strained as he trails his palms across my tummy.

I nod as I kiss Roman once again. "Yes, Daddy. It's what I want."

Roman lifts his hips upward and his big hard shaft slides into my passage.

I spread my legs, throwing my head back as Roman's giant rod stirs my insides.

"So perfect," I whine, clenching and unclenching against Roman's shaft as I place my palms on Roman's pecs. "Just what I needed. So safe inside me tonight."

Sweat beads on Roman's forehead as he wiggles his dick deeper into my ass.

He drags his hands up my belly and clamps his fingers on my nipples, pinching them as he grinds inside me.

Something bursts inside me and causes me to cry out, and I glance down between my legs and see my seven-inch cock leaking in tandem with Roman's thrusts, pressing against my belly and oozing pre-come.

"That's right, boy." Roman grips my hips and presses into me slow and steady. "This is what you were born for, angel. This is how excited you're getting Daddy as you ride his thick cock in bed. Grind those sexy hips against my ten-inch dick, boy. Take your time to flex that untouched ass around my hardness. Let your worries melt and give yourself over to Daddy tonight. Let Daddy brand you and claim you as his own. This is what you've been waiting for your entire life, Bentley. A Daddy to give you the best pleasures on Earth. A Daddy to help you meet your goals. A Daddy who will pleasure you with everything he has. Let Daddy stroke in that precious channel and bust out an orgasm deep inside your body. You were put on this Earth to ride Daddy's cock, boy. Messy come and orgasms all over Daddy's hairy chest. Sink your nails into my chest and let Daddy make you come."`

My trembling body burns as Roman anchors himself in my ass.

His carnivorous hands cup my man mounds, squeezing my nipples tight.

My nipples bead as Roman grinds into me, and I let out a cry when his engorged crown brushes against my prostate.

I burn with pleasure, and I thrust my legs out and straddle Roman desperately, rubbing my spot against Roman's crown.

A muffled scream escapes me as my hair cascades over my cheeks, and Roman clamps his palm down around my mouth, bucking into me with everything he has.

A garbled cry escapes me as Roman rolls his hips against my ass cheeks, and spit trickles out of my lips.

"Such a pretty young man." Roman pins me down with his dick, mashing hard against my prostate. "Let that angel come out, boy. Clench those sexy cheeks around Daddy's dick and let Daddy give you what you need."

Ecstasy blinds me as Roman's dirty words bring me over the edge.

My balls heave and throb.

I let out a feral scream and spurt all over Roman's chest.

Roman goes at full speed inside my passage, fucking my walls as he crushes his crown against my prostate.

Then Roman tugs his dick out of my crack and forces me to my knees.

"Suck my cock, boy." Roman breathes hard as he threads his fingers through my hair. "Wrap those lips around Daddy's dick and suck him off. This is what you wanted, boy. Daddy will give you what you need."

The gates of heaven open as I part my lips and let Roman shove his cock into my mouth.

Roman plunges himself into me, forcing himself down my throat with so much intensity it takes away my ability to breathe.

I grasp the sheets as Roman stretches out my throat with his giant member, gagging as he saws in and out of my lips.

"Just like that, boy." Roman pushes every inch of his dick into my esophagus. "Let Daddy park this big Mack truck right in your little garage. You're Daddy's to own. Daddy's to fuck. Spread that throat and let Daddy give you what you need."

Roman's big dick shakes in my throat.

His giant balls jolt as they dump out squirt after squirt of hot white come into my throat.

I blink back tears as I suck up every squirt, feeling the hot spurts deep in my gut.

I gag as I extract the come out of Roman's dick, sucking hard to get every bit of seed.

I swirl my tongue around Roman's throbbing cock head, and slobber all over his dick as I swallow up everything.

A beat passes when Roman grabs my hair and forces my chin up.

Roman stares into my eyes and then plunges his tongue into my mouth.

My heart soars as Roman kisses me with so much passion and beauty, so much love.

I crush my lips against Roman's, love and desperation pouring out of me as I kiss my beautiful protector with everything I have.

"So perfect, Daddy." I pour my heart into Roman's mouth. "Just what I wanted. A true protector. Thank you."

"You're such a special boy, Bentley." Roman cradles my mouth. "I love you so much, baby boy."

"I love you too, Daddy."

Roman takes me into his firm arms and falls asleep.

Epilogue

One week later

TODAY'S THE DAY.

The biggest, scariest, craziest motherfucking day of my life.

Sweat beads under my armpits as I take Roman's hand and wait on the courthouse steps for the Manhattan DA to arrive.

Today's the day the Manhattan DA will let Roman know if he won his lawsuit against the state of New York for wrongful imprisonment.

Today's the day we'll find out if the bill Jericho and Roman sponsored will pass through the New York legislature.

A bolt of nervousness darts across me as I twine my fingers through Roman's and take a deep calming breath.

"I'm scared, Daddy," I say. "I'm worried that the District Attorney is going to send you and Jericho back to Rikers Island."

Roman brushes a strand of hair from my temple. "You're silly, boy. Jericho and I aren't going back to prison."

I sniffle and hold Señor Antlers tight. "Are you sure, Daddy?"

"Yes." Roman squeezes my waist. "Jericho and I are already out on parole. That part of our lives is over."

"Then why are we here today?"

"Today's the day we find out if District Attorney Michaels will give our lawsuit against the state of New York a gold stamp of approval," Roman explains. "That's what's going to happen today, sweet angel. We'll also find out if *Jericho's Law* passed to change the paths of so many people in this country who've been wrongfully imprisoned for hurting abusers."

Roman's words wash over me like snowflakes on a Christmas tree farm. "Thank you for explaining that to me, Daddy. I'm just nervous because I really don't want you to go back to prison. That would literally be the worst thing ever."

Roman lets out a laugh. "You're adorable, Bentley. But there's literally zero danger of me going back to prison. Winning this lawsuit will benefit underprivileged people who are victims of judicial corruption in this state, and that's why we're here."

My heart melts in my chest as I listen to every word my Daddy says.

Roman is so smart and even though I'm still nervous, deep down I know he's telling the truth.

I hide from the news stations pointing cameras at Roman and me and nuzzle up to Roman's chest.

Over the past week, news stations have called us relentlessly to try to get a statement about Roman's story.

Twenty TV stations called to do an exposé on Roman and the illegal experiences he suffered in Rikers Island.

Roman is a national hero and he's become the face of wrongful imprisonment in the USA.

I shake my head in amusement as butterflies flurry across my chest.

When I first ran into Roman four weeks ago, I was convinced he was the epitome of corruption in our legal system.

I thought he was a good-for-nothing, privileged Russian criminal who had billions of dollars at his disposal to buy his way out of prison.

Yes, Roman's a billionaire, and yes, he can definitely buy his way out of anything in this life, but he's also a man with a heart.

He helped me take down the evil bad guy who hurt my family all those years ago and protected me.

And now Roman's working to change millions of lives for the better in New York.

Roman's a national hero.

How amazing is that?

Roman places his palm on my lower back and gives me a comforting squeeze. "The District Attorney is about to come out now, baby boy. Just hold my hand tight and don't let your nerves overwhelm you."

I lean into Roman's arm and nod, even though all I want to do is crawl into bed and play with my soldiers. "Okay, Daddy. I'll listen to his announcement now."

I hold Señor Antlers tight under my arm and wait.

***

"Congratulations, Roman and Jericho," the District Attorney says, wrapping up his speech.

He retrieves a velvet box and opens it in front of my brother and my boyfriend.

"You won your lawsuit against the state of New York, Roman," the DA says. "*Jericho's Law* is in place to ensure that federal judges who accept bribes from mobsters will be sentenced to fifteen years in Rikers Island for corruption. You'll both receive medals for your heroism and we're giving you the keys to the city."

The DA removes gold medals from the velvet box and holds them up in the light.

He slides one of the beautiful medals around Roman's neck and then walks over to Jericho and does the same.

Jericho stares at the medal in shock and runs a shaky hand through his hair as he drags his fingers over the gold.

The medal shows a picture of Jericho smiling and waving and it glistens like it's the finest thing in the world.

"Thank you, DA Michaels." Jericho wipes a tear from his eye as he embraces the District Attorney in a hug. "I'm so grateful you listened to my story, Sir. It means so much to me."

The District Attorney pats Jericho's back. "You've suffered long enough, son. That man never had a right to do what he did all those years ago and it's a bastardization of justice that you were locked up in the most overcrowded prison in the country all those years. What your judge did to you was unjust because men aren't supposed to stay in Rikers Island for more than one year at a time. You deserve your freedom now. *Jericho's Law* will make sure that this never happens again."

The crowd on the courthouse steps bursts into applause as Jericho and Roman hug the DA.

A man in a Patagonia jacket holds up a camera and flashes a thumbs up at Roman.

"Congratulations, Roman and Jericho!" the man says. "You're both heroes!"

I blush. "Thank you, Sir."

A woman with blonde hair lets out a moan. "Fuck," she

drawls. "I'd let either of those studs pin me to the cell bars in Rikers Island."

Fierce protective instincts slam into me from every direction.

"No," I say, rushing to Roman's side and throwing my arms around my beautiful Daddy. "My Daddy is mine. He only needs his boy to make him happy. Buzz off, lady."

The newscasters laugh hysterically as they film my hug with Roman.

"That's a keeper," one newswoman says, winking at the camera as she gestures to Roman and me. "Bentley is one lucky dude, folks. Not only does he get to share Roman's five-million-dollar settlement against the state of New York, but he has the sexiest, growliest Daddy in Manhattan all to himself."

Roman trails his calloused thumb down my cheek. "I'm donating all of my money to my new fund to help prisoners who've been victims of judicial corruption in this state, ma'am. Not a penny of this money will stay in my pockets."

My heart floods with so much warmth as I look up into Roman's eyes.

Roman's act is so generous but it's also kind of hilarious because he doesn't need the money anyway.

Roman's billion-dollar bank account was officially unfrozen last week and he's now one of the richest men in New York City who can buy me anything he likes.

Last night, Roman booked us the penthouse suite at the Ritz Carleton and we flew in a private luxury helicopter all around New York City while we ate truffles dusted in edible diamonds.

We took Anastasia with us to see the Statue of Liberty up close and we even had a private photo shoot with the statue.

Anastasia was blown away and she recited ten million factoids about the Statue of Liberty because she loves it so much and waxed poetic about its artistic merit.

Anastasia's a little annoying to be around for more than five minutes without wanting to tear your head off but the night was still amazing.

"I love you so much, Daddy." I squeeze Roman tight and hug him with everything I have. "You're so brave and strong and you helped so many people. I'm so proud of you for fighting hard to make a difference."

I expect Roman to say something sweet in response but instead he does something that shocks me.

Roman pulls a box out of his pocket and drops to one knee.

"Sweet boy." Roman's voice is soft and caring as he opens up the velvet box and pulls out a glistening Cartier diamond ring. "When I first saw your picture in Rikers Island, I didn't know what to expect. I saw a beautiful twenty-year-old angel staring up at me with glistening curly locks and bashful blue eyes. You were the first beautiful man I'd seen in eight long years and it felt like I was looking into a bastion of truth and wonderment. But when I arrived on your Christmas tree farm, I quickly discovered that you were so much more to me. You weren't the type of boy who'd roll over or let someone push you around. No, you were a ferocious, headstrong young man who'd stop at nothing to make his opinions known. My plan to avoid you at all costs quickly fell to the wayside once I realized how truly amazing you were. You're a man who cares about justice and fighting for what's right and doing the right thing. You're a man who hates corruption and thinks it's disgusting when people get out on sweetheart deals they don't deserve. But you're also a man who cares about helping your grandparents whenever you can and bringing yummy cupcakes to the little old lady who lives across the street. You have so many sides to you, Bentley, and before I knew it, all my plans to avoid you were tossed out the window. When we went to cut down Christmas trees together with your Paw Paw's chainsaw, I knew it would be impossible to avoid you any longer. You're whip smart, snarky, and funny as hell, and I knew in that moment that I wanted to be with you for the rest of my life. And then when I caught you jerking off on my pillowcase, I knew I had to become your Daddy. I couldn't avoid it or run from my feelings anymore. You were horny for me, Bentley, so fucking horny — But the feelings I felt for you were so much more than lust. I feared that I was falling in love with you when you joined me on that carriage ride through the Christmas tree farm where we ate all those delicious treats and acted out on our physical attraction to each other for the first time. I tried to fight it, but love has a way of breaking down walls. No matter how hard I struggled to break away from you, your spunky personality and amazing character drew me back. They say that dogs bark at which they don't understand, and while you barked at me at first, Bentley, you melted like a Hershey's kiss when you realized my intentions were pure and that I could be a wonderful Daddy to you. You're my precious boy, Bentley, but today I need so much more from you. I need you to become my husband, Bentley. I must ask you the question that's been on my mind every day for the last week. Will you marry me?"

I accept the ring. "Yes," I cry out, thrusting my arms around Roman's neck. "Yes, Roman, you beautiful man. I'll freaking marry you."

My heart turns into a big melted candy cane as I stare into Roman's eyes. "When I first saw you in the doorway of my grandparents's farm house, I was confused as hell. I had no idea why my grandparents would ever invite a felon from Rikers Island to our tree farm for Christmas, and I was as mad as an elf who's had too much eggnog when I realized that you got a sweetheart deal. To me, Roman, you epitomized corruption in the legal system in this country, and you were everything that was wrong with the billionaire class. My brother Jericho never had the opportunities you had, and I took out my resentment on you. But over the course of the last four weeks, I discovered that you were so much more than a corrupt billion- aire who buys his way out of whatever he wants. You're a fighter. A protector. A true student of life. You studied hard before you came to my Christmas tree farm and you even memorized the Latin names of Christmas trees to impress me. You bought me meaningful treats for our first official date together and filled the carriage with so many delicious danishes and truffles that I can still taste them in my mouth to this day. And when you realized that I'd broken into your bedroom and done lewd things to your pillowcase, you didn't hold it against me at all. You could've reported me to the police but you didn't. You accepted me, all of me, from my sassy side to the sexual boy who needed you to make love to me. You accepted my little side, and played toy soldiers with me and fed my favorite reindeer stuffy Señor Antlers even though you were starving and really wanted to eat. You practiced true consent with me in the bedroom, and always made sure to ask for my permission before you tried anything. I was actually shocked that you did this because you're a felon who's spent so much time in Rikers Island, but I shouldn't have been surprised. You're a man who understands that being a Daddy is all about respecting his boy's wishes, and you took my needs and limits into consideration at all times. And you didn't just tolerate my curves and my little side – you adored them. You showed me that you thought I was amazing in unique ways. You're more open-minded than the boys I met at university who blabbed on and on about body positivity but left me on read. And I didn't even mention that you're donating the settlement you received today to the fund you set up for underprivileged convicts in this state. You're using your privilege for good in this life and I love you so much for it. You're a beautiful man in every way, and I'm so honored you want to marry me. Yes, Roman. I want to be your husband too. Put that beautiful ring on my finger, Daddy, and kiss me."

Roman slides the ring all the way onto my finger.

I melt into a giant puddle of Hershey's kisses when Roman plants a big beautiful kiss on my lips.

"I love you so much, Daddy!" I moan into Roman's lips, pressing my hips against him as he kisses me in front of the cameras. "My big beautiful protector. Adoring and loving me for who I am."

The crowd cheers as we make out on national TV.

"I'll have what he's having," Preston jokes, nudging Macon in the ribs.

Preston's monkey leaps on Macon's head and does a happy dance.

Roman lets out a laugh. "I love you so much, boy."

My heart swells with so much warmth as I kiss Roman with everything I have. "You're the best protector in the world, Daddy. I'm so excited to be your husband forever."

"Me too, boy."

I can only think one thing as I trail my eyes over the diamond ring shaped like a glistening Christmas tree on my finger.

Roman's my husband.

And I get to be with this beautiful man every single day for the rest of my life.

**

Thank you so much for reading this story!

I had SUCH a blast writing it and hope you enjoyed it as much as me!

I love reading about diverse characters and I'm so glad I finally got to incorporate a big boy into one of my stories after SO long!

drumroll please

There's going to be another book in the *Russian Protectors* series!! (Woohoo haha!)

Bodyguard Daddy is the next book scheduled for release and it will come out in early January 2022 (one month from now)!

It follows 18-year-old Preston Harmony who's been in love with his growly bodyguard Sasha for sooo long and wants to make Sasha his Daddy!

It also includes Daddy kink, age play, Macon and Bentley's weddings (they have a combined wedding on Bentley's Christmas tree farm!), Christian's brand-new ice cream theme park he opens in California, a boy band who loves to banter and tease their friend Preston about his crush, an adorable monkey who likes to throw bananas around, a Daddy who's determined to not act on his feelings for his boy, a broken jet that leads to some forced proximity fun, an evil Italian who's coming back to get Sasha after a dark thing that happened in the past, a suspense plot with lots of BANGS and BOOMS, and a guaranteed HEA packed with warm fuzzies!!

Turn the page for a sneak peak...

"BODYGUARD DADDY" SNEAK PEAK

Preston

One year earlier

"No, Sir. I already told you—"

The fist flies through the air and smashes into the paparazzo's jaw.

Crack.

"That's what you get, motherfucker," the biggest, roughest, growliest man I've ever seen in my life spits out to the paparazzo on the ground in front of me. "The boy said *no pictures.* Don't ask him again."

The monkey stuffy that I'm holding falls to my feet.

My head spins and my heart turns into a melted popsicle.

Holy. Fucking. Shit.

Did this man just... Rescue me?

Did he just... Save me from a camera wielding stalker who was trying to take pics of me to sell to TMZ?

"It's not my fault, man." The paparazzo lets out a cry. "The lead singer of the most famous boy band in the world should be used to unexpected pictures by now."

My knight in leather and prison tattoos tugs his gold rings off and rams his fist into the man's face once again.

Slam.

"You need a new bodyguard," my knight grunts after he finishes beating my stalker paparazzo into a pulp. "That man should have left you alone after you said no the first time."

Time freaking stops as I stare into my protector's eyes.

Holy. Fucking. Shit.

I was merely walking along Sunset Boulevard with my stuffed monkey under my arm to the rescue monkey I saw in the advertisement online.

The paparazzo with the camera leapt in front of me and ordered me to smile for a picture.

I begged him to stop because I really don't want pictures of my monkey stuffy ending up on the internet; Little Monkey is quite camera shy.

That's when my rescuer showed up and solved all my problems with his tattooed fists.

"Uhhhm," I joke, picking up my stuffy from the ground. "Please tell me someone didn't spike my apple juice this morning, because that was the most *amazing* thing I've ever seen."

"You shouldn't be on this street alone, boy." The man rams his Rolex back onto his wrist and adjusts his gold rings. "That man could've hurt you."

I can barely breathe as the man with the thick muscles, chiseled jaw, and menacing prison tattoos turns to me.

I gulp loudly and try not to stare at my rescuer's pecs.

Because *holy shit.*

Everything about this man screams *Dream Daddy.*

The man seriously looks like Goliath straight out of the

Bible story but also like he spends every goddamn hour of his life in the gym.

But I sense that this man is so much more than a gym aficionado.

After all, he beat up a stalker paparazzo for me and rescued my stuffy from the fate of tabloid bullying.

I rub my hands on my khakis. "I was just going to *Celebrity Animal Rescue* to pick up a baby monkey. I wasn't going to be out long."

The man stares at me. "Are you Preston Harmony? From *Wonder Rection*?"

"That's me," I confess, my cheeks turning pink. "The singer from the biggest boy band in the world."

"I recognized you at once," the man clips out. "The paparazzo obviously did too."

"Yeah, yeah," I groan, smoothing out Little Monkey's cowlick. "It's not his fault though. I'm a celebrity walking alone in LA and the paparazzo was only trying to do his job."

"That man was taking pictures of you without your consent." The man's voice is deadly. "A boy with your level of fame shouldn't be on Sunset Boulevard alone. You'll attract weirdos."

"I knooow," I say, standing on the balls of my feet. "I thought I could slip out of band practice for an hour to pick up my new furry friend. But apparently the weirdos out here noticed me."

"What's your name?" I ask.

"Sasha Antonov." Sasha's gaze is penetrating and deep.

I nod. "I've never met a Sasha before."

"It's Russian."

"Oh," I say, swallowing a giggle. "That makes more sense. You do have a silly accent."

"It was nice to meet you, Preston," Sasha barks in a deep voice. "I hope you rescue your monkey and get back to your bandmates in one piece."

Uhhhh.

I know this man really didn't just say he was leaving me, right?

Not after he knew just what to do when I was in danger, didn't pause, didn't hesitate, took matters into his own hand and protected me?

"Wait." I hurry to Sasha's side before he leaves my life forever. "I need to ask you something."

Sasha's jaw ticks. "Make it snappy. I'm heading to the gym to work out."

I clear my throat. "Are you... Looking for work at all?"

The man furrows his brow. "Tell me what you mean, boy."

I inhale a deep breath of air. "I think I probably do need a twenty-four seven bodyguard who could... Take me on tours, go out with me when I'm shopping, and keep me safe from the paparazzi. Singing in *Wonder Rection* is a lot of work and I didn't realize how dangerous it was getting in the spotlight."

Sasha lets out a sigh. "Here," he growls, reaching into his wallet. "Take my business card. I was a bouncer back in Russia before I moved to LA."

I nearly moan as relief washes over me from every angle. "Thank you, Sasha. I'll give this to my manager and give you a call."

"Have a good day."

As Sasha turns to walk away from me in the sexiest leather jacket I've ever seen, I can only think one thing.

Sasha's not just going to come work for me.

He's going to be my motherfucking Daddy.

I don't give a shit if I have to wait a year to make it happen.

Sasha will be mine whether he likes it or not.

PRE-ORDER BODYGUARD DADDY TODAY

PLEASE CONSIDER LEAVING A REVIEW

Did you love this book?

Please consider leaving a review on Amazon!

It doesn't matter how many stars you give.

Every review helps Amazon show my book to new readers.

Thank you :)

GET YOUR FREE STORY!

Do you like free Daddy stories?

Get a FREE 11K short that follows Riley (who you met in this book) as he meets his forever Daddy on a weekend trip to New York when you sign up for my newsletter :)

It is ONLY available on BookFunnel — claim your free copy today!

GET MY FREE STORY TODAY

JOIN THE FACEBOOK PARTY!

Are you on Facebook? I'd love to be friends with you!

I just started my brand-new Facebook group *Aster's Angels and Devils* where I post Daddy memes, funny jokes, and snippets from upcoming books!

It'd be SO cool if you joined the party :)

JOIN ASTER'S ANGELS AND DEVILS ON FACEBOOK!

RUSSIAN PROTECTORS

Hitman Daddy

Have you read the FIRST book in the *Russian Protectors* series?

It's called *Hitman Daddy* and it follows 19-year-old Christian as he meets a dark and deadly hitman named Nikolai in a LGBT nightclub in downtown NYC!

READ HITMAN DADDY

PRAISE FOR ASTER RAE

★ ★ ★ ★ ★ *"Eeekk! I adored the second book in Aster Rae's Russian Protectors series! So so good!!"* - **Haylee**

★ ★ ★ ★ ★ *"This is such a fun steamy book... The daddy characters are as ruthless as they are tender and the littles are sweet and sassy. This is the perfect cuddly rainy day read to escape into!"* - **Maria**

★ ★ ★ ★ ★ *"It's SO GOOD! I can't wait for people to meet Rowan. And scary Daddy Igor. They are going to LOVE him!"* - **B**

★ ★ ★ ★ ★ *"Totally dying here... This is perfect! I love mob humor."* - **CC**

★ ★ ★ ★ ★ *"I loved the fact that Rowan was able to be and stand up for himself, and express exactly what he needed. That was a great twist on the usual "boy" attitude."* - **Annie**

★ ★ ★ ★ ★ *"Igor was so growly...loved it!! Rowan seriously needed a protector and Igor could see that, but Igor also needed and wanted to take care of Rowan. I loved how Rowan tested Igor and Igor passed* with flying colors. The story was really well written, highly recommend!" - **Janet**

★ ★ ★ ★ ★ "Light and fluffy! Rowan is an absolutely darling little and Igor is a gruff grump of a Daddy with a heart of gold!" - **HMW**

★ ★ ★ ★ ★ "Igor is all cuddles on the inside! This is a sweet Daddy story with a mafia rivalry plot ongoing through the series. So many cute and funny moments. Excited for the next!" - **RA on Goodreads**

★ ★ ★ ★ ★ "Very determined little... An extremely smitten Mafia Daddy! Enjoyable Daddy/Little dynamic." - **Tammy on Goodreads**

★ ★ ★ ★ ★ "Thoroughly enjoyed the second book in this series. Really sweet story of Rowan getting his daddy!" - **Denise**

★ ★ ★ ★ ★ "Outstanding... I highly recommend this book to everyone looking for a touching storyline. I would love to live in their world and be their friend!" - **Missy**

ABOUT THE AUTHOR

Hi! I'm Aster Rae. I write MM Mafia stories with lots of love and heart. When I'm not writing, I can be found munching on dairy-free ice cream bars and daydreaming about my favorite Mafia hunks.

You can keep up with me by following me on BookBub!

Printed in Great Britain
by Amazon

71784110R00163